A
Texas Matchmaker

ANDY ADAMS

1ˢᵗ WORLD
LIBRARY
Literary Society

A Texas Matchmaker

Andy Adams

© 1st World Library – Literary Society, 2004
PO Box 2211
Fairfield, IA 52556
www.1stworldlibrary.org
First Edition

LCCN: 2005901127

Softcover ISBN: 1-4218-1105-7
Hardcover ISBN: 1-4218-1005-0
eBook ISBN: 1-4218-1205-3

Purchase *"A Texas Matchmaker"*
as a traditional bound book at:
www.1stWorldLibrary.org/purchase.asp?ISBN=1-4218-1105-7

1st World Library Literary Society is a nonprofit organization dedicated to promoting literacy by:

- Creating a free internet library accessible from any computer worldwide.
- Hosting writing competitions and offering book publishing scholarships.

Readers interested in supporting literacy through sponsorship, donations or membership please contact:
literacy@1stworldlibrary.org
Check us out at: www.1stworldlibrary.ORG
and start downloading free ebooks today.

A Texas Matchmaker
contributed by Tim, Ed & Rodney
in support of
1st World Library Literary Society

CONTENTS

CHAPTER I

LANCE LOVELACE

When I first found employment with Lance Lovelace, a Texas cowman, I had not yet attained my majority, while he was over sixty. Though not a native of Texas, "Uncle Lance" was entitled to be classed among its pioneers, his parents having emigrated from Tennessee along with a party of Stephen F. Austin's colonists in 1821. The colony with which his people reached the state landed at Quintana, at the mouth of the Brazos River, and shared the various hardships that befell all the early Texan settlers, moving inland later to a more healthy locality. Thus the education of young Lovelace was one of privation. Like other boys in pioneer families, he became in turn a hewer of wood or drawer of water, as the necessities of the household required, in reclaiming the wilderness. When Austin hoisted the new-born Lone Star flag, and called upon the sturdy pioneers to defend it, the adventurous settlers came from every quarter of the territory, and among the first who responded to the call to arms was young Lance Lovelace. After San Jacinto, when the fighting was over and the victory won, he laid down his arms, and returned to ranching with the same zeal and energy. The first legislature assembled voted to those who had borne arms in behalf of the new republic, lands in payment for their services. With this land scrip for his pay, young Lovelace, in company with others, set out for the territory lying south of the Nueces. They were a band of daring spirits. The country was primitive and fascinated them, and they remained. Some settled on the Frio River, though the majority crossed the Nueces, many going as far south as the Rio Grande. The country was as large as the men were daring, and there was elbow room for all and to spare. Lance Lovelace located a ranch a few miles south of the Nueces River, and, from the cooing of the doves in the encinal, named it Las Palomas.

"When I first settled here in 1838," said Uncle Lance to me one morning, as we rode out across the range, "my nearest neighbor lived forty miles up the river at Fort Ewell. Of course there were some Mexican families nearer, north on the Frio, but they don't count. Say, Tom, but she was a purty country then! Why, from those hills yonder, any morning you could see a thousand antelope in a band going into the river to drink. And wild turkeys? Well, the first few years we lived here, whole flocks roosted every night in that farther point of the encinal. And in the winter these prairies were just flooded with geese and brant. If you wanted venison, all you had to do was to ride through those mesquite thickets north of the river to jump a hundred deer in a morning's ride. Oh, I tell you she was a land of plenty."

The pioneers of Texas belong to a day and generation which has almost gone. If strong arms and daring spirits were required to conquer the wilderness, Nature seemed generous in the supply; for nearly all were stalwart types of the inland viking. Lance Lovelace, when I first met him, would have passed for a man in middle life. Over six feet in height, with a rugged constitution, he little felt his threescore years, having spent his entire lifetime in the outdoor occupation of a ranchman. Living on the wild game of the country, sleeping on the ground by a camp-fire when his work required it, as much at home in the saddle as by his ranch fireside, he was a romantic type of the strenuous pioneer.

He was a man of simple tastes, true as tested steel in his friendships, with a simple honest mind which followed truth and right as unerringly as gravitation. In his domestic affairs, however, he was unfortunate. The year after locating at Las Palomas, he had returned to his former home on the Colorado River, where he had married Mary Bryan, also of the family of

Austin's colonists. Hopeful and happy they returned to their new home on the Nueces, but before the first anniversary of their wedding day arrived, she, with her first born, were laid in the same grave. But grief does not kill, and the young husband bore his loss as brave men do in living out their allotted day. But to the hour of his death the memory of Mary Bryan mellowed him into a child, and, when unoccupied, with every recurring thought of her or the mere mention of her name, he would fall into deep reverie, lasting sometimes for hours. And although he contracted two marriages afterward, they were simply marriages of convenience, to which, after their termination, he frequently referred flippantly, sometimes with irreverence, for they were unhappy alliances.

On my arrival at Las Palomas, the only white woman on the ranch was "Miss Jean," a spinster sister of its owner, and twenty years his junior. After his third bitter experience in the lottery of matrimony, evidently he gave up hope, and induced his sister to come out and preside as the mistress of Las Palomas. She was not tall like her brother, but rather plump for her forty years. She had large gray eyes, with long black eyelashes, and she had a trick of looking out from under them which was both provoking and disconcerting, and no doubt many an admirer had been deceived by those same roguish, laughing eyes. Every man, Mexican and child on the ranch was the devoted courtier of Miss Jean, for she was a lovable woman; and in spite of her isolated life and the constant plaguings of her brother on being a spinster, she fitted neatly into our pastoral life. It was these teasings of her brother that gave me my first inkling that the old ranchero was a wily matchmaker, though he religiously denied every such accusation. With a remarkable complacency, Jean Lovelace met and parried her tormentor, but her brother never tired of his hobby while there was a third person to listen.

Though an unlettered man, Lance Lovelace had been a close observer of humanity. The big book of Life had been open always before him, and he had profited from its pages. With my advent at Las Palomas, there were less than half a dozen books on the ranch, among them a copy of Bret Harte's poems and a large Bible.

"That book alone," said he to several of us one chilly evening, as we sat around the open fireplace, "is the greatest treatise on humanity ever written. Go with me to-day to any city in any country in Christendom, and I'll show you a man walk up the steps of his church on Sunday who thanks God that he's better than his neighbor. But you needn't go so far if you don't want to. I reckon if I could see myself, I might show symptoms of it occasionally. Sis here thanks God daily that she is better than that Barnes girl who cut her out of Amos Alexander. Now, don't you deny it, for you know it's gospel truth! And that book is reliable on lots of other things. Take marriage, for instance. It is just as natural for men and women to mate at the proper time, as it is for steers to shed in the spring. But there's no necessity of making all this fuss about it. The Bible way discounts all these modern methods. 'He took unto himself a wife' is the way it describes such events. But now such an occurrence has to be announced, months in advance. And after the wedding is over, in less than a year sometimes, they are glad to sneak off and get the bond dissolved in some divorce court, like I did with my second wife."

All of us about the ranch, including Miss Jean, knew that the old ranchero's views on matrimony could be obtained by leading up to the question, or differing, as occasion required. So, just to hear him talk on his favorite theme, I said: "Uncle Lance, you must recollect this is a different generation. Now, I've read books" -

"So have I. But it's different in real life. Now, in those novels you have read, the poor devil is nearly worried to death for fear he'll not get her. There's a hundred things happens; he's thrown off the scent one day and cuts it again the next, and one evening he's in a heaven of bliss and before the dance ends a rival looms up and there's hell to pay, - excuse me, Sis, - but he gets her in the end. And that's the way it goes in the books. But getting down to actual cases - when the money's on the table and the game's rolling - it's as simple as picking a sire and a dam to raise a race horse. When they're both willing, it don't require any expert to see it - a one-eyed or a blind man can tell the symptoms. Now, when any of you boys get into that fix, get it over with as soon as possible."

"From the drift of your remarks," said June Deweese very innocently, "why wouldn't it be a good idea to go back to the old method of letting the parents make the matches?"

"Yes; it would be a good idea. How in the name of common sense could you expect young sap-heads like you boys to understand anything about a woman? I know what I'm talking about. A single woman never shows her true colors, but conceals her imperfections. The average man is not to be blamed if he fails to see through her smiles and Sunday humor. Now, I was forty when I married the second time, and forty-five the last whirl. Looks like I'd a-had some little sense, now, don't it? But I didn't. No, I didn't have any more show than a snowball in - Sis, hadn't you better retire. You're not interested in my talk to these boys. - Well, if ever any of you want to get married you have my consent. But you'd better get my opinion on her dimples when you do. Now, with my sixty odd years, I'm worth listening to. I can take a cool, dispassionate view of a woman now, and pick every good point about her, just as if she was a cow horse that I was buying for my own saddle."

Miss Jean, who had a ready tongue for repartee, took advantage of the first opportunity to remark: "Do you know, brother, matrimony is a subject that I always enjoy hearing discussed by such an oracle as yourself. But did it never occur to you what an unjust thing it was of Providence to reveal so much to your wisdom and conceal the same from us babes?"

It took some little time for the gentle reproof to take effect, but Uncle Lance had an easy faculty of evading a question when it was contrary to his own views. "Speaking of the wisdom of babes," said he, "reminds me of what Felix York, an old '36 comrade of mine, once said. He had caught the gold fever in

'49, and nothing would do but he and some others must go to California. The party went up to Independence, Missouri, where they got into an overland emigrant train, bound for the land of gold. But it seems before starting, Senator Benton had made a speech in that town, in which he made the prophecy that one day there would be a railroad connecting the Missouri River with the Pacific Ocean. Felix told me this only a few years ago. But he said that all the teamsters made the prediction a byword. When, crossing some of the mountain ranges, the train halted to let the oxen blow, one bull-whacker would say to another: 'Well, I'd like to see old Tom Benton get his railroad over *this* mountain.' When Felix told me this he said - 'There's a railroad to-day crosses those same mountain passes over which we forty-niners whacked our bulls. And to think I was a grown man and had no more sense or foresight than a little baby blinkin' its eyes in the sun.'"

With years at Las Palomas, I learned to like the old ranchero. There was something of the strong, primitive man about him which compelled a youth of my years to listen to his counsel. His confidence in me was a compliment which I appreciate to this day. When I had been in his employ hardly two years, an incident occurred which, though only one of many similar acts cementing our long friendship, tested his trust.

One morning just as he was on the point of starting on horseback to the county seat to pay his taxes, a Mexican arrived at the ranch and announced that he had seen a large band of *javalina* on the border of the chaparral up the river. Uncle Lance had promised his taxes by a certain date, but he was a true sportsman and owned a fine pack of hounds; moreover, the peccary is a migratory animal and does not wait upon the pleasure of the hunter. As I rode out from the corrals to learn what had brought the vaquero with such haste, the old ranchero cried, "Here, Tom, you'll have to go to the county seat. Buckle this money belt under your shirt, and if you lack enough gold to cover the taxes, you'll find silver here in my saddle-bags. Blow the horn, boys, and get the guns. Lead the way, Pancho. And say, Tom, better leave the road after crossing the Sordo, and strike through that mesquite country," he called back as he swung into the saddle and started, leaving me a sixty-mile ride in his stead. His warning to leave the road after crossing the creek was timely, for a ranchman had been robbed by bandits on that road the month before. But I made the ride in safety before sunset, paying the taxes, amounting to over a thousand dollars.

During all our acquaintance, extending over a period of twenty years, Lance Lovelace was a constant revelation to me, for he was original in all things. Knowing no precedent, he recognized none which had not the approval of his own conscience. Where others were content to follow, he blazed his own pathways - immaterial to him whether they were followed by others or even noticed. In his business relations and in his own way, he was exact himself and likewise exacting of others. Some there are who might criticise him for an episode which occurred about four years after my advent at Las Palomas.

Mr. Whitley Booth, a younger man and a brother-in-law of the old ranchero by his first wife, rode into the ranch one evening, evidently on important business. He was not a frequent caller, for he was also a ranchman, living about forty miles north and west on the Frio River, but was in the habit of bringing his family down to the Nueces about twice a year for a visit of from ten days to two weeks' duration. But this time, though we had been expecting the family for some little time, he came alone, remained over night, and at breakfast ordered his horse, as if expecting to return at once. The two ranchmen were holding a conference in the sitting-room when a Mexican boy came to me at the corrals and said I was wanted in the house. On my presenting myself, my employer said: "Tom, I want you as a witness to a business transaction. I'm lending Whit, here, a thousand dollars, and as we have never taken any notes between us, I merely want you as a witness. Go into my room, please, and bring out, from under my bed, one of those largest bags of silver."

The door was unlocked, and there, under the ranchero's bed, dust-covered, were possibly a dozen sacks of silver. Finding one tagged with the required amount, I brought it out and laid it on the table between the two men. But on my return I noticed Uncle Lance had turned his chair from the table and was gazing out of the window, apparently absorbed in thought. I saw at a glance that he was gazing into the past, for I had become used to these reveries on his part. I had not been excused, and an embarrassing silence ensued, which was only broken as he looked over his shoulder and said: "There it is, Whit; count it if you want to."

But Mr. Booth, knowing the oddities of Uncle Lance, hesitated. "Well - why - Look here, Lance. If you have any reason for not wanting to loan me this amount, why, say so."

"There's the money, Whit; take it if you want to. It'll pay for the hundred cows you are figuring on buying. But I was just thinking: can two men at our time of life, who have always been friends, afford to take the risk of letting a business transaction like this possibly make us enemies? You know I started poor here, and what I have made and saved is the work of my lifetime. You are welcome to the money, but if anything should happen that you didn't repay me, you know I wouldn't feel right towards you. It's probably my years that does it, but - now, I always look forward to the visits of your family, and Jean and I always enjoy our visits at your ranch. I think we'd be two old fools to allow anything to break up those pleasant relations." Uncle Lance turned in his chair, and, looking into the downcast countenance of Mr. Booth, continued: "Do you know, Whit, that youngest girl of yours reminds me of her aunt, my own Mary, in a hundred ways. I just love to have your girls tear around this old ranch - they seem to give me back certain glimpses of my youth that are priceless to an old man."

"That'll do, Lance," said Mr. Booth, rising and extending his hand. "I don't want the money now. Your view of the matter is right, and our friendship is worth more than a thousand cattle to me. Lizzie and the girls were anxious to come with me, and I'll go right back and send them down."

CHAPTER II

SHEPHERD'S FERRY

Within a few months after my arrival at Las Palomas, there was a dance at Shepherd's Ferry. There was no necessity for an invitation to such local meets; old and young alike were expected and welcome, and a dance naturally drained the sparsely settled community of its inhabitants from forty to fifty miles in every direction. On the Nueces in 1875, the amusements of the countryside were extremely limited; barbecues, tournaments, and dancing covered the social side of ranch life, and whether given up or down our home river, or north on the Frio, so they were within a day's ride, the white element of Las Palomas could always be depended on to be present, Uncle Lance in the lead.

Shepherd's Ferry is somewhat of a misnomer, for the water in the river was never over knee-deep to a horse, except during freshets. There may have been a ferry there once; but from my advent on the river there was nothing but a store, the keeper of which also conducted a road-house for the accommodation of travelers. There was a fine grove for picnic purposes within easy reach, which was also frequently used for camp-meeting purposes. Gnarly old live-oaks spread their branches like a canopy over everything, while the sea-green moss hung from every limb and twig, excluding the light and lazily waving with every vagrant breeze. The fact that these grounds were also used for camp-meetings only proved the broad toleration of the people. On this occasion I distinctly remember that Miss Jean introduced a lady to me, who was the wife of an Episcopal minister, then visiting on a ranch near Oakville, and

ANDY ADAMS

I danced several times with her and found her very amiable.

On receipt of the news of the approaching dance at the ferry, we set the ranch in order. Fortunately, under seasonable conditions work on a cattle range is never pressing. A programme of work outlined for a certain week could easily be postponed a week or a fortnight for that matter; for this was the land of "la manana," and the white element on Las Palomas easily adopted the easy-going methods of their Mexican neighbors. So on the day everything was in readiness. The ranch was a trifle over thirty miles from Shepherd's, which was a fair half day's ride, but as Miss Jean always traveled by ambulance, it was necessary to give her an early start. Las Palomas raised fine horses and mules, and the ambulance team for the ranch consisted of four mealy-muzzled brown mules, which, being range bred, made up in activity what they lacked in size.

Tiburcio, a trusty Mexican, for years in the employ of Uncle Lance, was the driver of the ambulance, and at an early morning hour he and his mules were on their mettle and impatient to start. But Miss Jean had a hundred petty things to look after. The lunch - enough for a round-up - was prepared, and was safely stored under the driver's seat. Then there were her own personal effects and the necessary dressing and tidying, with Uncle Lance dogging her at every turn.

"Now, Sis," said he, "I want you to rig yourself out in something sumptuous, because I expect to make a killing with you at this dance. I'm almost sure that that Louisiana mule-drover will be there. You know you made quite an impression on him when he was through here two years ago. Well, I'll take a hand in the game this time, and if there's any marry in him, he'll have to lead trumps. I'm getting tired of having my dear sister trifled with by every passing drover. Yes, I am! The next one that hangs around Las Palomas, basking in your smiles, has got to declare his intentions whether he buys mules or not. Oh, you've got a brother, Sis, that'll look out for you. But you must play your part. Now, if that mule-buyer's there, shall I" -

"Why, certainly, brother, invite him to the ranch," replied Miss Jean, as she busied herself with the preparations. "It's so kind of you to look after me. I was listening to every word you said, and I've got my best bib and tucker in that hand box. And just you watch me dazzle that Mr. Mule-buyer. Strange you didn't tell me sooner about his being in the country. Here, take these boxes out to the ambulance. And, say, I put in the middle-sized coffee pot, and do you think two packages of ground coffee will be enough? All right, then. Now, where's my gloves?"

We were all dancing attendance in getting the ambulance off, but Uncle Lance never relaxed his tormenting, "Come, now, hurry up," said he, as Jean and himself led the way to the gate where the conveyance stood waiting; "for I want you to look your best this evening, and you'll be all tired out if you don't get a good rest before the dance begins. Now, in case the mule-buyer don't show up, how about Sim Oliver? You see, I can put in a good word there just as easily as not. Of course, he's a widower like myself, but you're no spring pullet - you wouldn't class among the buds - besides Sim branded eleven hundred calves last year. And the very last time I was talking to him, he allowed he'd crowd thirteen hundred close this year - big calf crop, you see. Now, just why he should go to the trouble to tell me all this, unless he had his eye on you, is one too many for me. But if you want me to cut him out of your string of eligibles, say the word, and I'll chouse him out. You just bet, little girl, whoever wins you has got to score right. Great Scott! but you have good taste in selecting perfumery. Um-ee! it makes me half drunk to walk alongside of you. Be sure and put some of that ointment on your kerchief when you get there."

"Really," said Miss Jean, as they reached the ambulance, "I wish you had made a little memorandum of what I'm expected to do - I'm all in a flutter this morning. You see, without your help my case is hopeless. But I think I'll try for the mule-buyer. I'm getting tired looking at these slab-sided cowmen. Now, just look at those mules - haven't had a harness on in a month. And Tiburcio can't hold four of them, nohow. Lance, it looks like you'd send one of the boys to drive me down to the ferry."

"Why, Lord love you, girl, those mules are as gentle as kittens; and you don't suppose I'm going to put some gringo over a veteran like Tiburcio. Why, that old boy used to drive for Santa Anna during the invasion in '36. Besides, I'm sending Theodore and Glenn on horseback as a bodyguard. Las Palomas is putting her best foot forward this morning in giving you a stylish turnout, with outriders in their Sunday livery. And those two boys are the best ropers on the ranch, so if the mules run off just give one of your long, keen screams, and the boys will rope and hog-tie every mule in the team. Get in now and don't make any faces about it."

It was pettishness and not timidity that ailed Jean Lovelace, for a pioneer woman like herself had of course no fear of horse-flesh. But the team was acting in a manner to unnerve an ordinary woman. With me clinging to the bits of the leaders, and a man each holding the wheelers, as they pawed the ground and surged about in their creaking harness, they were anything but gentle; but Miss Jean proudly took her seat; Tiburcio fingered the reins in placid contentment; there was a parting volley of admonitions from brother and sister - the latter was telling us where we would find our white shirts - when Uncle Lance signaled to us; and we sprang away from the team. The ambulance gave a lurch, forward, as the mules started on a run, but Tiburcio dexterously threw them on to a heavy bed of sand, poured the whip into them as they labored through it; they crossed the sand bed, Glenn Gallup and Theodore Quayle, riding, at their heads, pointed the team into the road, and they were off.

The rest of us busied ourselves getting up saddle horses and dressing for the occasion. In the latter we had no little trouble, for dress occasions like this were rare with us. Miss Jean had been thoughtful enough to lay our clothes out, but there was a busy borrowing of collars and collar buttons, and a blacking of boots which made the sweat stand out on our foreheads in beads. After we were dressed and ready to start, Uncle Lance could not be induced to depart from his usual custom, and wear his trousers outside his boots. Then we had to pull the boots off and polish them clear up to the ears in order to make him presentable. But we were in no particular hurry about starting, as we expected to out across the country and would overtake the ambulance at the mouth of the Arroyo Seco in time for the noonday lunch. There were six in our party, consisting of Dan Happersett, Aaron Scales, John Cotton, June Deweese, Uncle Lance, and myself. With the exception of Deweese, who was nearly twenty-five years old, the remainder of the boys on the ranch were young fellows, several of whom besides myself had not yet attained their majority. On ranch work, in the absence of our employer, June was recognized as the *segundo* of Los Palomas, owing to his age and his long employment on the ranch. He was a trustworthy man, and we younger lads entertained no envy towards him.

It was about nine o'clock when we mounted our horses and started. We jollied along in a party, or separated into pairs in cross-country riding, covering about seven miles an hour. "I remember," said Uncle Lance, as we were riding in a group, "the first time I was ever at Shepherd's Ferry. We had been down the river on a cow hunt for about three weeks and had run out of bacon. We had been eating beef, and venison, and antelope for a week until it didn't taste right any longer, so I sent the outfit on ahead and rode down to the store in the hope of getting a piece of bacon. Shepherd had just established the place at the time, and when I asked him if he had any bacon, he said he had, 'But is it good?' I inquired, and before he could reply an eight-year-old boy of his stepped between us, and throwing back his tow head, looked up into my face and said: 'Mister, it's a little the best I ever tasted.'"

"Now, June," said Uncle Lance, as we rode along, "I want you to let Henry Annear's wife strictly alone to-night. You know what a stink it raised all along the river, just because you danced with her once, last San Jacinto day. Of course, Henry made a fool of himself by trying to borrow a six-shooter and otherwise getting on the prod. And I'll admit that it don't take the best of eyesight to see that his wife to-day thinks more of your old boot than she does of Annear's wedding suit, yet her husband will be the last man to know it. No man can figure to a certainty on a woman. Three guesses is not enough, for she will and she won't, and she'll straddle the question or take the fence, and when you put a copper on her to win, she loses. God made them just that way, and I don't want to criticise His handiwork. But if my name is Lance Lovelace, and I'm sixty-odd years old, and this a chestnut horse that I'm riding, then Henry Annear's wife is an unhappy woman. But that fact, son, don't give you any license to stir up trouble between man and wife. Now, remember, I've warned you not to dance, speak to, or even notice her on this occasion. The chances are that that locoed fool will come heeled this time, and if you give him any excuse, he may burn a little powder."

June promised to keep on his good behavior, saying: "That's just what I've made up my mind to do. But look'ee here: Suppose he goes on the war path, you can't expect me to show the white feather, nor let him run any sandys over me. I loved his wife once and am not ashamed of it, and he knows it. And much as I want to obey you, Uncle Lance, if he attempts to stand up a bluff on me, just as sure as hell's hot there'll be a strange face or two in heaven."

I was a new man on the ranch and unacquainted with the facts, so shortly afterwards I managed to drop to the rear with Dan Happersett, and got the particulars. It seems that June and Mrs. Annear had not only been sweethearts, but that they had been engaged, and that the engagement had been broken within a month of the day set for their wedding, and that she had married Annear on a three weeks' acquaintance. Little wonder Uncle Lance took occasion to read the riot act to his *segundo* in the interests of peace. This was all news to me, but secretly I wished June courage and a good aim if it ever came to a show-down between them.

We reached the Arroyo Seco by high noon, and found the ambulance in camp and the coffee pot boiling. Under the direction of Miss Jean, Tiburcio had removed the seats from the conveyance, so as to afford seating capacity for over half our number. The lunch was spread under an old live-oak on the bank of the Nueces, making a cosy camp. Miss Jean had the happy knack of a good hostess, our twenty-mile ride had whetted our appetites, and we did ample justice to her tempting spread. After luncheon was over and while the team was being harnessed in, I noticed Miss Jean enticing Deweese off on one side, where the two held a whispered conversation, seated on an old fallen tree. As they returned, June was promising something which she had asked of him. And if there was ever a woman lived who could exact a promise that would be respected, Jean Lovelace was that woman; for she was like an elder sister to us all.

In starting, the ambulance took the lead as before, and near the middle of the afternoon we reached the ferry. The merry-makers were assembling from every quarter, and on our arrival possibly a hundred had come, which number was doubled by the time the festivities began. We turned our saddle and work stock into a small pasture, and gave ourselves over to the fast-gathering crowd. I was delighted to see that Miss Jean and Uncle Lance were accorded a warm welcome by every one, for I was somewhat of a stray on this new range. But when it became known that I was a recent addition to Las Palomas, the welcome was extended to me, which I duly appreciated.

The store and hostelry did a rushing business during the evening hours, for the dance did not begin until seven. A Mexican orchestra, consisting of a violin, an Italian harp, and two guitars, had come up from Oakville to furnish the music for the occasion. Just before the dance commenced, I noticed Uncle Lance greet a late arrival, and on my inquiring of June who he might be, I learned that the man was Captain Frank Byler from Lagarto, the drover Uncle Lance had been teasing Miss Jean about in the morning, and a man, as I learned later, who drove herds of horses north on the trail during the summer and during the winter drove mules and horses to Louisiana, for sale among the planters. Captain Byler was a good-looking, middle-aged fellow, and I made up my mind at once that he was due to rank as the lion of the evening among the ladies.

It is useless to describe this night of innocent revelry. It was a rustic community, and the people assembled were, with few exceptions, purely pastoral. There may have been earnest vows spoken under those spreading oaks - who knows? But if there were, the retentive ear which listened, and the cautious tongue which spake the vows, had no intention of having their confidences profaned on this page. Yet it was a night long to be remembered. Timid lovers sat apart, oblivious to the gaze of the merry revelers. Matrons and maidens vied with each other in affability to the sterner sex. I had a most enjoyable time.

I spoke Spanish well, and made it a point to cultivate the acquaintance of the leader of the orchestra. On his learning that I also played the violin, he promptly invited me to play a certain new waltz which he was desirous of learning. But I had no sooner taken the violin in my hand than the lazy rascal lighted a cigarette and strolled away, absenting himself for nearly an hour. But I was familiar with the simple dance music of the country, and played everything that was called for. My talent was quite a revelation to the boys of our ranch, and especially to the owner and mistress of Las Palomas. The latter had me play several old Colorado River favorites of hers, and I noticed that when she had the dashing Captain Byler for her partner, my waltzes seemed never long enough to suit her.

After I had been relieved, Miss Jean introduced me to a number of nice girls, and for the remainder of the evening I had no lack of partners. But there was one girl there whom I had not been introduced to, who always avoided my glance when I looked at her, but who, when we were in the same set and I squeezed her hand, had blushed just too lovely. When that dance was over, I went to Miss Jean for an introduction, but she did not know her, so I appealed to Uncle Lance, for I knew he could give the birth date of every girl present. We took a stroll through the crowd, and when I described her by her big eyes, he said in a voice so loud that I felt sure she must hear: "Why, certainly, I know her. That's Esther McLeod. I've trotted her on my knee a hundred times. She's the youngest girl of old man Donald McLeod who used to ranch over on the mouth of the San Miguel, north on the Frio. Yes, I'll give you an interslaption." Then in a subdued tone: "And if you can drop your rope on her, son, tie her good and fast, for she's good stock."

I was made acquainted as his latest adopted son, and inferred the old ranchero's approbation by many a poke in the ribs from him in the intervals between dances; for Esther and I danced every dance together until dawn. No one could charge me with neglect or inattention, for I close-herded her like a hired hand. She mellowed nicely towards me after the ice was broken, and with the limited time at my disposal, I made hay. When the dance broke up with the first signs of day, I saddled her horse and assisted her to mount, when I received the cutest little invitation, 'if ever I happened over on the Sau Miguel, to try and call.' Instead of beating about the bush, I assured her bluntly that if she ever saw me on Miguel Creek, it would be intentional; for I should have made the ride purely to see her. She blushed again in a way which sent a thrill through me. But on the Nueces in '75, if a fellow took a fancy to a girl there was no harm in showing it or telling her so.

I had been so absorbed during the latter part of the night that I had paid little attention to the rest of the Las Palomas outfit, though I occasionally caught sight of Miss Jean and the drover, generally dancing, sometimes promenading, and once had a glimpse of them tete-a-tete on a rustic settee in a secluded corner. Our employer seldom danced, but kept his eye on June Deweese in the interests of peace, for Annear and his wife were both present. Once while Esther and I were missing a dance over some light refreshment, I had occasion to watch June as he and Annear danced in the same set. I thought the latter acted rather surly, though Deweese was the acme of geniality, and was apparently having the time of his life as he tripped through the mazes of the dance. Had I not known of the deadly enmity existing between them, I could never have suspected anything but friendship, he was acting the part so perfectly. But then I knew he had given his plighted word to the master and mistress, and nothing but an insult or indignity could tempt him to break it.

On the return trip, we got the ambulance off before sunrise, expecting to halt and breakfast again at the Arroyo Seco. Aaron Scales and Dan Happersett acted as couriers to Miss Jean's conveyance, while the rest dallied behind, for there was quite a cavalcade of young folks going a distance our way. This gave Uncle Lance a splendid chance to quiz the girls in the party. I was riding with a Miss Wilson from Ramirena, who had come up to make a visit at a near-by ranch and incidentally attend the dance at Shepherd's. I admit that I was a little too much absorbed over another girl to be very entertaining, but Uncle Lance helped out by joining us. "Nice morning overhead, Miss Wilson," said he, on riding up. "Say, I've waited just as long as I'm going to for that invitation to your wedding which you promised me last summer. Now, I don't know so much about the young men down about Ramirena, but when I was a youngster back on the Colorado, when a boy loved a girl he married her, whether it was Friday or Monday, rain or shine. I'm getting tired of being put off with promises. Why, actually, I haven't been to a wedding in three years. What are we coming to?"

On reaching the road where Miss Wilson and her party separated from us, Uncle Lance returned to the charge: "Now, no matter how busy I am when I get your invitation, I don't care if the irons are in the fire and the cattle in the corral, I'll drown the fire and turn the cows out. And if Las Palomas has a horse that'll carry me, I'll merely touch the high places in coming. And when I get there I'm willing to do anything, - give the bride away, say grace, or carve the turkey. And what's more, I never kissed a bride in my life that didn't have good luck. Tell your pa you saw me. Good-by, dear."

On overtaking the ambulance in camp, our party included about twenty, several of whom were young ladies; but Miss Jean insisted that every one remain for breakfast, assuring them that she had abundance for all. After the impromptu meal was disposed of, we bade our adieus and separated to the four quarters. Before we had gone far, Uncle Lance rode alongside of me and said: "Tom, why didn't you tell me you was a fiddler? God knows you're lazy enough to be a good one, and you ought to be good on a bee course. But what made me warm to you last night was the way you built to Esther McLeod. Son, you set her cush about right. If you can hold sight on a herd of beeves on a bad night like you did her, you'll be a foreman some day. And she's not only good blood herself, but she's got cattle and land. Old man Donald, her father, was killed in the Confederate army. He was an honest Scotchman who kept Sunday and everything else he could lay his hands on. In all my travels I never met a man who could offer a longer prayer or take a bigger drink of whiskey. I remember the first time I ever saw him. He was serving on the grand jury, and I was a witness in a cattle-stealing case. He was a stranger to me, and we had just sat down at the same table at a hotel for dinner. We were on the point of helping ourselves, when the old Scot arose and struck the table a blow that made the dishes rattle. 'You heathens,' said he, 'will you partake of the bounty of your Heavenly Father without returning thanks?' We laid down our knives and forks like boys caught in a watermelon patch, and the old man asked a blessing. I've been at his house often. He was a good man, but Secession caught him and he never came back. So, Quirk, you see, a son-in-law will be a handy man in the family, and with the start you made last night I hope for good results." The other boys seemed to enjoy my embarrassment, but I said nothing in reply, being a new man with the outfit. We reached the ranch an hour before noon, two hours in advance of the ambulance; and the sleeping we did until sunrise the next morning required no lullaby.

CHAPTER III

LAS PALOMAS

There is something about those large ranches of southern Texas that reminds one of the old feudal system. The pathetic attachment to the soil of those born to certain Spanish land grants can only be compared to the European immigrant when for the last time he looks on the land of his birth before sailing. Of all this Las Palomas was typical. In the course of time several such grants had been absorbed into its baronial acres. But it had always been the policy of Uncle Lance never to disturb the Mexican population; rather he encouraged them to remain in his service. Thus had sprung up around Las Palomas ranch a little Mexican community numbering about a dozen families, who lived in *jacals* close to the main ranch buildings. They were simple people, and rendered their new master a feudal loyalty. There were also several small *ranchites* located on the land, where, under the Mexican regime, there had been pretentious adobe buildings. A number of families still resided at these deserted ranches, content in cultivating small fields or looking after flocks of goats and a few head of cattle, paying no rental save a service tenure to the new owner.

The customs of these Mexican people were simple and primitive. They blindly accepted the religious teachings imposed with fire and sword by the Spanish conquerors upon their ancestors. A padre visited them yearly, christening the babes, marrying the youth, shriving the penitent, and saying masses for the repose of the souls of the departed. Their social customs were in many respects unique. For instance, in courtship a young man was never allowed in the presence of his inamorata, unless in company of others, or under the eye of a chaperon. Proposals, even among the nearest of neighbors or most intimate of friends, were always made in writing, usually by the father of the young man to the parents of the girl, but in the absence of such, by a godfather or *padrino*. Fifteen days was the term allowed for a reply, and no matter how desirable the match might be, it was not accounted good taste to answer before the last day. The owner of Las Palomas was frequently called upon to act as *padrino* for his people, and so successful had he always been that the vaqueros on his ranch preferred his services to those of their own fathers. There was scarcely a vaquero at the home ranch but, in time past, had invoked his good offices in this matter, and he had come to be looked on as their patron saint.

The month of September was usually the beginning of the branding season at Las Palomas. In conducting this work, Uncle Lance was the leader, and with the white element already enumerated, there were twelve to fifteen vaqueros included in the branding outfit. The dance at Shepherd's had delayed the beginning of active operations, and a large calf crop, to say nothing of horse and mule colts, now demanded our attention and promised several months' work. The year before, Las Palomas had branded over four thousand calves, and the range was now dotted with the crop, awaiting the iron stamp of ownership.

The range was an open one at the time, compelling us to work far beyond the limits of our employer's land. Fortified with our own commissary, and with six to eight horses apiece in our mount, we scoured the country for a radius of fifty miles. When approaching another range, it was our custom to send a courier in advance to inquire of the ranchero when it would be convenient for him to give us a rodeo. A day would be set, when our outfit and the vaqueros of that range rounded up all the cattle watering at given points. Then we cut out the Las Palomas brand, and held them under herd or started them for the home ranch, where the calves were to be branded. In this manner we visited all the adjoining ranches, taking over a month to make the circuit of the ranges.

In making the tour, the first range we worked was that of rancho Santa Maria, south of our range and on the head of Tarancalous Creek. On approaching the ranch, as was customary, we prepared to encamp and ask for a rodeo. But in the choice of a vaquero to be dispatched on this mission, a spirited rivalry sprang up. When Uncle Lance learned that the rivalry amongst the vaqueros was meant to embarrass Enrique Lopez, who was *oso* to Anita, the pretty daughter of the corporal of Santa Maria, his matchmaking instincts came to the fore. Calling Enrique to one side, he made the vaquero confess that he had been playing for the favor of the senorita at Santa Maria. Then he dispatched Enrique on the mission, bidding him carry the choicest compliments of Las Palomas to every Don and Dona of Santa Maria. And Enrique was quite capable of adding a few embellishments to the old matchmaker's extravagant flatteries.

Enrique was in camp next morning, but at what hour of the night he had returned is unknown. The rodeo had been granted for the following day; there was a pressing invitation to Don Lance - unless he was willing to offend - to spend the idle day as the guest of Don Mateo. Enrique elaborated the invitation with a thousand adornments. But the owner of Las Palomas had lived nearly forty years among the Spanish-American people on the Nueces, and knew how to make allowances for the exuberance of the Latin tongue. There was no telling to what extent Enrique could have kept on delivering messages, but to his employer he was avoiding the issue.

"But did you get to see Anita?" interrupted Uncle Lance. Yes, he had seen her, but that was about all. Did not Don Lance know the customs among the Castilians? There was her mother ever present, or if she must absent herself, there was a bevy of *tias comadres* surrounding her, until the Dona Anita dare not even raise her eyes to meet his. "To perdition with such customs, no?" The freedom of a cow camp is a splendid opportunity to relieve one's mind upon prevailing injustices.

"Don't fret your cattle so early in the morning, son," admonished the wary matchmaker. "I've handled worse cases than this before. You Mexicans are sticklers on customs, and we must deal with our neighbors carefully. Before I show my hand in this, there's just one thing I want to know - is the girl willing? Whenever you can satisfy me on that point, Enrique, just call on the old man. But before that I won't stir a step. You remember what a time I had over Tiburcio's Juan - that's so, you were too young then. Well, June here remembers it. Why, the girl just cut up shamefully. Called Juan an Indian peon, and bragged about her Castilian family until you'd have supposed she was a princess of the blood royal. Why, it took her parents and myself a whole day to bring the girl around to take a sensible view of matters. On my soul, except that I didn't want to acknowledge defeat, I felt a dozen times like telling her to go straight up. And when she did marry you, she was as happy as a lark - wasn't she, Juan? But I like to have the thing over with in - well, say half an hour's time. Then we can have refreshments, and smoke, and discuss the prospects of the young couple."

Uncle Lance's question was hard to answer. Enrique had known the girl for several years, had danced with her on many a feast day, and never lost an opportunity to whisper the old, old story in her willing ear. Others had done the like, but the dark-eyed senorita is an adept in the art of coquetry, and there you are. But Enrique swore a great oath he would know. Yes, he would. He would lay siege to her as he had never done before. He would become *un oso grande*. Just wait until the branding was over and the fiestas of the Christmas season were on, and watch him dog her every step until he received her signal of surrender. Witness, all the saints, this row of Enrique Lopez, that the Dona Anita should have no peace of mind, no, not for one little minute, until she had made a complete capitulation. Then Don Lauce, the *padrino* of Las Palomas, would at once write the letter which would command the hand of the corporal's daughter. Who could refuse such a request, and what was a daughter of Santa Maria compared to a son of Las Palomas?

Tarancalous Creek ran almost due east, and rancho Santa Maria was located near its source, depending more on its wells for water supply than on the stream which only flowed for a few months during the year. Where the watering facilities were so limited the rodeo was an easy matter. A number of small round-ups at each established watering point, a swift cutting out of everything bearing the Las Palomas brand, and we moved on to the next rodeo, for we had an abundance of help at Santa Maria. The work was finished by the middle of the afternoon. After sending, under five or six men, our cut of several hundred cattle westward on our course, our outfit rode into rancho Santa Maria proper to pay our respects. Our wagon had provided an abundant dinner for our assistants and ourselves; but it would have been, in Mexican etiquette, extremely rude on our part not to visit the rancho and partake of a cup of coffee and a cigarette, thanking the ranchero on parting for his kindness in granting us the rodeo.

So when the last round-up was reached, Don Mateo and Uncle Lance turned the work over to their corporals, and in advance rode up to Santa Maria. The vaqueros of our ranch were anxious to visit the rancho, so it devolved on the white element to take charge of the cut. Being a stranger to Santa Maria, I was allowed to accompany our *segundo*, June Deweese, on an introductory visit. On arriving at the rancho, the vaqueros scattered among the *jacals* of their *amigos*, while June and myself were welcomed at the *casa primero*. There we found Uncle Lance partaking of refreshment, and smoking a cigarette as though he had been born a Senor Don of some ruling hacienda. June and I were seated at another table, where we were served with coffee, wafers, and home-made cigarettes. This was perfectly in order, but I could hardly control myself over the extravagant Spanish our employer was using in expressing the amity existing between Santa Maria and Las Palomas. In ordinary conversation, such as cattle and ranch affairs, Uncle Lance had a good command of Spanish; but on social and delicate topics some of his efforts were ridiculous in the extreme. He was well aware of his shortcomings, and frequently appealed to me to assist him. As a boy my playmates had been Mexican children, so that I not only spoke Spanish fluently but could also readily read and write it. So it was no surprise to me that, before taking our departure, my employer should command my services as an interpreter in driving an entering wedge. He was particular to have me assure our host and hostess of his high regard for them, and his hope that in the future even more friendly relations might exist between the two ranches. Had Santa Maria no young cavalier for the hand of some daughter of Las Palomas? Ah! there was the true bond for future friendships. Well, well, if the soil of this rancho was so impoverished, then the sons of Las Palomas must take the bit in their teeth and come courting to Santa Maria. And let Dona Gregoria look well to her daughters, for the young men of Las Palomas, true to their race, were not only handsome fellows but ardent lovers, and would be hard to refuse.

After taking our leave and catching up with the cattle, we pushed westward for the Ganso, our next stream of water. This creek was a tributary to the Nueces, and we worked down it several days, or until we had nearly a thousand cattle and were within thirty miles of home. Turning this cut over to June Deweese and a few vaqueros to take in to the ranch and brand, the rest of us turned westward and struck the Nueces at least fifty miles above Las Palomas. For the next few days our dragnet took in both sides of the Nueces, and when, on reaching the mouth of the Ganso, we were met by Deweese and the vaqueros we had another bunch of nearly a thousand ready. Dan Happersett was dispatched with the second bunch for branding, when we swung north to Mr. Booth's ranch on the Frio, where we rested a day. But there is little recreation on a cow hunt, and we were soon under full headway again. By the time we had worked down the Frio, opposite headquarters, we had too large a herd to carry conveniently, and I was sent in home with them, never rejoining the outfit until they reached Shepherd's Ferry. This was a disappointment to me, for I had hopes that when the outfit worked the range around the mouth of San Miguel, I might find some excuse to visit the McLeod ranch and see Esther. But after turning back up the home river to within twenty miles of the ranch, we again turned southward, covering the intervening ranches rapidly until we struck the Tarancalous about twenty-five miles east of Santa Maria.

We had spent over thirty days in making this circle, gathering over five thousand cattle, about one third of which were cows with calves by their sides. On the remaining gap in the circle we lost two days in waiting for rodeos, or gathering independently along the Tarancalous, and, on nearing the Santa Maria range, we had nearly fifteen hundred cattle. Our herd passed within plain view of the rancho, but we did not turn aside, preferring to make a dry camp for the night, some five or six miles further on our homeward course. But since we had used the majority of our *remuda* very hard that day, Uncle Lance dispatched Enrique and myself, with our wagon and saddle horses, by way of Santa Maria, to water our saddle stock and refill our kegs for camping purposes. Of course, the compliments of our employer to the ranchero of Santa Maria went with the *remuda* and wagon.

I delivered the compliments and regrets to Don Mateo, and asked the permission to water our saddle stock, which was readily granted. This required some time, for we had about a hundred and twenty-five loose horses with us, and the water had to be raised by rope and pulley from the pommel of a saddle horse. After watering the team we refilled our kegs, and the cook pulled out to overtake the herd, Enrique and I staying to water the *remuda*. Enrique, who was riding the saddle horse, while I emptied the buckets as they were hoisted to the surface, was evidently killing time. By his dilatory tactics, I knew the young rascal was delaying in the hope of getting a word with the Dona Anita. But it was getting late, and at the rate we were hoisting darkness would overtake us before we could reach the herd. So I ordered Enrique to the bucket, while I took my own horse and furnished the hoisting power. We were making some headway with the work, when a party of women, among them the Dona Anita, came down to the well to fill vessels for house use.

This may have been all chance - and then again it may not. But the gallant Enrique now outdid himself, filling jar after jar and lifting them to the shoulder of the bearer with the utmost zeal and amid a profusion of compliments. I was annoyed at the interruption in our work, but I could see that Enrique was now in the highest heaven of delight. The Dona Anita's mother was present, and made it her duty to notice that only commonplace formalities passed between her daughter and the ardent vaquero. After the jars were all filled, the bevy of women started on their return; but Dona Anita managed to drop a few feet to the rear of the procession, and, looking back, quietly took up one corner of her mantilla, and with a little movement, apparently all innocence, flashed a message back to the entranced Enrique. I was aware of the flirtation, but before I had made more of it Enrique sprang down from the abutment of the well, dragged me from my horse, and in an ecstasy of joy, crouching behind the abutments, cried: Had I seen the sign? Had I not noticed her token? Was my brain then so befuddled? Did I not understand the ways of the senoritas among his people? - that they always answered by a wave of the handkerchief, or the mantilla? Ave Maria, Tomas! Such stupidity! Why, to be sure, they could talk all day with their eyes.

A setting sun finally ended his confidences, and the watering was soon finished, for Enrique lowered the bucket in a gallop. On our reaching the herd and while we were catching our night horses, Uncle Lance strode out to the rope corral, with the inquiry, what had delayed us. "Nothing particular," I replied, and looked at Enrique, who shrugged his shoulders and repeated my answer. "Now, look here, you young liars," said the old ranchero; "the wagon has been in camp over an hour, and, admitting it did start before you, you had plenty of time to water the saddle stock and overtake it before it could possibly reach the herd. I can tell a lie myself, but a good one always has some plausibility. You rascals were up to some mischief, I'll warrant."

I had caught out my night horse, and as I led him away to saddle up, Uncle Lance, not content with my evasive answer, followed me. "Go to Enrique," I whispered; "he'll just bubble over at a good chance to tell you. Yes; it was the Dona Anita who caused the delay." A smothered chuckling shook the old man's frame, as he sauntered over to where Enrique was saddling. As the two led off the horse to picket in the gathering dusk, the ranchero had his arm around the vaquero's neck, and I felt that the old matchmaker would soon be in possession of the facts. A hilarious guffaw that reached me as I was picketing my horse announced that the story was out, and as the two returned to the fire Uncle Lance was slapping Enrique on the back at every step and calling him a lucky dog. The news spread through the camp like wild-fire, even to the vaqueros on night herd, who instantly began chanting an old love song. While Enrique and I were eating our supper, our employer paced backward and forward in meditation like a sentinel on picket, and when we had finished our meal, he joined us around the fire, inquiring of Enrique how soon the demand should be made for the corporal's daughter, and was assured that it could not be done too soon. "The padre only came once a year," he concluded, "and they must be ready."

"Well, now, this is a pretty pickle," said the old matchmaker, as he pulled his gray mustaches; "there isn't pen or paper in the outfit. And then we'll be busy branding on the home range for a month, and I can't spare a vaquero a day to carry a letter to Santa Maria. And besides, I might not be at home when the reply came. I think I'll just take the bull by the horns; ride back in the morning and set these old precedents at defiance, by arranging the match verbally. I can make the talk that this country is Texas now, and that under the new regime American customs are in order. That's what I'll do - and I'll take Tom Quirk with me for fear I bog down in my Spanish."

But several vaqueros, who understood some English, advised Enrique of what the old matchmaker proposed to do, when the vaquero threw his hands in the air and began sputtering Spanish in terrified disapproval. Did not Don Lance know that the marriage usages among his people were their most cherished customs? "Oh, yes, son," languidly replied Uncle Lance. "I'm some strong on the cherish myself, but not when it interferes with my plans. It strikes me that less than a month ago I heard you condemning to perdition certain customs of your people. Now, don't get on too high a horse - just leave it to Tom and me. We may stay a week, but when we come back we'll bring your betrothal with us in our vest pockets. There was never a Mexican born who can outhold me on palaver; and we'll eat every chicken on Santa Maria unless they surrender."

As soon as the herd had started for home the next morning, Uncle Lance and I returned to Santa Maria. We were extended a cordial reception by Don Mateo, and after the chronicle of happenings since the two rancheros last met had been reviewed, the motive of our sudden return was mentioned. By combining the vocabularies of my employer and myself, we mentioned our errand as delicately as possible, pleading guilty and craving every one's pardon for our rudeness in verbally conducting the negotiations. To our surprise, - for to Mexicans customs are as rooted as Faith, - Don Mateo took no offense and summoned Dona Gregoria. I was playing a close second to the diplomat of our side of the house, and when his Spanish failed him and he had recourse to English, it is needless to say I handled matters to the best of my ability. The Spanish is a musical, passionate language and well suited to love making, and though this was my first use of it for that purpose, within half an hour we had won the ranchero and his wife to our side of the question.

Then, at Don Mateo's orders, the parents of the girl were summoned. This involved some little delay, which permitted coffee being served, and discussion, over the cigarettes, of the commonplace matters of the country. There was beginning to be a slight demand for cattle to drive to the far north on the trails, some thought it was the sign of a big development, but neither of the rancheros put much confidence in the movement, etc., etc. The corporal and his wife suddenly made their appearance, dressed in their best, which accounted for the delay, and all cattle conversation instantly ceased. Uncle Lance arose and greeted the husky corporal and his timid wife with warm cordiality. I extended my greetings to the Mexican foreman, whom I had met at the rodeo about a month before. We then resumed our seats, but the corporal and his wife remained standing, and with an elegant command of his native tongue Don Mateo informed the couple of our mission. They looked at each other in bewilderment. Tears came into the wife's eyes. For a moment I pitied her. Indeed, the pathetic was not lacking. But the hearty corporal reminded his better half that her parents, in his interests, had once been asked for her hand under similar circumstances, and the tears disappeared. Tears are womanly; and I have since seen them shed, under less provocation, by fairer-skinned women than this simple, swarthy daughter of Mexico.

It was but natural that the parents of the girl should feign surprise and reluctance if they did not feel it. The Dona Anita's mother offered several trivial objections. Her daughter had never taken her into her confidence over any suitor. And did Anita really love Enrique Lopez of Las Palomas? Even if she did, could he support her, being but a vaquero? This brought Uncle Lance to the front. He had known Enrique since the day of his birth. As a five-year-old, and naked as the day he was born, had he not ridden a colt at branding time, twice around the big corral without being thrown? At ten, had he not thrown himself across a gateway and allowed a *caballada* of over two hundred wild range horses to jump over his prostrate body as they passed in a headlong rush through the gate? Only the year before at branding, when an infuriated bull had driven every vaquero out of the corrals, did not Enrique mount his horse, and, after baiting the bull out into the open, play with him like a kitten with a mouse? And when the bull, tiring, attempted to make his escape, who but Enrique had lassoed the animal by the fore feet, breaking his neck in the throw? The diplomat of Las Palomas dejectedly admitted that the bull was a prize animal, but could not deny that he himself had joined in the plaudits to the daring vaquero. But if there were a possible doubt that the Dona Anita did not love this son of Las Palomas, then Lance Lovelace himself would oppose the union. This was an important matter. Would Don Mateo be so kind as to summon the senorita?

The senorita came in response to the summons. She was a girl of possibly seventeen summers, several inches taller than her mother, possessing a beautiful complexion with large lustrous eyes. There was something fawnlike in her timidity as she gazed at those about the table. Dona Gregoria broke the news, informing her that the ranchero of Las Palomas had asked her hand in marriage for Enrique, one of his vaqueros. Did she love the man and was she willing to marry him? For reply the girl hid her face in the mantilla of her mother. With commendable tact Dona Gregoria led the mother and daughter into another room, from which the two elder women soon returned with a favorable reply. Uncle Lance arose and assured the corporal and his wife that their daughter would receive his special care and protection; that as long as water ran and grass grew, Las Palomas would care for her own children.

We accepted an invitation to remain for dinner, as several hours had elapsed since our arrival. In company with the corporal, I attended to our horses, leaving the two rancheros absorbed in a discussion of Texas fever, rumors of which were then attracting widespread attention in the north along the cattle trails. After dinner we took our leave of host and hostess, promising to send Enrique to Santa Maria at the earliest opportunity.

It was a long ride across country to Las Palomas, but striking a free gait, unencumbered as we were, we covered the country rapidly. I had somewhat doubted the old matchmaker's sincerity in making this match, but as we rode along he told me of his own marriage to Mary Bryan, and the one happy year of life which it brought him, mellowing into a mood of

　　　　ANDY ADAMS

seriousness which dispelled all doubts. It was almost sunset when we sighted in the distance the ranch buildings at Las Palomas, and half an hour later as we galloped up to assist the herd which was nearing the corrals, the old man stood in his stirrups and, waving his hat, shouted to his outfit: "Hurrah for Enrique and the Dona Anita!" And as the last of the cattle entered the corral, a rain of lassos settled over the smiling rascal and his horse, and we led him in triumph to the house for Miss Jean's blessing.

CHAPTER IV

CHRISTMAS

The branding on the home range was an easy matter. The cattle were compelled to water from the Nueces, so that their range was never over five or six miles from the river. There was no occasion even to take out the wagon, though we made a one-night camp at the mouth of the Ganso, and another about midway between the home ranch and Shepherd's Ferry, pack mules serving instead of the wagon. On the home range, in gathering to brand, we never disturbed the mixed cattle, cutting out only the cows and calves. On the round-up below the Ganso, we had over three thousand cattle in one rodeo, finding less than five hundred calves belonging to Las Palomas, the bulk on this particular occasion being steer cattle. There had been little demand for steers for several seasons and they had accumulated until many of them were fine beeves, five and six years old.

When the branding proper was concluded, our tally showed nearly fifty-one hundred calves branded that season, indicating about twenty thousand cattle in the Las Palomas brand. After a week's rest, with fresh horses, we re-rode the home range in squads of two, and branded any calves we found with a running iron. This added nearly a hundred more to our original number. On an open range like ours, it was not expected that everything would be branded; but on quitting, it is safe to say we had missed less than one per cent of our calf crop.

The cattle finished, we turned our attention to the branding of the horse stock. The Christmas season was approaching, and we wanted to get the work well in hand for the usual holiday festivities. There were some fifty *manadas* of mares belonging to Las Palomas, about one fourth of which were used for the rearing of mules, the others growing our saddle horses for ranch use. These bands numbered twenty to twenty-five brood mares each, and ranged mostly within twenty miles of the home ranch. They were never disturbed except to brand the colts, market surplus stock, or cut out the mature geldings to be broken for saddle use. Each *manada* had its own range, never trespassing on others, but when they were brought together in the corral there was many a battle royal among the stallions.

I was anxious to get the work over in good season, for I intended to ask for a two weeks' leave of absence. My parents lived near Cibollo Ford on the San Antonio River, and I made it a rule to spend Christmas with my own people. This year, in particular, I had a double motive in going home; for the mouth of San Miguel and the McLeod ranch lay directly on my route. I had figured matters down to a fraction; I would have a good excuse for staying one night going and another returning. And it would be my fault if I did not reach the ranch at an hour when an invitation to remain over night would be simply imperative under the canons of Texas hospitality. I had done enough hard work since the dance at Shepherd's to drive every thought of Esther McLeod out of my mind if that were possible, but as the time drew nearer her invitation to call was ever uppermost in my thoughts.

So when the last of the horse stock was branded and the work was drawing to a close, as we sat around the fireplace one night and the question came up where each of us expected to spend Christmas, I broached my plan. The master and mistress were expected at the Booth ranch on the Frio. Nearly all the boys, who had homes within two or three days' ride, hoped to improve the chance to make a short visit to their people. When, among the others, I also made my application for leave of absence, Uncle Lance turned in his chair with apparent surprise. "What's that? You want to go home? Well, now, that's a new one on me. Why, Tom, I never knew you had any folks; I got the idea, somehow, that you was won on a horse race. Here I had everything figured out to send you down to Santa Maria with Enrique. But I reckon with the ice broken, he'll have to swim out or drown. Where do your folks live?" I explained that they lived on the San Antonio River, northeast about one hundred and fifty miles. At this I saw my employer's face brighten. "Yes, yes, I see," said he musingly; "that will carry you past the widow McLeod's. You can go, son, and good luck to you."

I timed my departure from Las Palomas, allowing three days for the trip, so as to reach home on Christmas eve. By making a slight deviation, there was a country store which I could pass on the last day, where I expected to buy some presents for my mother and sisters. But I was in a pickle as to what to give Esther, and on consulting Miss Jean, I found that motherly elder sister had everything thought out in advance. There was an old Mexican woman, a pure Aztec Indian, at a ranchita belonging to Las Palomas, who was an expert in Mexican drawn work. The mistress of the home ranch had been a good patron of this old woman, and the next morning we drove over to the ranchita, where I secured half a dozen ladies' hand-kerchiefs, inexpensive but very rare.

I owned a private horse, which had run idle all summer, and naturally expected to ride him on this trip. But Uncle Lance evidently wanted me to make a good impression on the widow McLeod, and brushed my plans aside, by asking me as a favor to ride a certain black horse belonging to his private string. "Quirk," said he, the evening before my departure, "I wish you would ride Wolf, that black six-year-old in my mount. When that rascal of an Enrique saddle-broke him for me, he always mounted him with a free head and on the move, and now when I use him he's always on the fidget. So you just ride him over to the San Antonio and back, and see if you can't cure him of that restlessness. It may be my years, but I just despise a horse that's always dancing a jig when I want to mount him."

Glenn Gallup's people lived in Victoria County, about as far from Las Palomas as mine, and the next morning we set out down the river. Our course together only led a short distance, but we jogged along until noon, when we rested an hour and parted, Glenn going on down the river for Oakville, while I turned almost due north across country for the mouth of San Miguel. The black carried me that afternoon as though the saddle was empty. I was constrained to hold him in, in view of the long journey before us, so as not to reach the McLeod ranch too early. Whenever we struck cattle on our course, I rode through them to pass away the time, and just about sunset I cantered up to the McLeod ranch with a dash. I did not know a soul on the place, but put on a bold front and asked for Miss Esther. On catching sight of me, she gave a little start, blushed modestly, and greeted me cordially.

Texas hospitality of an early day is too well known to need comment; I was at once introduced to the McLeod household. It was rather a pretentious ranch, somewhat dilapidated in appearance - appearances are as deceitful on a cattle ranch as in the cut of a man's coat. Tony Hunter, a son-in-law of the widow, was foreman on the ranch, and during the course of the evening in the discussion of cattle matters, I innocently drew out the fact that their branded calf crop of that season amounted to nearly three thousand calves. When a similar question was asked me, I reluctantly admitted that the Las Palomas crop was quite a disappointment this year, only branding sixty-five hundred calves, but that our mule and horse colts ran nearly a thousand head without equals in the Nueces valley.

I knew there was no one there who could dispute my figures, though Mrs. McLeod expressed surprise at them. "Ye dinna say," said my hostess, looking directly at me over her spectacles, "that Las Palomas branded that mony calves thi' year? Why, durin' ma gudeman's life we always branded mair calves than did Mr. Lovelace. But then my husband would join the army, and I had tae depend on greasers tae do ma work, and oor kye grew up mavericks." I said nothing in reply, knowing it to be quite natural for a woman or inexperienced person to feel always the prey of the fortunate and far-seeing.

The next morning before leaving, I managed to have a nice private talk with Miss Esther, and thought I read my title clear, when she surprised me with the information that her mother contemplated sending her off to San Antonio to a private school for young ladies. Her two elder sisters had married against her mother's wishes, it seemed, and Mrs. McLeod was determined to give her youngest daughter an education and fit her for something better than being the wife of a common cow hand. This was the inference from the conversation which passed between us at the gate. But when Esther thanked me for the Christmas remembrance I had brought her, I felt that I would take a chance on her, win or lose. Assuring her that I would make it a point to call on my return, I gave the black a free rein and galloped out of sight.

I reached home late on Christmas eve. My two elder brothers, who also followed cattle work, had arrived the day before, and the Quirk family were once more united, for the first time in two years. Within an hour after my arrival, I learned from my brothers that there was to be a dance that night at a settlement about fifteen miles up the river. They were going, and it required no urging on their part to insure the presence of Quirk's three boys. Supper over, a fresh horse was furnished me, and we set out for the dance, covering the distance in less than two hours. I knew nearly every one in the settlement, and got a cordial welcome. I played the fiddle, danced with my former sweethearts, and, ere the sun rose in the morning, rode home in time for breakfast. During that night's revelry, I contrasted my former girl friends on the San Antonio with another maiden, a slip of the old Scotch stock, transplanted and nurtured in the sunshine and soil of the San Miguel. The comparison stood all tests applied, and in my secret heart I knew who held the whip hand over the passions within me.

As I expected to return to Las Palomas for the New Year, my time was limited to a four days' visit at home. But a great deal can be said in four days; and at the end I was ready to saddle my black, bid my adieus, and ride for the southwest. During my visit I was careful not to betray that I had even a passing thought of a sweetheart, and what parents would suspect that a rollicking, carefree young fellow of twenty could have any serious intentions toward a girl? With brothers too indifferent, and sisters too young, the secret was my own, though Wolf, my mount, as he put mile after mile behind us, seemed conscious that his mission to reach the San Miguel without loss of time was of more than ordinary moment. And a better horse never carried knight in the days of chivalry.

On reaching the McLeod ranch during the afternoon of the second day, I found Esther expectant; but the welcome of her mother was of a frigid order. Having a Scotch mother myself, I knew something of arbitrary natures, and met Mrs. McLeod's coolness with a fund of talk and stories; yet I could see all too plainly that she was determinedly on the defensive. I had my favorite fiddle with me which I was taking back to Las Palomas, and during the evening I played all the old Scotch ballads I knew and love songs of the highlands, hoping to soften her from the decided stand she had taken against me and my intentions. But her heritage of obstinacy was large, and her opposition strong, as several well-directed thrusts which reached me in vulnerable places made me aware, but I smiled as if they were flattering compliments. Several times I mentally framed replies only to smother them, for I was the stranger within her gates, and if she saw fit to offend a guest she was still within her rights.

But the next morning as I tarried beyond the reasonable hour for my departure, her wrath broke out in a torrent. "If ye dinna ken the way hame, Mr. Quirk, I'll show it ye," she said as she joined Esther and me at the hitch-rack, where we had been loitering for an hour. "And I dinna care muckle whaur ye gang, so ye get oot o' ma sight, and stay oot o' it. I thocht ye waur a ceevil stranger when ye bided wi' us last week, but noo I ken ye are something mair, ridin' your fine horses an' makin' presents tae ma lassie. That's a' the guid that comes o' lettin' her rin tae every dance at Shepherd's Ferry. Gang ben the house tae your wark, ye jade, an' let me attend tae this fine gentleman. Noo, sir, gin ye ony business onywhaur else, ye 'd aye better be ridin' tae it, for ye are no wanted here, ye ken."

"Why, Mrs. McLeod," I broke in politely. "You hardly know anything about me."

"No, an' I dinna wish it. You are frae Las Palomas, an' that's aye enough for me. I ken auld Lance Lovelace, an' those that bide wi' him. Sma' wonder he brands sae mony calves and sells mair kye than a' the ither ranchmen in the country. Ay, man, I ken him well."

I saw that I had a tartar to deal with, but if I could switch her invective on some one absent, it would assist me in controlling myself. So I said to the old lady: "Why, I've known Mr. Lovelace now almost a year, and over on the Nueces he is well liked, and considered a cowman whose word is as good as gold. What have you got against him?"

"Ower much, ma young freend. I kent him afore ye were born. I'm sorry tae say that while ma gudeman was alive, he was a frequent visitor at oor place. But we dinna see him ony mair. He aye keeps awa' frae here, and camps wi' his wagons when he's ower on the San Miguel to gather cattle. He was no content merely wi' what kye drifted doon on the Nueces, but warked a big outfit the year around, e'en comin' ower on the Frio an' San Miguel maverick huntin'. That's why he brands twice the calves that onybody else does, and owns a forty-mile front o' land on both sides o' the river. Ye see, I ken him weel."

"Well, isn't that the way most cowmen got their start?" I innocently inquired, well knowing it was. "And do you blame him for running his brand on the unowned cattle that roamed the range? I expect if Mr. Lovelace was my father instead of my employer, you wouldn't be talking in the same key," and with that I led my horse out to mount.

ANDY ADAMS

"Ye think a great deal o' yersel', because ye're frae Las Palomas. Aweel, no vaquero of auld Lance Lovelace can come sparkin' wi' ma lass. I've heard o' auld Lovelace's matchmaking. I'm told he mak's matches and then laughs at the silly gowks. I've twa worthless sons-in-law the noo, are here an' anither a stage-driver. Aye, they 're capital husbands for Donald McLeod's lassies, are they no? Afore I let Esther marry the first scamp that comes simperin' aroond here, I'll put her in a convent, an' mak' a nun o' the bairn. I gave the ither lassies their way, an' look at the reward. I tell ye I'm goin' to bar the door on the last one, an' the man that marries her will be worthy o' her. He winna be a vaquero frae Las Palomas either!"

I had mounted my horse to start, well knowing it was useless to argue with an angry woman. Esther had obediently retreated to the safety of the house, aware that her mother had a tongue and evidently willing to be spared its invective in my presence. My horse was fidgeting about, impatient to be off, but I gave him the rowel and rode up to the gate, determined, if possible, to pour oil on the troubled waters. "Mrs. McLeod," said I, in humble tones, "possibly you take the correct view of this matter. Miss Esther and I have only been acquainted a few months, and will soon forget each other. Please take me in the house and let me tell her good-by."

"No, sir. Dinna set foot inside o' this gate. I hope ye know ye're no wanted here. There's your road, the one leadin' south, an' ye'd better be goin', I'm thinkin'."

I held in the black and rode off in a walk. This was the first clean knock-out I had ever met. Heretofore I had been egotistical enough to hold my head rather high, but this morning it drooped. Wolf seemed to notice it, and after the first mile dropped into an easy volunteer walk. I never noticed the passing of time until we reached the river, and the black stopped to drink. Here I unsaddled for several hours; then went on again in no cheerful mood. Before I came within sight of Las Palomas near evening, my horse turned his head and nickered, and in a few minutes Uncle Lance and June Deweese galloped up and overtook me. I had figured out several very plausible versions of my adventure, but this sudden meeting threw me off my guard - and Lance Lovelace was a hard man to tell an undetected, white-faced lie. I put on a bold front, but his salutation penetrated it at a glance.

"What's the matter, Tom; any of your folks dead?"

"No."

"Sick?"

"No."

"Girl gone back on you?"

"I don't think."

"It's the old woman, then?"

"How do you know?"

"Because I know that old dame. I used to go over there occasionally when old man Donald was living, but the old lady - excuse me! I ought to have posted you, Tom, but I don't suppose it would have done any good. Brought your fiddle with you, I see. That's good. I expect the old lady read my title clear to you."

My brain must have been under a haze, for I repeated every charge she had made against him, not even sparing the accusation that he had remained out of the army and added to his brand by mavericking cattle.

"Did she say that?" inquired Uncle Lance, laughing. "Why, the old hellion! She must have been feeling in fine fettle!"

CHAPTER V

A PIGEON HUNT

The new year dawned on Las Palomas rich in promise of future content. Uncle Lance and I had had a long talk the evening before, and under the reasoning of the old optimist the gloom gradually lifted from my spirits. I was glad I had been so brutally blunt that evening, regarding what Mrs. McLeod had said about him; for it had a tendency to increase the rancher's aggressiveness in my behalf. "Hell, Tom," said the old man, as we walked from the corrals to the house, "don't let a little thing like this disturb you. Of course she'll four-flush and bluff you if she can, but you don't want to pay any more attention to the old lady than if she was some *pelado*. To be sure, it would be better to have her consent, but then" -

Glenn Gallup also arrived at the ranch on New Year's eve. He brought the report that wild pigeons were again roosting at the big bend of the river. It was a well-known pigeon roost, but the birds went to other winter feeding grounds, except during years when there was a plentiful sweet mast. This bend was about midway between the ranch and Shepherd's, contained about two thousand acres, and was heavily timbered with ash, pecan, and hackberry. The feeding grounds lay distant, extending from the encinal ridges on the Las Palomas lands to live-oak groves a hundred miles to the southward. But however far the pigeons might go for food, they always returned to the roosting place at night.

"That means pigeon pie," said Uncle Lance, on receiving Glenn's report. "Everybody and the cook can go. We only have a sweet mast about every three or four years in the encinal, but it always brings the wild pigeons. We'll take a couple of pack mules and the little and the big pot and the two biggest Dutch ovens on the ranch. Oh, you got to parboil a pigeon if you want a tender pie. Next to a fish fry, a good pigeon pie makes the finest eating going. I've made many a one, and I give notice right now that the making of the pie falls to me or I won't play. And another thing, not a bird shall be killed more than we can use. Of course we'll bring home a mess, and a few apiece for the Mexicans."

We had got up our horses during the forenoon, and as soon as dinner was over the white contingent saddled up and started for the roost. Tiburcio and Enrique accompanied us, and, riding leisurely, we reached the bend several hours before the return of the birds. The roost had been in use but a short time, but as we scouted through the timber there was abundant evidence of an immense flight of pigeons. The ground was literally covered with feathers; broken limbs hung from nearly every tree, while in one instance a forked hackberry had split from the weight of the birds.

We made camp on the outskirts of the timber, and at early dusk great flocks of pigeons began to arrive at their roosting place. We only had four shotguns, and, dividing into pairs, we entered the roost shortly after dark. Glenn Gallup fell to me as my pardner. I carried the gunny sack for the birds, not caring for a gun in such unfair shooting. The flights continued to arrive for fully an hour after we entered the roost, and in half a dozen shots we bagged over fifty birds. Remembering the admonition of Uncle Lance, Gallup refused to kill more, and we sat down and listened to the rumbling noises of the grove. There was a constant chattering of the pigeons, and as they settled in great flights in the trees overhead, whipping the branches with their wings in search of footing, they frequently fell to the ground at our feet.

Gallup and I returned to camp early. Before we had skinned our kill the others had all come in, disgusted with the ease with which they had filled their bags. We soon had two pots filled and on the fire parboiling, while Tiburcio lined two ovens with pastry, all ready for the baking. In a short time two horsemen, attracted by our fire, crossed the river below our camp and rode up.

"Hello, Uncle Lance," lustily shouted one of them, as he dismounted. "It's you, is it, that's shooting my pigeons? All right, sir, I'll stay all night and help you eat them. I had figured on riding back to the Frio to-night, but I've changed my mind. Got any horse hobbles here?" The two men, George Nathan and Hugh Trotter, were accommodated with hobbles, and after an exchange of commonplace news of the country, we settled down to story-telling. Trotter was a convivial acquaintance of Aaron Scales, quite a vagabond and consequently a story-teller. After Trotter had narrated a late dream, Scales unlimbered and told one of his own.

"I remember a dream I had several years ago, and the only way I can account for it was, I had been drinking more or less during the day. I dreamt I was making a long ride across a dreary desert, and towards night it threatened a bad storm. I began to look around for some shelter. I could just see the tops of a clump of trees beyond a hill, and rode hard to get to them, thinking that there might be a house amongst them. How I did ride! But I certainly must have had a poor horse, for I never seemed to get any nearer that timber. I rode and rode, but all this time, hours and hours it seemed, and the storm gathering and scattering raindrops falling, the timber seemed scarcely any nearer.

"At last I managed to reach the crest of the hill. Well, sir, there wasn't a tree in sight, only, under the brow of the hill, a deserted adobe *jacal*, and I rode for that, picketed my horse and went in. The *jacal* had a thatched roof with several large holes in it, and in the fireplace burned a roaring fire. That was some strange, but I didn't mind it and I was warming my hands before the fire and congratulating myself on my good luck, when a large black cat sprang from the outside into an open window, and said: 'Pardner, it looks like a bad night outside.'

"I eyed him a little suspiciously; but, for all that, if he hadn't spoken, I wouldn't have thought anything about it, for I like cats. He walked backward and forward on the window sill, his spine and tail nicely arched, and rubbed himself on either window jamb. I watched him some little time, and finally concluded to make friends with him. Going over to the window, I put out my hand to stroke his glossy back, when a gust of rain came through the window and the cat vanished into the darkness.

"I went back to the fire, pitying the cat out there in the night's storm, and was really sorry I had disturbed him. I didn't give the matter overmuch attention but sat before the fire, wondering who could have built it and listening to the rain outside, when all of a sudden Mr. Cat walked between my legs, rubbing himself against my boots, purring and singing. Once or twice I thought of stroking his fur, but checked myself on remembering he had spoken to me on the window sill. He would walk over and rub himself against the jambs of the fireplace, and then come back and rub himself against my boots friendly like. I saw him just as clear as I see those pots on the fire or these saddles lying around here. I was noting every move of his as he meandered around, when presently he cocked up an eye at me and remarked: 'Old sport, this is a fine fire we have here.'

"I was beginning to feel a little creepy, for I'd seen mad dogs and skunks, and they say a cat gets locoed likewise, and the cuss was talking so cleverly that I began to lose my regard for him. After a little while I concluded to pet him, for he didn't seem a bit afraid; but as I put out my hand to catch him, he nimbly hopped into the roaring fire and vanished. Then I did feel foolish. I had a good six-shooter, and made up my mind if he showed up again I'd plug him one for luck. I was growing sleepy, and it was getting late, so I concluded to spread down my saddle blankets and slicker before the fire and go to sleep.

While I was making down my bed, I happened to look towards the fire, when there was my black cat, with not even a hair singed. I drew my gun quietly and cracked away at him, when he let out the funniest little laugh, saying: 'You've been drinking, Aaron; you're nervous; you couldn't hit a flock of barns.'

"I was getting excited by this time, and cut loose on him rapidly, but he dodged every shot, jumping from the hearth to the mantel, from the mantel to an old table, from there to a niche in the wall, and from the niche clear across the room and out of the window. About then I was some nervous, and after a while lay down before the fire and tried to go to sleep.

"It was a terrible night outside - one of those nights when you can hear things; and with the vivid imagination I was enjoying then, I was almost afraid to try to sleep. But just as I was going into a doze, I raised up my head, and there was my cat walking up and down my frame, his back arched and his tail flirting with the slow sinuous movement of a snake. I reached for my gun, and as it clicked in cocking, he began raking my legs, sharpening his claws and growling like a tiger. I gave a yell and kicked him off, when he sprang up on the old table and I could see his eyes glaring at me. I emptied my gun at him a second time, and at every shot he crouched lower and crept forward as if getting ready to spring. When I had fired the last shot I jumped up and ran out into the rain, and hadn't gone more than a hundred yards before I fell into a dry wash. When I crawled out there was that d - d cat rubbing himself against my boot leg. I stood breathless for a minute, thinking what next to do, and the cat remarked: 'Wasn't that a peach of a race we just had!'

"I made one or two vicious kicks at him and he again vanished. Well, fellows, in that dream I walked around that old *jacal* all night in my shirt sleeves, and it raining pitchforks. A number of times I peeped in through the window or door, and there sat the cat on the hearth, in full possession of the shack, and me out in the weather. Once when I looked in he was missing, but while I was watching he sprang through a hole in the roof, alighting in the fire, from which he walked out gingerly, shaking his feet as if he had just been out in the wet. I shot away every cartridge I had at him, but in the middle of the shooting he would just coil up before the fire and snooze away.

"That night was an eternity of torment to me, and I was relieved when some one knocked on the door, and I awoke to find myself in a good bed and pounding my ear on a goose-hair pillow in a hotel in Oakville. Why, I wouldn't have another dream like that for a half interest in the Las Palomas brand. No, honest, if I thought drinking gave me that hideous dream, here would be one lad ripe for reform."

"It strikes me," said Uncle Lance, rising and lifting a pot lid, "that these birds are parboiled by this time. Bring me a fork, Enrique. Well, I should say they were. I hope hell ain't any hotter than that fire. Now, Tiburcio, if you have everything ready, we'll put them in the oven, and bake them a couple of hours."

Several of us assisted in fixing the fire and properly coaling the ovens. When this had been attended to, and we had again resumed our easy positions around the fire, Trotter remarked: "Aaron, you ought to cut drinking out of your amusements; you haven't the constitution to stand it. Now with me it's different. I can drink a week and never sleep; that's the kind of a build to have if you expect to travel and meet all comers. Last year I was working for a Kansas City man on the trail, and after the cattle were delivered about a hundred miles beyond, - Ellsworth, up in Kansas, - he sent us home by way of Kansas City. In fact, that was about the only route we could take. Well, it was a successful trip, and as this man was plum white, anyhow, he concluded to show us the sights around his burg. He was interested in a commission firm out at the stockyards, and the night we reached there all the office men, including the old man himself, turned themselves loose to show us a good time.

"We had been drinking alkali water all summer, and along about midnight they began to drop out until there was no one left to face the music except a little cattle salesman and myself. After all the others quit us, we went into a feed trough on a back street, and had a good supper. I had been drinking everything like a good fellow, and at several places there was no salt to put in the beer. The idea struck me that I would buy a sack of salt from this eating ranch and take it with me. The landlord gave me a funny look, but after some little parley went to the rear and brought out a five-pound sack of table salt.

"It was just what I wanted, and after paying for it the salesman and I started out to make a night of it. This yard man was a short, fat Dutchman, and we made a team for your whiskers. I carried the sack of salt under my arm, and the quantity of beer we killed before daylight was a caution. About daybreak, the salesman wanted me to go to our hotel and go to bed, but as I never drink and sleep at the same time, I declined. Finally he explained to me that he would have to be at the yards at eight o'clock, and begged me to excuse him. By this time he was several sheets in the wind, while I could walk a chalk line without a waver. Somehow we drifted around to the hotel where the outfit were supposed to be stopping, and lined up at the bar for a final drink. It was just daybreak, and between that Dutch cattle salesman and the barkeeper and myself, it would have taken a bookkeeper to have kept a check on the drinks we consumed - every one the last.

"Then the Dutchman gave me the slip and was gone, and I wandered into the office of the hotel. A newsboy sold me a paper, and the next minute a bootblack wanted to give me a shine. Well, I took a seat for a shine, and for two hours I sat there as full as a tick, and as dignified as a judge on the bench. All the newsboys and bootblacks caught on, and before any of the outfit showed up that morning to rescue me, I had bought a dozen papers and had my boots shined for the tenth time. If I'd been foxy enough to have got rid of that sack of salt, no one could have told I was off the reservation; but there it was under my arm. If ever I make another trip over the trail, and touch at Kansas City returning, I'll hunt up that cattle salesman, for he's the only man I ever met that can pace in my class."

"Did you hear that tree break a few minutes ago?" inquired Mr. Nathan. "There goes another one. It hardly looks possible that enough pigeons could settle on a tree to break it down. Honestly, I'd give a purty to know how many birds are in that roost to-night. More than there are cattle in Texas, I'll bet. Why, Hugh killed, with both barrels, twenty-two at one shot."

We had brought blankets along, but it was early and no one thought of sleeping for an hour yet. Mr. Nathan was quite a sportsman, and after he and Uncle Lance had discussed the safest method of hunting *javalina*, it again devolved on the boys to entertain the party with stories.

"I was working on a ranch once," said Glenn Gallup, "out on the Concho River. It was a stag outfit, there being few women then out Concho way. One day two of the boys were riding in home when an accident occurred. They had been shooting more or less during the morning, and one of them, named Bill Cook, had carelessly left the hammer of his six-shooter on a cartridge. As Bill jumped his horse over a dry *arroyo*, his pistol was thrown from its holster, and, falling on the hard ground, was discharged. The bullet struck him in the ankle, ranged upward, shattering the large bone in his leg into fragments, and finally lodged in the saddle.

"They were about five miles from camp when the accident happened. After they realized how bad he was hurt, Bill remounted his horse and rode nearly a mile; but the wound bled so then that the fellow with him insisted on his getting off and lying on the ground while he went into the ranch for a wagon. Well, it's to be supposed that he lost no time riding in, and I was sent to San Angelo for a doctor. It was just noon when I got off. I had to ride thirty miles. Talk about your good horses - I had one that day. I took a free gait from the start, but the last ten miles was the fastest, for I covered the entire distance in less than three hours. There was a doctor in the town who'd been on the frontier all of his life, and was used to such calls. Well, before dark that evening we drove into the ranch.

"They had got the lad into the ranch, had checked the flow of blood and eased the pain by standing on a chair and pouring water on the wound from a height. But Bill looked pale as a ghost from the loss of blood. The doctor gave the leg a single look, and, turning to us, said: 'Boys, she has to come off.'

"The doctor talked to Bill freely and frankly, telling him that it was the only chance for his life. He readily consented to the operation, and while the doctor was getting him under the influence of opiates we fixed up an operating table. When all was ready, the doctor took the leg off below the knee, cursing us generally for being so sensitive to cutting and the sight of blood. There was quite a number of boys at the ranch, but it affected them all alike. It was interesting to watch him cut and tie arteries and saw the bones, and I think I stood it better than any of them. When the operation was over, we gave the fellow the best bed the ranch afforded and fixed him up comfortable. The doctor took the bloody stump and wrapped it up in an old newspaper, saying he would take it home with him.

"After supper the surgeon took a sleep, saying we would start back to town by two o'clock, so as to be there by daylight. He gave instructions to call him in case Bill awoke, but he hoped the boy would take a good sleep. As I had left my horse in town, I was expected to go back with him. Shortly after midnight the fellow awoke, so we aroused the doctor, who reported him doing well. The old Doc sat by his bed for an hour and told him all kinds of stories. He had been a surgeon in the Confederate army, and from the drift of his talk you'd think it was impossible to kill a man without cutting off his head.

"'Now take a young fellow like you,' said the doctor to his

patient, 'if he was all shot to pieces, just so the parts would hang together, I could fix him up and he would get well. You have no idea, son, how much lead a young man can carry.' We had coffee and lunch before starting, the doctor promising to send me back at once with necessary medicines.

"We had a very pleasant trip driving back to town that night. The stories he could tell were like a song with ninety verses, no two alike. It was hardly daybreak when we reached San Angelo, rustled out a sleepy hostler at the livery stable where the team belonged, and had the horses cared for; and as we left the stable the doctor gave me his instrument case, while he carried the amputated leg in the paper. We both felt the need of a bracer after our night's ride, so we looked around to see if any saloons were open. There was only one that showed any signs of life, and we headed for that. The doctor was in the lead as we entered, and we both knew the barkeeper well. This barkeeper was a practical joker himself, and he and the doctor were great hunting companions. We walked up to the bar together, when the doctor laid the package on the counter and asked: 'Is this good for two drinks?' The barkeeper, with a look of expectation in his face as if the package might contain half a dozen quail or some fresh fish, broke the string and unrolled it. Without a word he walked straight from behind the bar and out of the house. If he had been shot himself he couldn't have looked whiter.

"The doctor went behind the bar and said: 'Glenn, what are you going to take?' 'Let her come straight, doctor,' was my reply, and we both took the same. We had the house all to ourselves, and after a second round of drinks took our leave. As we left by the front door, we saw the barkeeper leaning against a hitching post half a block below. The doctor called to him as we were leaving: 'Billy, if the drinks ain't on you, charge them to me.'"

The moon was just rising, and at Uncle Lance's suggestion we each carried in a turn of wood. Piling a portion of it on the fire, the blaze soon lighted up the camp, throwing shafts of light far into the recesses of the woods around us. "In another hour," said Uncle Lance, recoaling the oven lids, "that smaller pie will be all ready to serve, but we'll keep the big one for breakfast. So, boys, if you want to sit up awhile longer, we'll have a midnight lunch, and then all turn in for about forty winks." As the oven lid was removed from time to time to take note of the baking, savory odors of the pie were wafted to our anxious nostrils. On the intimation that one oven would be ready in an hour, not a man suggested blankets, and, taking advantage of the lull, Theodore Quayle claimed attention.

"Another fellow and myself," said Quayle, "were knocking around Fort Worth one time seeing the sights. We had drunk until it didn't taste right any longer. This chum of mine was queer in his drinking. If he ever got enough once, he didn't want any more for several days: you could cure him by offering him plenty. But with just the right amount on board, he was a hail fellow. He was a big, ambling, awkward cuss, who could be led into anything on a hint or suggestion. We had been knocking around the town for a week, until there was nothing new to be seen.

"Several times as we passed a millinery shop, kept by a little blonde, we had seen her standing at the door. Something - it might have been his ambling walk, but, anyway, something - about my chum amused her, for she smiled and watched him as we passed. He never could walk along beside you for any distance, but would trail behind and look into the windows. He could not be hurried - not in town. I mentioned to him that he had made a mash on the little blond milliner, and he at once insisted that I should show her to him. We passed down on the opposite side of the street and I pointed out the place. Then we walked by several times, and finally passed when she was standing in the doorway talking to some customers. As we came up he straightened himself, caught her eye, and tipped his hat with the politeness of a dancing master. She blushed to the roots of her hair, and he walked on very erect some little distance, then we turned a corner and held a confab. He was for playing the whole string, discount or no discount, anyway.

"An excuse to go in was wanting, but we thought we could invent one; however, he needed a drink or two to facilitate his thinking and loosen his tongue. To get them was easier than the excuse; but with the drinks the motive was born. 'You wait here,' said he to me, 'until I go round to the livery stable and get my coat off my saddle.' He never encumbered himself with extra clothing. We had not seen our horses, saddles, or any of our belongings during the week of our visit. When he returned he inquired, 'Do I need a shave?'

"'Oh, no,' I said, 'you need no shave. You may have a drink too many, or lack one of having enough. It's hard to make a close calculation on you.'

"'Then I'm all ready,' said he, 'for I've just the right gauge of steam.' He led the way as we entered. It was getting dark and the shop was empty of customers. Where he ever got the manners, heaven only knows. Once inside the door we halted, and she kept a counter between us as she approached. She ought to have called the police and had us run in. She was probably scared, but her voice was fairly steady as she spoke. 'Gentlemen, what can I do for you?'

"'My friend here,' said he, with a bow and a wave of the hand, 'was unfortunate enough to lose a wager made between us. The terms of the bet were that the loser was to buy a new hat for one of the dining-room girls at our hotel. As we are leaving town to-morrow, we have just dropped in to see if you have anything suitable. We are both totally incompetent to decide on such a delicate matter, but we will trust entirely to your judgment in the selection.' The milliner was quite collected by this time, as she asked: 'Any particular style? - and about what price?'

"'The price is immaterial,' said he disdainfully. 'Any man who will wager on the average weight of a train-load of cattle, his own cattle, mind you, and miss them twenty pounds, ought to pay for his lack of judgment. Don't you think so, Miss - er - er. Excuse me for being unable to call your name - but - but - '

'De Ment is my name,' said she with some little embarrassment.

"'Livingstone is mine,' said he with a profound bow,' and this gentleman is Mr. Ochiltree, youngest brother of Congressman Tom. Now regarding the style, we will depend entirely upon your selection. But possibly the loser is entitled to some choice in the matter. Mr. Ochiltree, have you any preference in regard to style?'

"'Why, no, I can generally tell whether a hat becomes a lady or not, but as to selecting one I am at sea. We had better depend on Miss De Ment's judgment. Still, I always like an abundance of flowers on a lady's hat. Whenever a girl walks down the street ahead of me, I like to watch the posies, grass, and buds on her hat wave and nod with the motion of her walk. Miss De Ment, don't you agree with me that an abundance of flowers becomes a young lady? And this girl can't be over twenty.'

"'Well, now,' said she, going into matters in earnest, 'I can scarcely advise you. Is the young lady a brunette or blonde?'

"'What difference does that make?' he innocently asked.

"'Oh,' said she, smiling, 'we must harmonize colors. What would suit one complexion would not become another. What color is her hair?'

"'Nearly the color of yours,' said he. 'Not so heavy and lacks the natural wave which yours has - but she's all right. She can ride a string of my horses until they all have sore backs. I tell you she is a cute trick. But, say, Miss De Ment, what do you think of a green hat, broad brimmed, turned up behind and on one side, long black feathers run round and turned up behind, with a blue bird on the other side swooping down like a pigeon hawk, long tail feathers and an arrow in its beak? That strikes me as about the mustard. What do you think of that kind of a hat, dear?'

"'Why, sir, the colors don't harmonize,' she replied, blushing.

"'Theodore, do you know anything about this harmony of colors? Excuse me, madam, - and I crave your pardon, Mr. Ochiltree, for using your given name, - but really this harmony of colors is all French to me.'

"'Well, if the young lady is in town, why can't you have her drop in and make her own selection?' suggested the blond milliner. He studied a moment, and then awoke as if from a trance. 'Just as easy as not; this very evening or in the morning. Strange we didn't think of that sooner. Yes; the landlady of the hotel can join us, and we can count on your assistance in selecting the hat.' With a number of comments on her attractive place, inquiries regarding trade, and a flattering compliment on having made such a charming acquaintance, we edged towards the door. 'This evening then, or in the morning at the farthest, you may expect another call, when my friend must pay the penalty of his folly by settling the bill. Put it on heavy.' And he gave her a parting wink.

"Together we bowed ourselves out, and once safe in the street he said: 'Didn't she help us out of that easy? If she wasn't a blonde, I'd go back and buy her two hats for suggesting it as she did.'

"'Rather good looking too,' I remarked.

"'Oh, well, that's a matter of taste. I like people with red blood in them. Now if you was to saw her arm off, it wouldn't bleed; just a little white water might ooze out, possibly. The best-looking girl I ever saw was down in the lower Rio Grande country, and she was milking a goat. Theodore, my dear fellow, when I'm led blushingly to the altar, you'll be proud of my choice. I'm a judge of beauty.'"

It was after midnight when we disposed of the first oven of pigeon pot-pie, and, wrapping ourselves in blankets, lay down around the fire. With the first sign of dawn, we were aroused by Mr. Nathan and Uncle Lance to witness the return flight of the birds to their feeding grounds. Hurrying to the nearest opening, we saw the immense flight of pigeons blackening the sky overhead. Stiffened by their night's rest, they flew low; but the beauty and immensity of the flight overawed us, and we stood in mute admiration, no one firing a shot. For fully a half-hour the flight continued, ending in a few scattering birds.

CHAPTER VI

SPRING OF '76

The spring of '76 was eventful at Las Palomas. After the pigeon hunt, Uncle Lance went to San Antonio to sell cattle for spring delivery. Meanwhile, Father Norquin visited the ranch and spent a few days among his parishioners, Miss Jean acting the hostess in behalf of Las Palomas. The priest proved a congenial fellow of the cloth, and among us, with Miss Jean's countenance, it was decided not to delay Enrique's marriage; for there was no telling when Uncle Lance would return. All the arrangements were made by the padre and Miss Jean, the groom-to-be apparently playing a minor part in the preliminaries. Though none of the white element of the ranch were communicants of his church, the priest apparently enjoyed the visit. At parting, the mistress pressed a gold piece into his chubby palm as the marriage fee for Enrique; and, after naming a day for the ceremony, the padre mounted his horse and left us for the Tarancalous, showering his blessings on Las Palomas and its people.

During the intervening days before the wedding, we overhauled an unused *jacal* and made it habitable for the bride and groom. The *jacal* is a crude structure of this semi-tropical country, containing but a single room with a shady, protecting stoop. It is constructed by standing palisades on end in a trench. These constitute the walls. The floor is earthen, while the roof is thatched with the wild grass which grows rank in the overflow portions of the river valley. It forms a serviceable shelter for a warm country, the peculiar roofing equally defying rain and the sun's heat. Under the leadership of the mistress of the ranch, assisted by the Mexican women, the *jacal* was transformed into a rustic bower; for Enrique was not only a favorite among the whites, but also among his own people. A few gaudy pictures of Saints and the Madonna ornamented the side walls, while in the rear hung the necessary crucifix. At the time of its building the *jacal* had been blessed, as was customary before occupancy, and to Enrique's reasoning the potency of the former sprinkling still held good.

Weddings were momentous occasions among the Mexican population at Las Palomas. In outfitting the party to attend Enrique's wedding at Santa Maria, the ranch came to a stand-still. Not only the regular ambulance but a second conveyance was required to transport the numerous female relatives of the groom, while the men, all in gala attire, were mounted on the best horses on the ranch. As none of the whites attended, Deweese charged Tiburcio with humanity to the stock, while the mistress admonished every one to be on his good behavior. With greetings to Santa Maria, the wedding party set out. They were expected to return the following evening, and the ranch was set in order to give the bride a rousing reception on her arrival at Las Palomas. The largest place on the ranch was a warehouse, and we shifted its contents in such a manner as to have quite a commodious ball-room. The most notable decoration of the room was an immense heart-shaped figure, in which was worked in live-oak leaves the names of the two ranches, flanked on either side with the American and Mexican flags. Numerous other decorations, expressing welcome to the bride, were in evidence on every hand. Tallow was plentiful at Las Palomas, and candles were fastened at every possible projection.

The mounted members of the wedding party returned near the middle of the afternoon. According to reports, Santa Maria had treated them most hospitably. The marriage was simple, but the festivities following had lasted until dawn. The returning guests sought their *jacals* to snatch a few hours' sleep before the revelry would be resumed at Las Palomas. An hour before sunset the four-mule ambulance bearing the bride and groom drove into Las Palomas with a flourish. Before leaving the bridal couple at their own *jacal*, Tiburcio halted the ambulance in front of the ranch-house for the formal welcome. In the absence of her brother, Miss Jean officiated in behalf of Las Palomas, tenderly caressing the bride. The boys monopolized her with their congratulations and welcome, which delighted Enrique. As for the bride, she seemed at home from the first, soon recognizing me as the *padrino segundo* at the time of her betrothal.

Quite a delegation of the bride's friends from Santa Maria accompanied the party on their return, from whom were chosen part of the musicians for the evening - violins and guitars in the hands of the native element of the two ranches making up a pastoral orchestra. I volunteered my services; but so much of the music was new to me that I frequently excused myself for a dance with the senoritas. In the absence of Uncle Lance, our *segundo*, June Deweese, claimed the first dance of the evening with the bride. Miss Jean lent only the approval of her presence, not participating, and withdrawing at an early hour. As all the American element present spoke Spanish slightly, that became the language of the evening. But, further than to countenance with our presence the festivities, we were out of place, and, ere midnight, all had excused themselves with the exception of Aaron Scales and myself. On the pleadings of Enrique, I remained an hour or two longer, dancing with his bride, or playing some favorite selection for the delighted groom.

Several days after the wedding Uncle Lance returned. He had been successful in contracting a trail herd of thirty-five hundred cattle, and a *remuda* of one hundred and twenty-five saddle horses with which to handle them. The contract called for two thousand two-year-old steers and fifteen hundred threes. There was a difference of four dollars a head in favor of the older cattle, and it was the ranchero's intention to fill the latter class entirely from the Las Palomas brand. As to the younger cattle, neighboring ranches would be invited to deliver twos in filling the contract, and if any were lacking, the home ranch would supply the deficiency. Having ample range, the difference in price was an inducement to hold the younger cattle. To keep a steer another year cost nothing, while the ranchero returned convinced that the trail might soon furnish an outlet for all surplus cattle. In the matter of the horses, too, rather than reduce our supply of saddle stock below the actual needs of the ranch, Uncle Lance concluded to buy fifty head in making up the *remuda*. There were several hundred geldings on the ranch old enough for saddle purposes, but they would be as good as useless in handling cattle the first year after breaking.

As this would be the first trail herd from Las Palomas, we naturally felt no small pride in the transaction. According to contract, everything was to be ready for final delivery on the twenty-fifth of March. The contractors, Camp & Dupree, of Fort Worth, Texas, were to send their foreman two weeks in advance to receive, classify, and pass upon the cattle and saddle stock. They were exacting in their demands, yet humane and reasonable. In making up the herd no cattle were to be corralled at night, and no animal would be received which had been roped. The saddle horses were to be treated likewise. These conditions would put into the saddle every available man on the ranch as well as on the ranchitas. But we looked eagerly forward to the putting up of the herd. Letters were written and dispatched to a dozen ranches within striking distance, inviting them to turn in two-year-old steers at the full contract price. June Deweese was sent out to buy fifty saddle horses, which would fill the required standard, "fourteen hands or better, serviceable and gentle broken." I was dispatched to Santa Maria, to invite Don Mateo Gonzales to participate in the contract. The range of every saddle horse on the ranch was located, so that we could gather them, when wanted, in a day. Less than a month's time now remained before the delivery day, though we did not expect to go into camp for actual gathering until the arrival of the trail foreman.

In going and returning from San Antonio my employer had traveled by stage. As it happened, the driver of the up-stage out of Oakville was Jack Martin, the son-in-law of Mrs. McLeod. He and Uncle Lance being acquainted, the old ranchero's matchmaking instincts had, during the day's travel, again forged to the front. By roundabout inquiries he had elicited the information that Mrs. McLeod had, immediately after the holidays, taken Esther to San Antonio and placed her in school. By innocent artful suggestions of his interest in the welfare of the family, he learned the name of the private school of which Esther was a pupil. Furthermore, he cultivated the good will of the driver in various ways over good cigars, and at parting assured him on returning he would take the stage so as to have the pleasure of his company on the return trip - the highest compliment that could be paid a stage-driver.

From several sources I had learned that Esther had left the ranch for the city, but on Uncle Lance's return I got the full particulars. As a neighboring ranchman, and bearing self-invented messages from the family, he had the assurance to call at the school. His honest countenance was a passport any-where, and he not only saw Esther but prevailed on her teachers to give the girl, some time during his visit in the city, a half holiday. The interest he manifested in the girl won his request, and the two had spent an afternoon visiting the parks and other points of interest. It is needless to add that he made hay in my behalf during this half holiday. But the most encouraging fact that he unearthed was that Esther was disgusted with her school life and was homesick. She had declared that if she ever got away from school, no power on earth could force her back again.

"Shucks, Tom," said he, the next morning after his return, as we were sitting in the shade of the corrals waiting for the *remuda* to come in, "that poor little country girl might as well be in a penitentiary as in that school. She belongs on these prairies, and you can't make anything else out of her. I can read between the lines, and any one can see that her education is finished. When she told me how rudely her mother had treated you, her heart was an open book and easily read. Don't you lose any sleep on how you stand in her affections - that's all serene. She'll he home on a spring vacation, and that'll be your chance. If I was your age, I'd make it a point to see that she didn't go back to school. She'll run off with you rather than that. In the game of matrimony, son, you want to play your cards boldly and never hesitate to lead trumps."

To further matters, when returning by stage my employer had ingratiated himself into the favor of the driver in many ways, and urged him to send word to Mrs. McLeod to turn in her two-year-olds on his contract. A few days later her foreman and son-in-law, Tony Hunter, rode down to Las Palomas, anxious for the chance to turn in cattle. There had been little opportunity for several years to sell steers, and when a chance like this came, there would have been no trouble to fill half a dozen contracts, as supply far exceeded demand.

Uncle Lance let Mrs. McLeod's foreman feel that in allotting her five hundred of the younger cattle, he was actuated by old-time friendship for the family. As a mark of special consideration he promised to send the trail foreman to the San Miguel to pass on the cattle on their home range, but advised the foreman to gather at least seven hundred steers, allowing for two hundred to be culled or cut back. Hunter remained over night, departing the next morning, delighted over his allowance of cattle and the liberal terms of the contract.

It was understood that, in advance of his outfit, the trail foreman would come down by stage, and I was sent into Oakville with an extra saddle horse to meet him. He had arrived the day previous, and we lost no time in starting for Las Palomas. This trail foreman was about thirty years of age, a quiet red-headed fellow, giving the name of Frank Nancrede, and before we had covered half the distance to the ranch I was satisfied that he was a cowman. I always prided myself on possessing a good eye for brands, but he outclassed me, reading strange brands at over a hundred yards, and distinguishing cattle from horse stock at a distance of three miles.'

We got fairly well acquainted before reaching the ranch, but it was impossible to start him on any subject save cattle. I was able to give him a very good idea of the *remuda*, which was then under herd and waiting his approval, and I saw the man brighten into a smile for the first time on my offering to help him pick out a good mount for his own saddle. I had a vague idea of what the trail was like, and felt the usual boyish attraction for it; but when I tried to draw him out in regard to it, he advised me, if I had a regular job on a ranch, to let trail work alone.

We reached the ranch late in the evening and I introduced Nancrede to Uncle Lance, who took charge of him. We had established a horse camp for the trail *remuda*, north of the river, and the next morning the trail foreman, my employer, and June Deweese, rode over to pass on the saddle stock. The *remuda* pleased him, being fully up to the contract standard, and he accepted it with but a single exception. This exception tickled Uncle Lance, as it gave him an opportunity to annoy his sister about Nancrede, as he did about every other cowman or drover who visited the ranch. That evening, as I was chatting with Miss Jean, who was superintending the Mexican help milking at the cow pen, Uncle Lance joined us.

"Say, Sis," said he, "our man Nancrede is a cowman all right. I tried to ring in a 'hipped' horse on him this morning, - one hip knocked down just the least little bit, - but he noticed it and refused to accept him. Oh, he's got an eye in his head all right. So if you say so, I'll give him the best horse on the ranch in old Hippy's place. You're always making fun of slab-sided cowmen; he's pony-built enough to suit you, and I kind o' like the color of his hair myself. Did you notice his neck? - he'll never tie it if it gets broken. I like a short man; if he stubs his toe and falls down he doesn't reach halfway home. Now, if he has as good cow sense in receiving the herd as he had on the *remuda*, I'd kind o' like to have him for a brother-in-law. I'm getting a little too old for active work and would like to retire, but June, the durn fool, won't get married, and about the only show I've got is to get a husband for you. I'd as lief live in Hades as on a ranch without a woman on it. What do you think of him?"

"Why, I think he's an awful nice fellow, but he won't talk. And besides, I'm not baiting my hook for small fish like trail foremen; I was aiming to keep my smiles for the contractors. Aren't they coming down?"

"Well, they might come to look the herd over before it starts out. Now, Dupree is a good cowman, but he's got a wife already. And Camp, the financial man of the firm, made his money peddling Yankee clocks. Now, you don't suppose for a moment I'd let you marry him and carry you away from Las Palomas. Marry an old clock peddler? - not if he had a million! The idea! If they come down here and I catch you smiling on old Camp, I'll set the hounds on you. What you want to do is to set your cap for Nancrede. Of course, you're ten years the elder, but that needn't cut any figure. So just burn a few smiles on the red-headed trail foreman! You know you can count on your loving brother to help all he can."

The conversation was interrupted by our *segundo* and the trail foreman riding up to the cow pen. The two had been up the river during the afternoon, looking over the cattle on the range, for as yet we had not commenced gathering. Nancrede was very reticent, discovering a conspicuous lack of words to express his opinion of what cattle Deweese had shown him.

The second day after the arrival of the trail foreman, we divided our forces into two squads and started out to gather our three-year-olds. By the ranch records, there were over two thousand steers of that age in the Las Palomas brand. Deweese took ten men and half of the ranch saddle horses and went up above the mouth of the Ganso to begin gathering. Uncle Lance took the remainder of the men and horses and went down the river nearly to Shepherd's, leaving Dan Happersett and three Mexicans to hold and night-herd the trail *remuda.* Nancrede declined to stay at the ranch and so joined our outfit on the down-river trip. We had postponed the gathering until the last hour, for every day improved the growing grass on which our mounts must depend for subsistence, and once we started, there would be little rest for men or horses.

The younger cattle for the herd were made up within a week after the invitations were sent to the neighboring ranches. Naturally they would be the last cattle to be received and would come in for delivery between the twentieth and the last of the month. With the plans thus outlined, we started our gathering. Counting Nancrede, we had twelve men in the saddle in our down-river outfit. Taking nothing but three-year-olds, we did not accumulate cattle fast; but it was continuous work, every man, with the exception of Uncle Lance, standing a guard on night-herd. The first two days we only gathered about five hundred steers. This number was increased by about three hundred on the third day, and that evening Dan Happersett with a vaquero rode into camp and reported that Nancrede's outfit had arrived from San Antonio. He had turned the *remuda* over to them on their arrival, sending the other two Mexicans to join Deweese above on the river.

The fourth day finished the gathering. Nancrede remained with us to the last, making a hand which left no doubt in any one's mind that he was a cowman from the ground up. The last round-up on the afternoon of the fourth day, our outriders sighted the vaqueros from Deweese's outfit, circling and drifting in the cattle on their half of the circle. The next morning the two camps were thrown together on the river opposite the ranch. Deweese had fully as many cattle as we had, and when the two cuts had been united and counted, we lacked but five head of nineteen hundred. Several of Nancrede's men joined us that morning, and within an hour, under the trail foreman's directions, we cut back the overplus, and the cattle were accepted.

Under the contract we were to road-brand them, though Nancrede ordered his men to assist us in the work. Under ordinary circumstances we should also have vented the ranch brand, but owing to the fact that this herd was to be trailed to

Abilene, Kansas, and possibly sold beyond that point, it was unnecessary and therefore omitted. We had a branding chute on the ranch for grown cattle, and the following morning the herd was corralled and the road-branding commenced. The cattle were uniform in size, and the stamping of the figure '4' over the holding "Lazy L" of Las Palomas, moved like clockwork. With a daybreak start and an abundance of help the last animal was ironed up before sundown. As a favor to Nancrede's outfit, their camp being nearly five miles distant, we held them the first night after branding.

No sooner had the trail foreman accepted our three-year-olds than he and Glen Gallup set out for the McLeod ranch on the San Miguel. The day our branding was finished, the two returned near midnight, reported the San Miguel cattle accepted and due the next evening at Las Palomas. By dawn Nancrede and myself started for Santa Maria, the former being deficient in Spanish, the only weak point, if it was one, in his make-up as a cowman. We were slightly disappointed in not finding the cattle ready to pass upon at Santa Maria. That ranch was to deliver seven hundred, and on our arrival they had not even that number under herd. Don Mateo, an easy-going ranchero, could not understand the necessity of such haste. What did it matter if the cattle were delivered on the twenty-fifth or twenty-seventh? But I explained as delicately as I could that this was a trail man, whose vocabulary did not contain *manana*. In interpreting for Nancrede, I learned something of the trail myself: that a herd should start with the grass and move with it, keeping the freshness of spring, day after day and week after week, as they trailed northward. The trail foreman assured Don Mateo that had his employers known that this was to be such an early spring, the herd would have started a week sooner.

By impressing on the ranchero the importance of not delaying this trail man, we got him to inject a little action into his corporal. We asked Don Mateo for horses and, joining his outfit, made three rodeos that afternoon, turning into the cattle under herd nearly two hundred and fifty head by dark that evening. Nancrede spent a restless night, and at dawn, as the cattle were leaving the bed ground, he and I got an easy count on them and culled them down to the required number before breakfasting. We had some little trouble explaining to Don Mateo the necessity of giving the bill of sale to my employer, who, in turn, would reconvey the stock to the contractors. Once the matter was made clear, the accepted cattle were started for Las Palomas. When we overtook them an hour afterward, I instructed the corporal, at the instance of the red-headed foreman, to take a day and a half in reaching the ranch; that tardiness in gathering must not be made up by a hasty drive to the point of delivery; that the animals must be treated humanely.

On reaching the ranch we found that Mr. Booth and some of his neighbors had arrived from the Frio with their contingent. They had been allotted six hundred head, and had brought down about two hundred extra cattle in order to allow some choice in accepting. These were the only mixed brands that came in on the delivery, and after they had been culled down and accepted, my employer appointed Aaron Scales as clerk. There were some five or six owners, and Scales must catch the brands as they were freed from the branding chute. Several of the owners kept a private tally, but not once did they have occasion to check up the Marylander's decisions. Before the branding of this hunch was finished, Wilson, from Ramirena, rode into the ranch and announced his cattle within five miles of Las Palomas. As these were the last two hundred to be passed upon, Nancrede asked to have them in sight of the ranch by sun-up in the morning.

On the arrival of the trail outfit from San Antonio, they brought a letter from the contractors, asking that a conveyance meet them at Oakville, as they wished to see the herd before it started. Tiburcio went in with the ambulance to meet them, and they reached the ranch late at night. On their arrival twenty-six hundred of the cattle had already been passed upon, branded, and were then being held by Nancrede's outfit across the river at their camp. Dupree, being a practical cowman, understood the situation; but Camp was restless and uneasy as if he expected to find the cattle in the corrals at the ranch. Camp was years the older of the two, a pudgy man with a florid complexion and nasal twang, and kept the junior member busy answering his questions. Uncle Lance enjoyed the situation, jollying his sister about the elder contractor and quietly inquiring of the red-haired foreman how and where Dupree had picked him up.

The contractors had brought no saddles with them, so the ambulance was the only mode of travel. As we rode out to receive the Wilson cattle the next morning, Uncle Lance took advantage of the occasion to jolly Nancrede further about the senior member of the firm, the foreman smiling appreciatingly. "The way your old man talked last night," said he, "you'd think he expected to find the herd in the front yard. Too bad to disappoint him; for then he could have looked them over with a lantern from the gallery of the house. Now, if they had been Yankee clocks instead of cattle, why, he'd been right at home, and could have taken them in the house and handled them easily. It certainly beats the dickens why some men want to break into the cattle business. It won't surprise me if he asks you to trail the herd past the ranch so he can see them. Well, you and Dupree will have to make him some *dinero* this summer or you will lose him for a partner. I can see that sticking out."

We received and branded the two hundred Wilson cattle that forenoon, sending them to the main herd across the river. Mr. Wilson and Uncle Lance were great cronies, and as the latter was feeling in fine fettle over the successful fulfillment of his contract, he was tempted also to jolly his neighbor ranchero over his cattle, which, by the way, were fine. "Nate," said he to Mr. Wilson, "it looks like you'd quit breeding goats and rear cattle instead. Honest, if I didn't know your brand, I'd swear some Mexican raised this bunch. These Fort Worth cowmen are an easy lot, or yours would never have passed under the classification."

An hour before noon, Tomas Martines, the corporal of Santa Maria, rode up to inquire what time we wished his cattle at the corrals. They were back several miles, and he could deliver them on an hour's notice. One o'clock was agreed upon, and, never dismounting, the corporal galloped away to his herd. "Quirk," said Nancrede to me, noticing the Mexican's unaccustomed air of enterprise, "if we had that fellow under us awhile we'd make a cow-hand out of him. See the wiggle he gets on himself now, will you?" Promptly at the hour, the herd were counted and corralled, Don Mateo Gonzales not troubling to appear, which was mystifying to the North Texas men, but Uncle Lance explained that a mere incident like selling seven hundred cattle was not sufficient occasion to arouse the ranchero of Santa Maria when his corporal could attend to the business.

That evening saw the last of the cattle branded. The herd was completed and ready to start the following morning. The two contractors were driven across the river during the afternoon to look over the herd and *remuda*. At the instance of my employer, I wrote a letter of congratulation to Don Mateo, handing it to his corporal, informing him that in the course of ten days a check would he sent him in payment. Uncle Lance had fully investigated the financial standing of the contractors, but it was necessary for him to return with them to San Antonio for a final settlement.

The ambulance made an early start for Oakville on the morning of the twenty-sixth, carrying the contractors and my employer, and the rest of us rode away to witness the start of the herd. Nancrede's outfit numbered fifteen, - a cook, a horse wrangler, himself, and twelve outriders. They comprised an odd mixture of men, several barely my age, while others were gray-haired and looked like veteran cow-hands. On leaving the Nueces valley, the herd was strung out a mile in length, and after riding with them until they reached the first hills, we bade them good-by. As we started to return Frank Nancrede made a remark to June Deweese which I have often recalled: "You fellows may think this is a snap; but if I had a job on as good a ranch as Las Palomas, you'd never catch me on a cattle trail."

CHAPTER VII

SAN JACINTO DAY

A few days later, when Uncle Lance returned from San Antonio, we had a confidential talk, and he decided not to send me with the McLeod check to the San Miguel. He had reasons of his own, and I was dispatched to the Frio instead, while to Enrique fell the pleasant task of a similar errand to Santa Maria. In order to grind an axe, Glenn Gallup was sent down to Wilson's with the settlement for the Ramirena cattle, which Uncle Lance made the occasion of a jovial expression of his theory of love-making. "Don't waste any words with old man Nate," said he, as he handed Glenn the check; "but build right up to Miss Jule. Holy snakes, boy, if I was your age I would make her dizzy with a big talk. Tell her you're thinking of quitting Las Palomas and driving a trail herd yourself next year. Tell it big and scary. Make her eyes fairly bulge out, and when you can't think of anything else, tell her she's pretty."

I spent a day or two at the Booth ranch, and on my return found the Las Palomas outfit in the saddle working our horse stock. Yearly we made up new *manadas* from the two-year-old fillies. There were enough young mares to form twelve bands of about twenty-five head each. In selecting these we were governed by standard colors, bays, browns, grays, blacks, and sorrels forming separate *manadas*, while all mongrel colors went into two bands by themselves. In the latter class there was a tendency for the colors of the old Spanish stock, - coyotes, and other hybrid mixtures, - after being dormant for generations, to crop out again. In breaking these fillies into new bands, we added a stallion a year or two older and of

ANDY ADAMS

acceptable color, and they were placed in charge of a trusty vaquero, whose duty was to herd them for the first month after being formed. The Mexican in charge usually took the band round the circuit of the various ranchitas, corralling his charge at night, drifting at will, so that by the end of the month old associations would be severed, and from that time the stallion could be depended on as herdsman.

In gathering the fillies, we also cut out all the geldings three years old and upward to break for saddle purposes. There were fully two hundred of these, and the month of April was spent in saddle-breaking this number. They were a fine lot of young horses, and under the master eye of two perfect horsemen, our *segundo* and employer, every horse was broken with intelligence and humanity. Since the day of their branding as colts these geldings had never felt the touch of a human hand; and it required more than ordinary patience to overcome their fear, bring them to a condition of submission, and make serviceable ranch horses out of them. The most difficult matter was in overcoming their fear. It was also necessary to show the mastery of man over the animal, though this process was tempered with humanity. We had several circular, sandy corrals into which the horse to be broken was admitted for the first saddling. As he ran round, a lasso skillfully thrown encircled his front feet and he came down on his side. One fore foot was strapped up, a hackamore or bitless bridle was adjusted in place, and he was allowed to arise. After this, all depended on the patience and firmness of the handler. Some horses yielded to kind advances and accepted the saddle within half an hour, not even offering to pitch, while others repelled every kindness and fought for hours. But in handling the gelding of spirit, we could always count on the help of an extra saddler.

While this work was being done, the herd of geldings was held close at hand. After the first riding, four horses were the daily allowance of each rider. With the amount of help available, this allowed twelve to fifteen horses to the man, so that every animal was ridden once in three or four days. Rather than corral, we night-herded, penning them by dawn and riding our first horse before sun-up. As they gradually yielded, we increased our number to six a day and finally before the breaking was over to eight. When the work was finally over they were cut into *remudas* of fifty horses each, furnished a gentle bell mare, when possible with a young colt by her side, and were turned over to a similar treatment as was given the fillies in forming *manadas*. Thus the different *remudas* at Las Palomas always took the name of the bell mare, and when we were at work, it was only necessary for us to hobble the princess at night to insure the presence of her band in the morning.

When this month's work was two thirds over, we enjoyed a holiday. All good Texans, whether by birth or adoption, celebrate the twenty-first of April, - San Jacinto Day. National holidays may not always he observed in sparsely settled communities, but this event will remain a great anniversary until the sons and daughters of the Lone Star State lose their patriotism or forget the blessings of liberty. As Shepherd's Ferry was centrally located, it became by common consent the meeting-point for our local celebration. Residents from the Frio and San Miguel and as far south on the home river as Lagarto, including the villagers of Oakville, usually lent their presence on this occasion. The white element of Las Palomas was present without an exception. As usual, Miss Jean went by ambulance, starting the afternoon before and spending the night at a ranch above the ferry. Those remaining made a daybreak start, reaching Shepherd's by ten in the morning.

While on the way from the ranch to the ferry, I was visited with some misgivings as to whether Esther McLeod had yet returned from San Antonio. At the delivery of San Miguel's cattle at Las Palomas, Miss Jean had been very attentive to Tony Hunter, Esther's brother-in-law, and through him she learned that Esther's school closed for the summer vacation on the fifteenth of April, and that within a week afterward she was expected at home. Shortly after our reaching the ferry, a number of vehicles drove in from Oakville. One of these conveyances was an elaborate six-horse stage, owned by Bethel & Oxenford, star route mail contractors between San Antonio and Brownsville, Texas. Seated by young Oxenford's side in the driver's box sat Esther McLeod, while inside the coach was her sister, Mrs. Martin, with the senior member of the firm, his wife, and several other invited guests. I had heard something of the gallantry of young Jack Oxenford, who was the nephew of a carpet-bag member of Congress, and prided himself on being the best whip in the country. In the latter field I would gladly have yielded him all honors, but his attentions to Esther were altogether too marked to please either me or my employer. I am free to admit that I was troubled by this turn of affairs. The junior mail contractor made up in egotism what he lacked in appearance, and no doubt had money to burn, as star route mail contracting was profitable those days, while I had nothing but my monthly wages. To make matters more embarrassing, a blind man could have read Mrs. Martin's approval of young Oxenford.

The programme for the forenoon was brief - a few patriotic songs and an oration by a young lawyer who had come up from Corpus Christi for the occasion. After listening to the opening song, my employer and I took a stroll down by the river, as we were too absorbed in the new complications to pay proper attention to the young orator.

"Tom," said Uncle Lance, as we strolled away from the grove, "we are up against the real thing now. I know young Oxenford, and he's a dangerous fellow to have for a rival, if he really is one. You can't tell much about a Yankee, though, for he's usually egotistical enough to think that every girl in the country is breaking her neck to win him. The worst of it is, this young fellow is rich - he's got dead oodles of money and he's making more every hour out of his mail contracts. One good thing is, we understand the situation, and all's fair in love and war. You can see, though, that Mrs. Martin has dealt herself a hand in the game. By the dough on her fingers she proposes to have a fist in the pie. Well, now, son, we'll give them a run for their money or break a tug in the effort. Tom, just you play to my lead to-day and we'll see who holds the high cards or knows best how to play them. If I can cut him off, that'll be your chance to sail in and do a little close-herding yourself."

We loitered along the river bank until the oration was concluded, my employer giving me quite an interesting account of my rival. It seems that young Oxenford belonged to a family then notoriously prominent in politics. He had inherited quite a sum of money, and, through the influence of his congressional uncle, had been fortunate enough to form a partnership with Bethel, a man who knew all the ropes in mail contracting. The senior member of the firm knew how to shake the tree, while the financial resources of the junior member and the political influence of his uncle made him a valuable man in gathering the plums on their large field of star route contracts. Had not exposure interrupted, they were due to have made a large fortune out of the government.

On our return to the picnic grounds, the assembly was dispersing for luncheon. Miss Jean had ably provided for the occasion, and on reaching our ambulance on the outer edge of the grove, Tiburcio had coffee all ready and the boys from the home ranch began to straggle in for dinner. Miss Jean had prevailed on Tony Hunter and his wife, who had come down on horseback from the San Miguel, to take luncheon with us, and from the hearty greetings which Uncle Lance extended to the guests of his sister, I could see that the owner and mistress of Las Palomas were diplomatically dividing the house of McLeod. I followed suit, making myself agreeable to Mrs. Hunter, who was but very few years the elder of Esther. Having spent a couple of nights at their ranch, and feeling a certain comradeship with her husband, I decided before dinner was over that I had a friend and ally in Tony's wife. There was something romantic about the young matron, as any one could see, and since the sisters favored each other in many ways, I had hopes that Esther might not overvalue Jack Oxenford's money.

After luncheon, as we were on our way to the dancing arbor, we met the Oakville party with Esther in tow. I was introduced to Mrs. Martin, who, in turn, made me acquainted with her friends, including her sister, perfectly unconscious that we were already more than mere acquaintances. From the demure manner of Esther, who accepted the introduction as a matter of course, I surmised she was concealing our acquaintance from her sister and my rival. We had hardly reached the arbor before Uncle Lance created a diversion and interested the mail contractors with a glowing yarn about a fine lot of young mules he had at the ranch, large enough for stage purposes. There was some doubt expressed by the stage men as to their size and weight, when my employer invited them to the outskirts of the grove, where he would show them a sample in our ambulance team. So he led them away, and I saw that the time had come to play to my employer's lead. The music striking up, I claimed Esther for the first dance, leaving Mrs. Martin, for the time being, in charge of her sister and Miss Jean. Before the first waltz ended I caught sight of all three of the ladies mingling in the dance. It was a source of no small satisfaction to me to see my two best friends, Deweese and Gallup, dancing with the married sisters, while Miss Jean was giving her whole attention to her partner, Tony Hunter. With the entire Las Palomas crowd pulling strings in my interest, and Father, in the absence of Oxenford, becoming extremely gracious, I grew bold and threw out my chest like the brisket on a beef steer.

I permitted no one to separate me from Esther. We started the second dance together, but no sooner did I see her sister, Mrs. Martin, whirl by us in the polka with Dan Happersett, than I suggested that we drop out and take a stroll. She consented, and we were soon out of sight, wandering in a labyrinth of lover's lanes which abounded throughout this live-oak grove. On reaching the outskirts of the picnic grounds, we came to an extensive opening in which our saddle horses were picketed. At a glance Esther recognized Wolf, the horse I had ridden the Christmas before when passing their ranch. Being a favorite saddle horse of the old ranchero, he was reserved for special occasions, and Uncle Lance had ridden him down to Shepherd's on this holiday. Like a bird freed from a cage, the ranch girl took to the horses and insisted on a little ride. Since her proposal alone prevented my making a similar suggestion, I allowed myself to be won over, but came near getting caught in protesting. "But you told me at the ranch that Wolf was one of ten in your Las Palomas mount," she poutingly protested.

"He is," I insisted, "but I have loaned him to Uncle Lance for the day."

"Throw the saddle on him then - I'll tell Mr. Lovelace when we return that I borrowed his horse when he wasn't looking."

Had she killed the horse, I felt sure that the apology would have been accepted; so, throwing saddles on the black and my own mount, we were soon scampering down the river. The inconvenience of a man's saddle, or the total absence of any, was a negligible incident to this daughter of the plains. A mile down the river, we halted and watered the horses. Then, crossing the stream, we spent about an hour circling slowly about on the surrounding uplands, never being over a mile from the picnic grounds. It was late for the first flora of the season, but there was still an abundance of blue bonnets. Dismounting, we gathered and wove wreaths for our horses' necks, and wandered picking the Mexican strawberries which grew plentifully on every hand.

But this was all preliminary to the main question. When it came up for discussion, this one of Quirk's boys made the talk of his life in behalf of Thomas Moore. Nor was it in vain. When Esther apologized for the rudeness her mother had shown me at her home, that afforded me the opening for which I was longing. We were sitting on a grassy hummock, weaving garlands, when I replied to the apology by declaring my intention of marrying her, with or without her mother's consent. Unconventional as the declaration was, to my surprise she showed neither offense nor wonderment. Dropping the flowers with which we were working, she avoided my gaze, and, turning slightly from me, began watching our horses, which had strayed away some distance. But I gave her little time for meditation, and when I aroused her from her reverie, she rose, saying, "We'd better go back - they'll miss us if we stay too long."

Before complying with her wish, I urged an answer; but she, artfully avoiding my question, insisted on our immediate return. Being in a quandary as to what to say or do, I went after the horses, which was a simple proposition. On my return, while we were adjusting the garlands about the necks of our mounts, I again urged her for an answer, but in vain. We stood for a moment between the two horses, and as I lowered my hand on my knee to afford her a stepping-stone in mounting, I thought she did not offer to mount with the same alacrity as she had done before. Something flashed through my addled mind, and, withdrawing the hand proffered as a mounting block, I clasped the demure maiden closely in my arms. What transpired has no witnesses save two saddle horses, and as Wolf usually kept an eye on his rider in mounting, I dropped the reins and gave him his freedom rather than endure his scrutiny. When we were finally aroused from this delicious trance, the horses had strayed away fully fifty yards, but I had received a favorable answer, breathed in a voice so low and tender that it haunts me yet.

As we rode along, returning to the grove, Esther requested that our betrothal be kept a profound secret. No doubt she had good reasons, and it was quite possible that there then existed some complications which she wished to conceal, though I avoided all mention of any possible rival. Since she was not due to return to her school before September, there seemed ample time to carry out our intentions of marrying. But as we jogged along, she informed me that after spending a few weeks with her sister in Oakville, it was her intention to return to the San Miguel for the summer. To allay her mother's distrust, it would be better for me not to call at the ranch. But this was easily compensated for when she suggested making several visits during the season with the Vaux girls, chums of hers, who lived on the Frio about thirty miles due north of Las Palomas. This was fortunate, since the Vaux ranch and ours were on the most friendly terms.

We returned by the route by which we had left the grounds. I repicketed the horses and we were soon mingling again with the revelers, having been absent little over an hour. No one seemed to have taken any notice of our absence. Mrs. Martin, I rejoiced to see, was still in tow of her sister and Miss Jean, and from the circle of Las Palomas courtiers who surrounded the ladies, I felt sure they had given her no opportunity even to miss her younger sister. Uncle Lance was the only member of our company absent, but I gave myself no uneasiness about him, since the mail contractors were both likewise missing. Rejoining our friends and assuming a nonchalant air, I flattered myself that my disguise was perfect.

During the remainder of the afternoon, in view of the possibility that Esther might take her sister, Mrs. Martin, into our secret and win her as an ally, I cultivated that lady's acquaintance, dancing with her and leaving nothing undone to foster her friendship. Near the middle of the afternoon, as the three sisters, Miss Jean, and I were indulging in light refreshment at a booth some distance from the dancing arbor, I sighted my employer, Dan Happersett, and the two stage men returning from the store. They passed near, not observing us, and from the defiant tones of Uncle Lance's voice, I knew they had been tampering with the 'private stock' of the merchant at Shepherd's. "Why, gentlemen," said he, "that ambulance team is no exception to the quality of mules I'm raising at Las Palomas. Drive up some time and spend a few days and take a look at the stock we're breeding. If you will, and I don't show you fifty mules fourteen and a half hands or better, I'll round up five hundred head and let you pick fifty as a pelon for your time and trouble. Why, gentlemen, Las Palomas has sold mules to the government."

On the return of our party to the arbor, Happersett claimed a dance with Esther, thus freeing me. Uncle Lance was standing some little distance away, still entertaining the mail contractors, and I edged near enough to notice Oxenford's florid face and leery eye. But on my employer's catching sight of me, he excused himself to the stage men, and taking my arm led me off. Together we promenaded out of sight of the crowd. "How do you like my style of a man herder?" inquired the old matchmaker, once we were out of hearing. "Why, Tom, I'd have held those mail thieves until dark, if Dan hadn't drifted in and given me the wink. Shepherd kicked like a bay steer on letting me have a second quart bottle, but it took that to put the right glaze in the young Yank's eye. Oh, I had him going south all right! But tell me, how did you and Esther make it?"

We had reached a secluded spot, and, seating ourselves on an old fallen tree trunk, I told of my success, even to the using of his horse. Never before or since did I see Uncle Lance give way to such a fit of hilarity as he indulged in over the perfect working out of our plans. With his hat he whipped me, the ground, the log on which we sat, while his peals of laughter rang out like the reports of a rifle. In his fit of ecstasy, tears of joy streaming from his eyes, he kept repeating again and again, "Oh, sister, run quick and tell pa to come!"

As we neared the grounds returning, he stopped me and we had a further brief confidential talk together. I was young and egotistical enough to think that I could defy all the rivals in existence, but he cautioned me, saying: "Hold on, Tom. You're young yet; you know nothing about the weaker sex, absolutely nothing. It's not your fault, but due to your mere raw youth. Now, listen to me, son: Don't underestimate any rival, particularly if he has gall and money, most of all, money. Humanity is the same the world over, and while you may not have seen it here among the ranches, it is natural for a woman to rave over a man with money, even if he is only a pimply excuse for a creature. Still, I don't see that we have very much to fear. We can cut old lady McLeod out of the matter entirely. But then there's the girl's sister, Mrs. Martin, and I look for her to cut up shameful when she smells the rat, which she's sure to do. And then there's her husband to figure on. If the ox knows his master's crib, it's only reasonable to suppose that Jack Martin knows where his bread and butter comes from. These stage men will stick up for each other like thieves. Now, don't you be too crack sure. Be just a trifle leary of every one, except, of course, the Las Palomas outfit."

I admit that I did not see clearly the reasoning behind much of this lecture, but I knew better than reject the advice of the old matchmaker with his sixty odd years of experience. I was still meditating over his remarks when we rejoined the crowd and were soon separated among the dancers. Several urged me to play the violin; but I was too busy looking after my own fences, and declined the invitation. Casting about for the Vaux girls, I found the eldest, with whom I had a slight acquaintance, being monopolized by Theodore Quayle and John Cotton, friendly rivals and favorites of the young lady. On my imploring the favor of a dance, she excused herself, and joined me on a promenade about the grounds, missing one dance entirely. In arranging matters with her to send me word on the arrival of Esther at their ranch, I attempted to make her show some preference between my two comrades, under the pretense of knowing which one to bring along, but she only smiled and maintained an admirable neutrality.

After a dance I returned the elder Miss Vaux to the tender care of John Cotton, and caught sight of my employer leaving the arbor for the refreshment booth with a party of women, including Mrs. Martin and Esther McLeod, to whom he was paying the most devoted attention. Witnessing the tireless energy of the old matchmaker, and in a quarter where he had little hope of an ally, brought me to thinking that there might be good cause for alarm in his warnings not to be over-confident. Miss Jean, whom I had not seen since luncheon, aroused me from my reverie, and on her wishing to know my motive for cultivating the acquaintance of Miss Vaux and neglecting my own sweetheart, I told her the simple truth. "Good idea, Tom," she assented. "I think I'll just ask Miss Frances home with me to spend Sunday. Then you can take her across to the Frio on horseback, so as not to offend either

John or Theodore. What do you think?"

I thought it was a good idea, and said so. At least the taking of the young lady home would be a pleasanter task for me than breaking horses. But as I expressed myself so, I could not help thinking, seeing Miss Jean's zeal in the matter, that the matchmaking instinct was equally well developed on both sides of the Lovelace family.

The afternoon was drawing to a close. The festivities would conclude by early sundown. Miss Jean would spend the night again at the halfway ranch, returning to Las Palomas the next morning; we would start on our return with the close of the amusements. Many who lived at a distance had already started home. It lacked but a few minutes of the closing hour when I sought out Esther for the "Home, Sweet Home" waltz, finding her in company of Oxenford, chaperoned by Mrs. Martin, of which there was need. My sweetheart excused herself with a poise that made my heart leap, and as we whirled away in the mazes of the final dance, rivals and all else passed into oblivion. Before we could realize the change in the music, the orchestra had stopped, and struck into "My Country, 'tis of Thee," in which the voice of every patriotic Texan present swelled the chorus until it echoed throughout the grove, befittingly closing San Jacinto Day.

CHAPTER VIII

A CAT HUNT ON THE FRIO

The return of Miss Jean the next forenoon, accompanied by Frances Vaux, was an occasion of more than ordinary moment at Las Palomas. The Vaux family were of creole extraction, but had settled on the Frio River nearly a generation before. Under the climatic change, from the swamps of Louisiana to the mesas of Texas, the girls grew up fine physical specimens of rustic Southern beauty. To a close observer, certain traces of the French were distinctly discernible in Miss Frances, notably in the large, lustrous eyes, the swarthy complexion, and early maturity of womanhood. Small wonder then that our guest should have played havoc among the young men of the countryside, adding to her train of gallants the devoted Quayle and Cotton of Las Palomas.

Aside from her charming personality, that Miss Vaux should receive a cordial welcome at Las Palomas goes without saying, since there were many reasons why she should. The old ranchero and his sister chaperoned the young lady, while I, betrothed to another, became her most obedient slave. It is needless to add that there was a fair field and no favor shown by her hosts, as between John and Theodore. The prize was worthy of any effort. The best man was welcome to win, while the blessings of master and mistress seemed impatient to descend on the favored one.

In the work in hand, I was forced to act as a rival to my friends, for I could not afford to lower my reputation for horsemanship before Miss Frances, when my betrothed was

ANDY ADAMS

shortly to be her guest. So it was not to be wondered at that Quayle and Cotton should abandon the *medeno* in mounting their unbroken geldings, and I had to follow suit or suffer by comparison. The other rascals, equal if not superior to our trio in horsemanship, including Enrique, born with just sense enough to be a fearless vaquero, took to the heavy sand in mounting vicious geldings; but we three jauntily gave the wildest horses their heads and even encouraged them to buck whenever our guest was sighted on the gallery. What gave special vim to our work was the fact that Miss Frances was a horsewoman herself, and it was with difficulty that she could be kept away from the corrals. Several times a day our guest prevailed on Uncle Lance to take her out to witness the roping. From a safe vantage place on the palisades, the old ranchero and his protege would watch us catching, saddling, and mounting the geldings. Under those bright eyes, lariats encircled the feet of the horse to be ridden deftly indeed, and he was laid on his side in the sand as daintily as a mother would lay her babe in its crib. Outside of the trio, the work of the gang was bunglesome, calling for many a protest from Uncle Lance, - they had no lady's glance to spur them on, - while ours merited the enthusiastic plaudits of Miss Frances.

Then came Sunday and we observed the commandment. Miss Jean had planned a picnic for the day on the river. We excused Tiburcio, and pressed the ambulance team into service to convey the party of six for the day's outing among the fine groves of elm that bordered the river in several places, and afforded ample shade from the sun. The day was delightfully spent. The chaperons were negligent and dilatory. Uncle Lance even fell asleep for several hours. But when we returned at twilight, the ambulance mules were garlanded as if for a wedding party.

The next morning our guest was to depart, and to me fell the pleasant task of acting as her escort. Uncle Lance prevailed on Miss Frances to ride a spirited chestnut horse from his mount, while I rode a *grulla* from my own. We made an early start, the old ranchero riding with us as far as the river. As he held the hand of Miss Vaux in parting, he cautioned her not to detain me at their ranch, as he had use for me at Las Palomas. "Of course," said he, "I don't mean that you shall hurry him right off to-day or even to-morrow. But these lazy rascals of mine will hang around a girl a week, if she'll allow it. Had John or Theodore taken you home, I shouldn't expect to see either of them in a fortnight. Now, if they don't treat you right at home, come back and live with us. I'll adopt you as my daughter. And tell your pa that the first general rain that falls, I'm coming over with my hounds for a cat hunt with him. Good-by, sweetheart."

It was a delightful ride across to the Frio. Mounted on two splendid horses, we put the Nueces behind us as the hours passed. Frequently we met large strings of cattle drifting in towards the river for their daily drink, and Miss Frances insisted on riding through the cows, noticing every brand as keenly as a vaquero on the lookout for strays from her father's ranch. The young calves scampered out of our way, but their sedate mothers permitted us to ride near enough to read the brands as we met and passed. Once we rode a mile out of our way to look at a *manada*. The stallion met us as we approached as if to challenge all intruders on his domain, but we met him defiantly and he turned aside and permitted us to examine his harem and its frolicsome colts.

But when cattle and horses no longer served as a subject, and the wide expanse of flowery mesa, studded here and there with Spanish daggers whose creamy flowers nodded to us as we passed, ceased to interest us, we turned to the ever interesting subject of sweethearts. But try as I might, I could never wring any confession from her which even suggested a preference among her string of admirers. On the other hand, when she twitted me about Esther, I proudly plead guilty of a Platonic friendship which some day I hoped would ripen into something more permanent, fully realizing that the very first time these two chums met there would be an interchange of confidences. And in the full knowledge that during these whispered admissions the truth would be revealed, I stoutly

ANDY ADAMS

denied that Esther and I were even betrothed.

But during that morning's ride I made a friend and ally of Frances Vaux. There was some talk of a tournament to be held during the summer at Campbellton on the Atascosa. She promised that she would detain Esther for it and find a way to send me word, and we would make up a party and attend it together. I had never been present at any of these pastoral tourneys and was hopeful that one would be held within reach of our ranch, for I had heard a great deal about them and was anxious to see one. But this was only one of several social outings which she outlined as on her summer programme, to all of which I was cordially invited as a member of her party. There was to be a dance on St. John's Day at the Mission, a barbecue in June on the San Miguel, and other local meets for the summer and early fall. By the time we reached the ranch, I was just beginning to realize that, socially, Shepherd's Ferry and the Nueces was a poky place.

The next morning I returned to Las Palomas. The horse-breaking was nearing an end. During the month of May we went into camp on a new tract of land which had been recently acquired, to build a tank on a dry *arroyo* which crossed this last landed addition to the ranch. It was a commercial peculiarity of Uncle Lance to acquire land but never to part with it under any consideration. To a certain extent, cows and land had become his religion, and whenever either, adjoining Las Palomas, was for sale, they were looked upon as a safe bank of deposit for any surplus funds. The last tract thus secured was dry, but by damming the *arroyo* we could store water in this tank or reservoir to tide over the dry spells. All the Mexican help on the ranch was put to work with wheelbarrows, while six mule teams ploughed, scraped, and hauled rock, one four-mule team being constantly employed in hauling water over ten miles for camp and stock purposes. This dry stream ran water, when conditions were favorable, several months in the year, and by building the tank our cattle capacity would be largely increased.

One evening, late in the month, when the water wagon returned, Tiburcio brought a request from Miss Jean, asking me to come into the ranch that night. Responding to the summons, I was rewarded by finding a letter awaiting me from Frances Vaux, left by a vaquero passing from the Frio to Santa Maria. It was a dainty missive, informing me that Esther was her guest; that the tournament would not take place, but to be sure and come over on Sunday. Personally the note was satisfactory, but that I was to bring any one along was artfully omitted. Being thus forced to read between the lines, on my return to camp the next morning by dawn, without a word of explanation, I submitted the matter to John and Theodore. Uncle Lance, of course, had to know what had called me in to the ranch, and, taking the letter from Quayle, read it himself.

"That's plain enough," said he, on the first reading. "John will go with you Sunday, and if it rains next month, I'll take Theodore with me when I go over for a cat hunt with old man Pierre. I'll let him act as master of the horse, - no, of the hounds, - and give him a chance to toot his own horn with Frances. Honest, boys, I'm getting disgusted with the white element of Las Palomas. We raise most everything here but white babies. Even Enrique, the rascal, has to live in camp now to hold down his breakfast. But you young whites - with the country just full of young women - well, it's certainly discouraging. I do all I can, and Sis helps a little, but what does it amount to - what are the results? That poem that Jean reads to us occasionally must be right. I reckon the Caucasian is played out."

Before the sun was an hour high, John Cotton and myself rode into the Vaux ranch on Sunday morning. The girls gave us a cheerful welcome. While we were breakfasting, several other lads and lasses rode up, and we were informed that a little picnic for the day had been arranged. As this was to our liking, John and I readily acquiesced, and shortly afterward a mounted party of about a dozen young folks set out for a hackberry grove, up the river several miles. Lunch baskets were taken along, but no chaperons. The girls were all dressed in cambric and muslin and as light in heart as the fabrics and ribbons they flaunted. I was gratified with the boldness of Cotton, as he cantered away with Frances, and with the day before him there was every reason to believe that his cause would he advanced. As to myself, with Esther by my side the livelong day, I could not have asked the world to widen an inch.

It was midnight when we reached Las Palomas returning. As we rode along that night, John confessed to me that Frances was a tantalizing enigma. Up to a certain point, she offered every encouragement, but beyond that there seemed to be a dead line over which she allowed no sentiment to pass. It was plain to be seen that he was discouraged, but I told him I had gone through worse ordeals.

Throughout southern Texas and the country tributary to the Nueces River, we always looked for our heaviest rainfall during the month of June. This year in particular, we were anxious to see a regular downpour to start the *arroyo* and test our new tank. Besides, we had sold for delivery in July, twelve hundred beef steers for shipment at Rockport on the coast. If only a soaking rain would fall, making water plentiful, we could make the drive in little over a hundred miles, while a dry season would compel; us to follow the river nearly double the distance.

We were riding our range thoroughly, locating our fattest beeves, when one evening as June Deweese and I were on the way back from the Ganso, a regular equinoctial struck us, accompanied by a downpour of rain and hail. Our horses turned their backs to the storm, but we drew slickers over our heads, and defied the elements. Instead of letting up as darkness set in, the storm seemed to increase in fury and we were forced to seek shelter. We were at least fifteen miles from the ranch, and it was simply impossible to force a horse against that sheeting rain. So turning to catch the storm in our backs, we rode for a ranchita belonging to Las Palomas. By the aid of flashes of lightning and the course of the storm, we reached the little ranch and found a haven. A steady rain fell all night, continuing the next day, but we saddled early and rode for our new reservoir on the *arroyo*. Imagine our surprise on sighting the embankment to see two horsemen ride up from the opposite direction and halt at the dam. Giving rein to our horses and galloping up, we found they were Uncle Lance and Theodore Quayle. Above the dam the *arroyo* was running like a mill-tail. The water in the reservoir covered several acres and had backed up stream nearly a quarter mile, the deepest point in the tank reaching my saddle skirts. The embankment had settled solidly, holding the gathering water to our satisfaction, and after several hours' inspection we rode for home.

With this splendid rain, Las Palomas ranch took on an air of activity. The old ranchero paced the gallery for hours in great glee, watching the downpour. It was too soon yet by a week to gather the beeves. But under the glowing prospect, we could not remain inert. The next morning the *segunao* took all the teams and returned to the tank to watch the dam and haul rock to rip-rap the flanks of the embankment. Taking extra saddle horses with us, Uncle Lance, Dan Happersett, Quayle, and myself took the hounds and struck across for the Frio. On reaching the Vaux ranch, as showers were still falling and the underbrush reeking with moisture, wetting any one to the skin who dared to invade it, we did not hunt that afternoon. Pierre Vaux was enthusiastic over the rain, while his daughters were equally so over the prospects of riding to the hounds, there being now nearly forty dogs in the double pack.

At the first opportunity, Frances confided to me that Mrs. McLeod had forbidden Esther visiting them again, since some busybody had carried the news of our picnic to her ears. But she promised me that if I could direct the hunt on the morrow within a few miles of the McLeod ranch, she would entice my sweetheart out and give me a chance to meet her. There was a roguish look in Miss Frances's eye during this disclosure which I was unable to fathom, but I promised during the few days' hunt to find some means to direct the chase within striking distance of the ranch on the San Miguel.

ANDY ADAMS

I promptly gave this bit of news in confidence to Uncle Lance, and was told to lie low and leave matters to him. That evening, amid clouds of tobacco smoke, the two old rancheros discussed the best hunting in the country, while we youngsters danced on the gallery to the strains of a fiddle. I heard Mr. Vaux narrating a fight with a cougar which killed two of his best dogs during the winter just passed, and before we retired it was understood that we would give the haunts of this same old cougar our first attention.

CHAPTER IX

THE ROSE AND ITS THORN

Dawn found the ranch astir and a heavy fog hanging over the Frio valley. Don Pierre had a *remuda* corralled before sun-up, and insisted on our riding his horses, an invitation which my employer alone declined. For the first hour or two the pack scouted the river bottoms with no success, and Uncle Lance's verdict was that the valley was too soggy for any animal belonging to the cat family, so we turned back to the divide between the Frio and San Miguel. Here there grew among the hills many Guajio thickets, and from the first one we beat, the hounds opened on a hot trail in splendid chorus. The pack led us through thickets for over a mile, when they suddenly turned down a ravine, heading for the river. With the ground ill splendid condition for trailing, the dogs in full cry, the quarry sought every shelter possible; but within an hour of striking the scent, the pack came to bay in the encinal. On coming up with the hounds, we found the animal was a large catamount. A single shot brought him from his perch in a scraggy oak, and the first chase of the day was over. The pelt was worthless and was not taken.

It was nearly noon when the kill was made, and Don Pierre insisted that we return to the ranch. Uncle Lance protested against wasting the remainder of the day, but the courteous Creole urged that the ground would be in fine condition for hunting at least a week longer; this hunt he declared was merely preliminary - to break the pack together and give them a taste of the chase before attacking the cougar. "Ah," said Don Pierre, with a deprecating shrug of the shoulders, "you have nothing to hurry you home. I come by your rancho an' stay one hol' week. You come by mine, al' time hurry. Sacre! Let de li'l dogs rest, an' in de mornin', mebbe we hunt de cougar. Ah, Meester Lance, we must haff de pack fresh for him. By Gar, he was one dam' wil' fellow. Mek one two pass, so. Biff! two dog dead."

Uncle Lance yielded, and we rode back to the ranch. The next morning our party included the three daughters of our host. Don Pierre led the way on a roan stallion, and after two hours' riding we crossed the San Miguel to the north of his ranch. A few miles beyond we entered some chalky hills, interspersed with white chaparral thickets which were just bursting into bloom, with a fragrance that was almost intoxicating. Under the direction of our host, we started to beat a long chain of these thickets, and were shortly rewarded by hearing the pack give mouth. The quarry kept to the cover of the thickets for several miles, impeding the chase until the last covert in the chain was reached, where a fight occurred with the lead hound. Don Pierre was the first to reach the scene, and caught several glimpses of a monster puma as he slunk away through the Brazil brush, leaving one of the Don's favorite hounds lacerated to the bone. But the pack passed on, and, lifting the wounded dog to a vaquero's saddle, we followed, lustily shouting to the hounds.

The spoor now turned down the San Miguel, and the pace was such that it took hard riding to keep within hearing. Mr. Vaux and Uncle Lance usually held the lead, the remainder of the party, including the girls, bringing up the rear. The chase continued down stream for fully an hour, until we encountered some heavy timber on the main Frio, our course having carried us several miles to the north of the McLeod ranch. Some distance below the juncture with the San Miguel the river made a large horseshoe, embracing nearly a thousand acres, which was covered with a dense growth of ash, pecan, and cypress. The trail led into this jungle, circling it several times before leading away. We were fortunately able to keep track of the chase from the baying of the hounds without entering the timber, and were watching its course, when suddenly it changed; the pack followed the scent across a bridge of driftwood on the Frio, and started up the river in full cry.

As the chase down the San Miguel passed beyond the mouth of the creek, Theodore Quayle and Frances Vaux dropped out and rode for the McLeod ranch. It was still early in the day, and understanding their motive, I knew they would rejoin us if their mission was successful. By the sudden turn of the chase, we were likely to pass several miles south of the home of my sweetheart, but our location could be easily followed by the music of the pack. Within an hour after leaving us, Theodore and Frances rejoined the chase, adding Tony Hunter and Esther to our numbers. With this addition, I lost interest in the hunt, as the course carried us straightaway five miles up the stream. The quarry was cunning and delayed the pack at every thicket or large body of timber encountered. Several times he craftily attempted to throw the hounds off the scent by climbing leaning trees, only to spring down again. But the pack were running wide and the ruse was only tiring the hunted. The scent at times left the river and circled through outlying mesquite groves, always keeping well under cover. On these occasions we rested our horses, for the hunt was certain to return to the river.

From the scattering order in which we rode, I was afforded a good opportunity for free conversation with Esther. But the information I obtained was not very encouraging. Her mother's authority had grown so severe that existence under the same roof was a mere armistice between mother and daughter, while this day's sport was likely to break the already strained relations. The thought that her suffering was largely on my account, nerved me to resolution.

The kill was made late in the day, in a bend of the river, about fifteen miles above the Vaux ranch, forming a jungle of several thousand acres. In this thickety covert the fugitive made his final stand, taking refuge in an immense old live-oak, the mossy festoons of which partially screened him from view. The larger portion of the cavalcade remained in the open, but the rest of us, under the leadership of the two rancheros, forced our horses through the underbrush and reached the hounds. The pack were as good as exhausted by the long run, and, lest the animal should spring out of the tree and escape, we circled it at a distance. On catching a fair view of the quarry, Uncle Lance called for a carbine. Two shots through the shoulders served to loosen the puma's footing, when he came down by easy stages from limb to limb, spitting and hissing defiance into the upturned faces of the pack. As he fell, we dashed in to beat off the dogs as a matter of precaution, but the bullets had done their work, and the pack mouthed the fallen feline with entire impunity.

Dan Happersett dragged the dead puma out with a rope over the neck for the inspection of the girls, while our horses, which had had no less than a fifty-mile ride, were unsaddled and allowed a roll and a half hour's graze before starting back. As we were watering our mounts, I caught my employer's ear long enough to repeat what I had learned about Esther's home difficulties. After picketing our horses, we strolled away from the remainder of the party, when Uncle Lance remarked: "Tom, your chance has come where you must play your hand and play it boldly. I'll keep Tony at the Vaux ranch, and if Esther has to go home to-night, why, of course, you'll have to take her. There's your chance to run off and marry. Now, Tom, you've never failed me yet; and this thing has gone far enough. We'll give old lady McLeod good cause to hate us from now on. I've got some money with me, and I'll rob the other boys, and to-night you make a spoon or spoil a horn. Sabe?"

I understood and approved. As we jogged along homeward, Esther and I fell to the rear, and I outlined my programme. Nor did she protest when I suggested that to-night was the accepted time. Before we reached the Vaux ranch every little detail was arranged. There was a splendid moon, and after supper she plead the necessity of returning home. Meanwhile every cent my friends possessed had been given me, and the two best horses of Las Palomas were under saddle for the start. Uncle Lance was arranging a big hunt for the morrow with Tony Hunter and Don Pierre, when Esther took leave of her friends, only a few of whom were cognizant of our intended elopement.

With fresh mounts under us, we soon covered the intervening distance between the two ranches. I would gladly have waived touching at the McLeod ranch, but Esther had torn her dress during the day and insisted on a change, and I, of necessity, yielded. The corrals were at some distance from the main buildings, and, halting at a saddle shed adjoining, Esther left me and entered the house. Fortunately her mother had retired, and after making a hasty change of apparel, she returned unobserved to the corrals. As we quietly rode out from the inclosure, my spirits soared to the moon above us. The night was an ideal one. Crossing the Frio, we followed the divide some distance, keeping in the open, and an hour before midnight forded the Nueces at Shepherd's. A flood of recollections crossed my mind, as our steaming horses bent their heads to drink at the ferry. Less than a year before, in this very grove, I had met her; it was but two months since, on those hills beyond, we had gathered flowers, plighted our troth, and exchanged our first rapturous kiss. And the thought that she was renouncing home and all for my sake, softened my heart and nerved me to every exertion.

Our intention was to intercept the south-bound stage at the first road house south of Oakville. I knew the hour it was due to leave the station, and by steady riding we could connect with it at the first stage stand some fifteen miles below. Lighthearted and happy, we set out on this last lap of our ride. Our horses seemed to understand the emergency, as they put the miles behind them, thrilling us with their energy and vigor. Never for a moment in our flight did my sweetheart discover a single qualm over her decision, while in my case all scruples were buried in the hope of victory. Recrossing the Nueces and entering the stage road, we followed it down several miles, sighting the stage stand about two o'clock in the morning. I was saddle weary from the hunt, together with this fifty-mile ride, and rejoiced in reaching our temporary destination. Esther, however, seemed little the worse for the long ride.

The welcome extended by the keeper of this relay station was gruff enough. But his tone and manner moderated when he learned we were passengers for Corpus Christi. When I made arrangements with him to look after our horses for a week or ten days at a handsome figure, he became amiable, invited us to a cup of coffee, and politely informed us that the stage was due in half an hour. But on its arrival, promptly on time, our hearts sank within us. On the driver's box sat an express guard holding across his knees a sawed-off, double-barreled shotgun. As it halted, two other guards stepped out of the coach, similarly armed. The stage was carrying an unusual amount of treasure, we were informed, and no passengers could be accepted, as an attempted robbery was expected between this and the next station.

Our situation became embarrassing. For the first time during our ride, Esther showed the timidity of her sex. The chosen destination of our honeymoon, nearly a hundred miles to the south, was now out of the question. To return to Oakville, where a sister and friends of my sweetheart resided, seemed the only avenue open. I had misgivings that it was unsafe, but Esther urged it, declaring that Mrs. Martin would offer no opposition, and even if she did, nothing now could come that would ever separate us. We learned from the keeper that Jack Martin was due to drive the north-bound stage out of Oakville that morning, and was expected to pass this relay station about daybreak. This was favorable, and we decided to wait and allow the stage to pass north before resuming our journey.

On the arrival of the stage, we learned that the down coach had been attacked, but the robbers, finding it guarded, had fled after an exchange of shots in the darkness. This had a further depressing effect on my betrothed, and only my encouragement to be brave and face the dilemma confronting us kept her up. Bred on the frontier, this little ranch girl was no weakling; but the sudden overturn of our well-laid plans had chilled my own spirits as well as hers. Giving the up stage a good start of us, we resaddled and started for Oakville, slightly crestfallen but still confident. In the open air Esther's fears gradually subsided, and, invigorated by the morning and the gallop, we reached our destination after our night's adventure with hopes buoyant and colors flying.

Mrs. Martin looked a trifle dumfounded at her early callers, but I lost no time in informing her that our mission was an elopement, and asked her approval and blessing. Surprised as she was, she welcomed us to breakfast, inquiring of our plans and showing alarm over our experience. Since Oakville was a county seat where a license could be secured, for fear of pursuit I urged an immediate marriage, but Mrs. Martin could see no necessity for haste. There was, she said, no one there whom she would allow to solemnize a wedding of her sister, and, to my chagrin, Esther agreed with her.

This was just what I had dreaded; but Mrs. Martin, with apparent enthusiasm over our union, took the reins in her own hands, and decided that we should wait until Jack's return, when we would all take the stage to Pleasanton, where an Episcopal minister lived. My heart sank at this, for it meant a delay of two days, and I stood up and stoutly protested. But now that the excitement of our flight had abated, my own Esther innocently sided with her sister, and I was at my wit's end. To all my appeals, the sisters replied with the argument that there was no hurry - that while the hunt lasted at the Vaux ranch Tony Hunter could be depended upon to follow the hounds; Esther would never be missed until his return; her mother would suppose she was with the Vaux girls, and would be busy preparing a lecture against her return.

Of course the argument of the sisters won the hour. Though dreading some unforeseen danger, I temporarily yielded. I knew the motive of the hunt well enough to know that the moment we had an ample start it would be abandoned, and the Las Palomas contingent would return to the ranch. Yet I dare not tell, even my betrothed, that there were ulterior motives in my employer's hunting on the Frio, one of which was to afford an opportunity for our elopement. Full of apprehension and alarm, I took a room at the village hostelry, for I had our horses to look after, and secured a much-needed sleep during the afternoon. That evening I returned to the Martin cottage, to urge again that we carry out our original programme by taking the south-bound stage at midnight. But all I could say was of no avail. Mrs. Martin was equal to every suggestion. She had all the plans outlined, and there was no occasion for me to do any thinking at all. Corpus Christi was not to be considered for a single moment, compared to Pleasanton and an Episcopalian service. What could I do?

At an early hour Mrs. Martin withdrew. The reaction from our escapade had left a pallor on my sweetheart's countenance, almost alarming. Noticing this, I took my leave early, hoping that a good night's rest would restore her color and her spirits. Returning to the hostelry, I resignedly sought my room, since there was nothing I could do but wait. Tossing and pitching on my bed, I upbraided myself for having returned to Oakville, where any interference with our plans could possibly develop.

The next morning at breakfast, I noticed that I was the object of particular attention, and of no very kindly sort. No one even gave me a friendly nod, while several avoided my glances. Supposing that some rumor of our elopement might be abroad, I hurriedly finished my meal and started for the Martins'. On reaching the door, I was met by its mistress, who, I had need to remind myself, was the sister of my betrothed. To my friendly salutation, she gave me a scornful, withering look.

"You're too late, young man," she said. "Shortly after you left last night, Esther and Jack Oxenford took a private conveyance for Beeville, and are married before this. You Las Palomas people are slow. Old Lance Lovelace thought he was playing it cute San Jacinto Day, but I saw through his little game. Somebody must have told him he was a matchmaker. Well, just give him my regards, and tell him he don't know the first principles of that little game. Tell him to drop in some time when he's passing; I may be able to give him some pointers that I'm not using at the moment. I hope your sorrow will not exceed my happiness. Good-morning, sir."

CHAPTER X

AFTERMATH

My memory of what happened immediately after Mrs. Martin's contemptuous treatment of me is as vague and indefinite as the vaporings of a fevered dream. I have a faint recollection of several friendly people offering their sympathy. The old stableman, who looked after the horses, cautioned me not to start out alone; but I have since learned that I cursed him and all the rest, and rode away as one in a trance. But I must have had some little caution left, for I remember giving Shepherd's a wide berth, passing several miles to the south.

The horses, taking their own way, were wandering home. Any exercise of control or guidance over them on my part was inspired by an instinct to avoid being seen. Of conscious direction there was none. Somewhere between the ferry and the ranch I remember being awakened from my torpor by the horse which I was leading showing an inclination to graze. Then I noticed their gaunted condition, and in sympathy for the poor brutes unsaddled and picketed them in a secluded spot. What happened at this halt has slipped from my memory. But I must have slept a long time; for I awoke to find the moon high overhead, and my watch, through neglect, run down and stopped. I now realized the better my predicament, and reasoned with myself whether I should return to Las Palomas or not. But there was no place else to go, and the horses did not belong to me. If I could only reach the ranch and secure my own horse, I felt that no power on earth could chain me to the scenes of my humiliation.

The horses decided me to return. Resaddling at an unknown hour, I rode for the ranch. The animals were refreshed and made good time. As I rode along I tried to convince myself that I could slip into the ranch, secure my own saddle horse, and meet no one except the Mexicans. There was a possibility that Deweese might still be in camp at the new reservoir, and I was hopeful that my employer might not yet be returned from the hunt on the Frio. After a number of hours' riding, the horse under saddle nickered. Halting him, I listened and heard the roosters crowing in a chorus at the ranch. Clouds had obscured the moon, and so by making a detour around the home buildings I was able to reach the Mexican quarters unobserved. I rode up to the house of Enrique, and quietly aroused him; told him my misfortune and asked him to hide me until he could get up my horse. We turned the animals loose, and, taking my saddle inside the *jacal*, held a whispered conversation. Deweese was yet at the tank. If the hunting party had returned, they had done so during the night. The distant range of my horse made it impossible to get him before the middle of the forenoon, but Enrique and Dona Anita assured me that my slightest wish was law to them. Furnishing me with a blanket and pillow, they made me a couch on a dry cowskin on the dirt floor at the foot of their bed, and before day broke I had fallen asleep.

On awakening, I found the sun had already risen. Enrique and his wife were missing from the room, but a peep through a crevice in the palisade wall revealed Dona Anita in the kitchen adjoining. She had detected my awakening, and soon brought me a cup of splendid coffee, which I drank with relish. She urged on me also some dainty dishes, which had always been favorites with me in Mexican cookery, but my appetite was gone. Throwing myself back on the cowskin, I asked Dona Anita how long Enrique had been gone in quest of my horse, and was informed that he left before dawn, not even waiting for his customary cup of coffee. With the kindness of a sister, the girl wife urged me to take their bed; but I assured her that comfort was the least of my concerns, complete effacement being my consuming thought.

Dona Anita withdrew, and as I lay pondering over the several possible routes of escape, I heard a commotion in the ranch. I was in the act of rising when Dona Anita burst into the *jacal* to tell me that Don Lance had been sighted returning. I was on my feet in an instant, heard the long-drawn notes of the horn calling in the hounds, and, peering through the largest crack, saw the cavalcade. As they approached, driving their loose mounts in front of them, I felt that my ill luck still hung over me; for among the unsaddled horses were the two which I had turned free but a few hours before. The hunters had met the gaunted animals between the ranch and the river, and were bringing them in to return them to their own *remuda*. But at the same time the horses were evidence that I was in the ranch. From the position of Uncle Lance, in advance, I could see that he was riding direct to the house, and my absence there would surely cause surprise. At best it was but a question of time until I was discovered.

In the face of this new development, I gave up. There was no escaping fate. Enrique might not return for two hours yet, and if he came, driving in my horse, it would only prove my presence. I begged Dona Anita to throw open the door and conceal nothing. But she was still ready to aid in my concealment until night, offering to deny my presence. But how could I conceal myself in a single room, and what was so simple a device to a worldly man of sixty years' experience? To me the case looked hopeless. Even before we had concluded our discussion, I saw Uncle Lance and the boys coming towards the Mexican quarters, followed by Miss Jean and the household contingent. The fact that the door of Enrique's *jacal* was closed, made it a shining mark for investigation. Opening the inner door, I started to meet the visitors; but Dona Anita planted herself at the outer entrance of the stoop, met the visitors, and within my hearing and without being asked stoutly denied my presence. "Hush up, you little liar," said a voice, and I heard a step and clanking spurs which I recognized. I had sat down on the edge of the bed, and was rolling a cigarette as the crowd filed into the *jacal*. A fortunate flush of anger came over me which served to steady my voice;

but I met their staring, after all, much as if I had been a culprit and they a vigilance committee.

"Well, young fellow, explain your presence here," demanded Uncle Lance. Had it not been for the presence of Miss Jean, I had on my tongue's end a reply, relative to the eleventh commandment, emphasized with sulphurous adjectives. But out of deference to the mistress of the ranch, I controlled my anger, and, taking out of my pocket a flint, a steel, and, a bit of *yesca,* struck fire and leisurely lighted my cigarette. Throwing myself back on the bed, as my employer repeated his demand, I replied, "Ask Anita." The girl understood, and, nothing abashed, told the story in her native tongue, continually referring to me as *pobre Tomas.* When her disconnected narrative was concluded, Uncle Lance turned on me, saying: -

"And this is the result of all our plans. You went into Oakville, did you? Tom, you haven't, got as much sense as a candy frog. Walked right into a trap with your head up and sassy. That's right - don't you listen to any one. Didn't I tell you that stage people would stick by each other like thieves? And you forgot all my warnings and deliberately" -

"Hold on," I interrupted. "You must recollect that the horses had had a fifty-mile forced ride, were jaded, and on the point of collapse. With the down stage refusing to carry us, and the girl on the point of hysteria, where else could I go?"

"Go to jail if necessary. Go anywhere but the place you went. The horses were jaded on a fifty-mile ride, were they? Either one of them was good for a hundred without unsaddling, and you know it. Haven't I told you that this ranch would raise horses when we were all dead and gone? Suppose you had killed a couple of horses? What would that have been, compared to your sneaking into the ranch this way, like a whipped cur with your tail between your legs? Now, the countryside will laugh at us both."

"The country may laugh," I answered, "but I'll not be here to hear it. Enrique has gone after my horse, and as soon as he gets in I'm leaving you for good."

"You'll do nothing of the kind. You think you're all shot to pieces, don't you? Well, you'll stay right here until all your wounds heal. I've taken all these degrees myself, and have lived to laugh at them afterward. And I have had lessons that I hope you'll never have to learn. When I found out that my third wife had known a gambler before she married me, I found out what the Bible means by rottenness of the bones with which it says an evil woman uncrowns her husband. I'll tell you about it some day. But you've not been scarred in this little side-play. You're not even powder burnt. Why, in less than a month you'll be just as happy again as if you had good sense."

Miss Jean now interrupted. "Clear right out of here," she said to her brother and the rest. "Yes, the whole pack of you. I want to talk with Tom alone. Yes, you too - you've said too much already. Run along out."

As they filed out, I noticed Uncle Lance pick up my saddle and throw it across his shoulder, while Theodore gathered up the rancid blankets and my fancy bridle, taking everything with them to the house. Waiting until she saw that her orders were obeyed, Miss Jean came over and sat down beside me on the bed. Anita stood like a fawn near the door, likewise fearing banishment, but on a sign from her mistress she spread a goatskin on the floor and sat down at our feet. Between two languages and two women, I was as helpless as an ironed prisoner. Not that Anita had any influence over me, but the mistress of the ranch had. In her hands I was as helpless as a baby. I had come to the ranch a stranger only a little over a year before, but had I been born there her interest could have been no stronger. Jean Lovelace relinquished no one, any more than a mother would one of her boys. I wanted to escape, to get away from observation; I even plead for a month's leave of absence. But my reasons were of no avail, and after arguing pro and con for over an hour, I went with her to the house. If the Almighty ever made a good woman and placed her among men for their betterment, then the presence of Jean Lovelace at Las Palomas savored of divine appointment.

On reaching the yard, we rested a long time on a settee under a group of china trees. The boys had dispersed, and after quite a friendly chat together, we saw Uncle Lance sauntering out of the house, smiling as he approached. "Tom's going to stay," said Miss Jean to her brother, as the latter seated himself beside us; "but this abuse and blame you're heaping on him must stop. He did what he thought was best under the circumstances, and you don't know what they were. He has given me his promise to stay, and I have given him mine that talk about this matter will be dropped. Now that your anger has cooled, and I have you both together, I want your word."

"Tom," said my employer, throwing his long bony arm around me, "I was disappointed, terribly put out, and I showed it in freeing my mind. But I feel better now - towards you, at least. I understand just how you felt when your plans were thwarted by an unforeseen incident. If I don't know everything, then, since the milk is spilt, I'm not asking for further particulars. If you did what you thought was best under the circumstances, why, that's all we ever ask of any one at Las Palomas. A mistake is nothing; my whole life is a series of errors. I've been trying, and expect to keep right on trying, to give you youngsters the benefit of my years; but if you insist on learning it for yourselves, well enough. When I was your age, I took no one's advice; but look how I've paid the fiddler. Possibly it was ordained otherwise, but it looks to me like a shame that I can't give you boys the benefit of my dearly bought experience. But whether you take my advice or not, we're going to be just as good friends as ever. I need young fellows like you on this ranch. I've sent Dan out after Deweese, and to-morrow we're going to commence gathering beeves. A few weeks' good hard work will do you worlds of good. In less than a year, you'll look back at this as a splendid lesson. Shucks! boy, a man is a narrow, calloused creature until he has been shook up a few times by love affairs. They develop him into the man he was intended to be. Come on into the house, Tom, and Jean will make us a couple of mint juleps."

What a blessed panacea for mental trouble is work! We were in the saddle by daybreak the next morning, rounding up *remudas*. Every available vaquero at the outlying ranchitas had been summoned. Dividing the outfit and horses, Uncle Lance took twelve men and struck west for the Ganso. With an equal number of men, Deweese pushed north for the Frio, which he was to work down below Shepherd's, thence back along the home river. From the ranch books, we knew there were fully two thousand beeves over five years old in our brand. These cattle had never known an hour's restraint since the day they were branded, and caution and cool judgment would be required in handling them. Since the contract only required twelve hundred, we expected to make an extra clean gathering, using the oldest and naturally the largest beeves.

During the week spent in gathering, I got the full benefit of every possible hour in the saddle. We reached the Ganso about an hour before sundown. The weather had settled; water was plentiful, and every one realized that the work in hand would require wider riding than under dry conditions. By the time we had caught up fresh horses, the sun had gone down. "Boys," said Uncle Lance, "we want to make a big rodeo on the head of this creek in the morning. Tom, you take two vaqueros and lay off to the southwest about ten miles, and make a dry camp to-night. Glenn may have the same help to the southeast; and every rascal of you be in your saddles by daybreak. There are a lot of big *ladino* beeves in those brushy hills to the south and west. Be sure and be in your saddles early enough to catch *all* wild cattle out on the prairies. If you want to, you can take a lunch in your pocket for breakfast. No; you need no blankets - you'll get up earlier if you sleep cold."

Taking Jose Pena and Pasquale Arispe with me, I struck off on our course in the gathering twilight. The first twitter of a bird in the morning brought me to my feet; I roused the others, and we saddled and were riding with the first sign of dawn in the east. Taking the outside circle myself, I gave every bunch of cattle met on my course a good start for the centre of the round-up. Pasquale and Jose followed several miles to my rear on inner circles, drifting on the cattle which I had started inward. As the sun arose, dispelling the morning mists, I could see other cattle coming down in long strings out of the hills to the eastward. Within an hour after starting, Gallup and I met. Our half circle to the southward was perfect, and each turning back, we rode our appointed divisions until the vaqueros from the wagon were sighted, throwing in cattle and closing up the northern portion of the circle. Before the sun was two hours high, the first rodeo of the day was together, numbering about three thousand mixed cattle. In the few hours since dawn, we had concentrated all animals in a territory at least fifteen miles in diameter.

Uncle Lance was in his element. Detailing two vaqueros to hold the beef cut within reach and a half dozen to keep the main herd compact, he ordered the remainder of us to enter and begin the selecting of beeves. There were a number of big wild steers in the round-up, but we left those until the cut numbered over two hundred. When every hoof over five years of age was separated, we had a nucleus for our beef herd numbering about two hundred and forty steers. They were in fine condition for grass cattle, and, turning the main herd free, we started our cut for the wagon, being compelled to ride wide of them as we drifted down stream towards camp, as there were a number of old beeves which showed impatience at the restraint. But by letting them scatter well, by the time they reached the wagon it required but two vaqueros to hold them.

The afternoon was but a repetition of the morning. Everything on the south side of the Nueces between the river and the wagon was thrown together on the second round-up of the day, which yielded less than two hundred cattle for our beef herd. But when we went into camp, dividing into squads for night-herding, the day's work was satisfactory to the ranchero. Dan Happersett was given five vaqueros and stood the first watch or until one A.M. Glenn Gallup and myself took the remainder of the men and stood guard until morning. When

Happersett called our guard an hour after midnight, he said to Gallup and me as we were pulling on our boots: "About a dozen big steers haven't laid down. There's only one of them that has given any trouble. He's a pinto that we cut in the first round-up in the morning. He has made two breaks already to get away, and if you don't watch him close, he'll surely give you the slip."

While riding to the relief, Glenn and I posted our vaqueros to be on the lookout for the pinto beef. The cattle were intentionally bedded loose; but even in the starlight and waning moon, every man easily spotted the *ladino* beef, uneasily stalking back and forth like a caged tiger across the bed ground. A half hour before dawn, he made a final effort to escape, charging out between Gallup and the vaquero following up on the same side. From the other side of the bed ground, I heard the commotion, but dare not leave the herd to assist. There was a mile of open country surrounding our camp, and if two men could not turn the beef on that space, it was useless for others to offer assistance. In the stillness of the morning hour, we could hear the running and see the flashes from six-shooters, marking the course of the outlaw. After making a half circle, we heard them coming direct for the herd. For fear of a stampede, we raised a great commotion around the sleeping cattle; but in spite of our precaution, as the *ladino* beef reentered the herd, over half the beeves jumped to their feet and began milling. But we held them until dawn, and after scattering them over several hundred acres, left them grazing contentedly, when, leaving two vaqueros with the feeding herd, we went back to the wagon. The camp had been astir some time, and when Glenn reported the incident of our watch, Uncle Lance said: "I thought I heard some shooting while I was cat-napping at daylight. Well, we can use a little fresh beef in this very camp. We'll kill him at noon. The wagon will move down near the river this morning, so we can make three rodeos from it without moving camp, and to-night we'll have a side of Pinto's ribs barbecued. My mouth is watering this very minute for a rib roast."

That morning after a big rodeo on the Nueces, well above the Ganso, we returned to camp. Throwing into our herd the cut of less than a hundred secured on the morning round-up, Uncle Lance, who had preceded us, rode out from the wagon with a carbine. Allowing the beeves to scatter, the old ranchero met and rode zigzagging through them until he came face to face with the pinto *ladino*. On noticing the intruding horseman, the outlaw threw up his head. There was a carbine report and the big fellow went down in his tracks. By the time the herd had grazed away, Tiburcio, who was cooking with our wagon, brought out all the knives, and the beef was bled, dressed, and quartered.

"You can afford to be extravagant with this beef," said Uncle Lance to the old cook, when the quarters had been carried in to the wagon. "I've been ranching on this river nearly forty years, and I've always made it a rule, where cattle cannot be safely handled, to beef them then and there. I've sat up many a night barbecuing the ribs of a *ladino*. If you have plenty of salt, Tiburcio, you can make a brine and jerk those hind quarters. It will make fine chewing for the boys on night herd when once we start for the coast."

Following down the home river, we made ten other rodeos before we met Deweese. We had something over a thousand beeves while he had less than eight hundred. Throwing the two cuts together, we made a count, and cut back all the younger and smaller cattle until the herd was reduced to the required number. Before my advent at Las Palomas, about the only outlet for beef cattle had been the canneries at Rockport and Fulton. But these cattle were for shipment by boat to New Orleans and other coast cities. The route to the coast was well known to my employer, and detailing twelve men for the herd, a horse wrangler and cook extra, we started for it, barely touching at the ranch on our course. It was a nice ten days' trip. After the first night, we used three guards of four men each. Grazing contentedly, the cattle quieted down until on our arrival half our numbers could have handled them. The herd was counted and received on the outlying prairies, and as no steamer was due for a few days, another outfit took charge of them.

Uncle Lance was never much of a man for towns, and soon after settlement the next morning we were ready to start home. But the payment, amounting to thirty thousand dollars, presented a problem, as the bulk of it came to us in silver. There was scarcely a merchant in the place who would assume the responsibility of receiving it even on deposit, and in the absence of a bank, there was no alternative but to take it home. The agent for the steamship company solicited the money for transportation to New Orleans, mentioning the danger of robbery, and referring to the recent attempt of bandits to hold up the San Antonio and Corpus Christi stage. I had good cause to remember that incident, and was wondering what my employer would do under the circumstances, when he turned from the agent, saying: -

"Well, we'll take it home just the same. I have no use for money in New Orleans. Nor do I care if every bandit in Texas knows we've got the money in the wagon. I want to buy a few new guns, anyhow. If robbers tackle us, we'll promise them a warm reception - and I never knew a thief who didn't think more of his own carcass than of another man's money."

The silver was loaded into the wagon in sacks, and we started on our return. It was rather a risky trip, but we never concealed the fact that we had every dollar of the money in the wagon. It would have been dangerous to make an attempt on us, for we were all well armed. We reached the ranch in safety, rested a day, and then took the ambulance and went on to San Antonio. Three of us, besides Tiburcio, accompanied our employer, each taking a saddle horse, and stopping by night at ranches where we were known. On the third day we reached the city in good time to bank the money, much to my relief.

As there was no work pressing at home, we spent a week in the city, thoroughly enjoying ourselves. Uncle Lance was negotiating for the purchase of a large Spanish land grant, which adjoined our range on the west, taking in the Ganso and several miles' frontage on both sides of the home river. This required his attention for a few days, during which time Deweese met two men on the lookout for stock cattle with which to start a new ranch on the Devil's River in Valverde County. They were in the market for three thousand cows, to be delivered that fall or the following spring. Our *segundo* promptly invited them to meet his employer that evening at our hotel. As the ranges in eastern Texas became of value for agriculture, the cowman moved westward, disposing of his cattle or taking them with him. It was men of this class whom Deweese had met during the day, and on filling their appointment in the evening, our employer and the buyers soon came to an agreement. References were exchanged, and the next afternoon a contract was entered into whereby we were to deliver, May first, at Las Palomas ranch, three thousand cows between the ages of two and four years.

There was some delay in perfecting the title to the land grant. "We'll start home in the morning, boys," said Uncle Lance, the evening after the contract was drawn. "You simply can't hurry a land deal. I'll get that tract in time, but there's over a hundred heirs now of the original Don. I'd just like to know what the grandee did for his king to get that grant. Tickled his royal nibs, I reckon, with some cock and bull story, and here I have to give up nearly forty thousand dollars of good honest money. Twenty years ago I was offered this same grant for ten cents an acre, and now I'm paying four bits. But I didn't have the money then, and I'm not sure I'd have bought it if I had. But I need it now, and I need it bad, and that's why I'm letting them hold me up for such a figure."

Stopping at the "last chance" road house on the outskirts of the city the next morning, for a final drink as we were leaving, Uncle Lance said to us over the cattle contract: "There's money in it - good money, too. But we're not going to fill it out of our home brand. Not in this year of our Lord. I think too much of my cows to part with a single animal. Boys, cows made Las Palomas what she is, and as long as they win for me,

I intend - to swear by them through thick and thin, in good and bad repute, fair weather or foul. So, June, just as soon as the fall branding is over, you can take Tom with you for an interpreter and start for Mexico to contract these cows. Las Palomas is going to branch out and spread herself. As a ranchman, I can bring the cows across for breeding purposes free of duty, and I know of no good reason why I can't change my mind and sell them. Dan, take Tiburcio out a cigar."

CHAPTER XI

A TURKEY BAKE

Deweese and I came back from Mexico during Christmas week. On reaching Las Palomas, we found Frank Nancrede and Add Tully, the latter being also a trail foreman, at the ranch. They were wintering in San Antonio, and were spending a few weeks at our ranch, incidentally on the lookout for several hundred saddle horses for trail purposes the coming spring. We had no horses for sale, but nevertheless Uncle Lance had prevailed on them to make Las Palomas head-quarters during their stay in the country.

The first night at the ranch, Miss Jean and I talked until nearly midnight. There had been so many happenings during my absence that it required a whole evening to tell them all. From the naming of Anita's baby to the rivalry between John and Theodore for the favor of Frances Vaux, all the latest social news of the countryside was discussed. Miss Jean had attended the dance at Shepherd's during the fall, and had heard it whispered that Oxenford and Esther were anything but happy. The latest word from the Vaux ranch said that the couple had separated; at least there was some trouble, for when Oxenford had attempted to force her to return to Oakville, and had made some disparaging remarks, Tony Hunter had crimped a six-shooter over his head. I pretended not to be interested in this, but secretly had I learned that Hunter had killed Oxenford, I should have had no very serious regrets.

Uncle Lance had promised Tully and Nancrede a turkey hunt during the holidays, so on our unexpected return it was decided to have it at once. There had been a heavy mast that year, and in the encinal ridges to the east wild turkeys were reported plentiful. Accordingly we set out the next afternoon for a camp hunt in some oak cross timbers which grew on the eastern border of our ranch lands. Taking two pack mules and Tiburcio as cook, a party of eight of us rode away, expecting to remain overnight. Uncle Lance knew of a fine camping spot about ten miles from the ranch. When within a few miles of the place, Tiburcio was sent on ahead with the pack mules to make camp. "Boys, we'll divide up here," said Uncle Lance, "and take a little scout through these cross timbers and try and locate some roosts. The camp will be in those narrows ahead yonder where that burnt timber is to your right. Keep an eye open for *javalina* signs; they used to be plentiful through here when there was good mast. Now, scatter out in pairs, and if you can knock down a gobbler or two we'll have a turkey bake to-night."

Dan Happersett knew the camping spot, so I went with him, and together we took a big circle through the encinal, keeping alert for game signs. Before we had gone far, evidence became plentiful, not only of turkeys, but of peccary and deer. Where the turkeys had recently been scratching, many times we dismounted and led our horses - but either the turkeys were too wary for us, or else we had been deceived as to the freshness of the sign. Several successive shots on our right caused us to hurry out of the timber in the direction of the reports. Halting in the edge of the timber, we watched the strip of prairie between us and the next cover to the south. Soon a flock of fully a hundred wild turkeys came running out of the encinal on the opposite side and started across to our ridge. Keeping under cover, we rode to intercept them, never losing sight of the covey. They were running fast; but when they were nearly halfway across the opening, there was another shot and they took flight, sailing into cover ahead of us, well out of range. But one gobbler was so fat that he was unable to fly over a hundred yards and was still in the open. We rode to cut him off. On sighting us, he attempted to rise; but his pounds were against him, and when we crossed his course he was so winded that our horses ran all around him. After we had both shot a few times, missing him, he squatted in some tall grass and stuck his head under a tuft. Dismounting, Dan sprang on to him like a fox, and he was ours. We wrung his neck, and agreed to report that we had shot him through the head, thus concealing, in the absence of bullet wounds, our poor marksmanship.

When we reached the camp shortly before dark, we found the others had already arrived, ours making the sixth turkey in the evening's bag. We had drawn ours on killing it, as had the others, and after supper Uncle Lance superintended the stuffing of the two largest birds. While this was in progress, others made a stiff mortar, and we coated each turkey with about three inches of the waxy play, feathers and all. Opening our camp-fire, we placed the turkeys together, covered them with ashes and built a heaping fire over and around them. A number of haunts had been located by the others, but as we expected to make an early hunt in the morning, we decided not to visit any of the roosts that night. After Uncle Lance had regaled us with hunting stories of an early day, the discussion innocently turned to my recent elopement. By this time the scars had healed fairly well, and I took the chaffing in all good humor. Tully told a personal experience, which, if it was the truth, argued that in time I might become as indifferent to my recent mishap as any one could wish.

"My prospects of marrying a few years ago," said Tully, lying full stretch before the fire, "were a whole lot better than yours, Quirk. But my ambition those days was to boss a herd up the trail and get top-notch wages. She was a Texas girl, just like yours, bred up in Van Zandt County. She could ride a horse like an Indian. Bad horses seemed afraid of her. Why, I saw her once when she was about sixteen, take a black stallion out of his stable, - lead him out with but a rope about his neck, - throw a half hitch about his nose, and mount him as though he was her pet. Bareback and without a bridle she rode him ten miles for a doctor. There wasn't a mile of the distance either but he felt the quirt burning in his flank and knew he was being ridden by a master. Her father scolded her at the time, and boasted about it later.

"She had dozens of admirers, and the first impression I ever made on her was when she was about twenty. There was a big tournament being given, and all the young bloods in many counties came in to contest for the prizes. I was a double winner in the games and contests - won a roping prize and was the only lad that came inside the time limit as a lancer, though several beat me on rings. Of course the tournament ended with a ball. Having won the lance prize, it was my privilege of crowning the 'queen' of the ball. Of course I wasn't going to throw away such a chance, for there was no end of rivalry amongst the girls over it. The crown was made of flowers, or if there were none in season, of live-oak leaves. Well, at the ball after the tournament I crowned Miss Kate with a crown of oak leaves. After that I felt bold enough to crowd matters, and things came my way. We were to be married during Easter week, but her mother up and died, so we put it off awhile for the sake of appearances.

"The next spring I got a chance to boss a herd up the trail for Jesse Ellison. It was the chance of my life and I couldn't think of refusing. The girl put up quite a mouth about it, and I explained to her that a hundred a month wasn't offered to every man. She finally gave in, but still you could see she wasn't pleased. Girls that way don't sabe cattle matters a little bit. She promised to write me at several points which I told her the herd would pass. When I bade her good-by, tears stood in her eyes, though she tried to hide them. I'd have gambled my life on her that morning.

"Well, we had a nice trip, good outfit and strong cattle. Uncle Jess mounted us ten horses to the man, every one fourteen hands or better, for we were contracted for delivery in Nebraska. It was a five months' drive with scarcely an incident on the way. Just a run or two and a dry drive or so. I had lots of time to think about Kate. When we reached the Chisholm crossing on Red River, I felt certain that I would find a letter, but I didn't. I wrote her from there, but when we reached Caldwell, nary a letter either. The same luck at Abilene. Try as I might, I couldn't make it out. Something was wrong, but what it was, was anybody's guess.

"At this last place we got our orders to deliver the cattle at the junction of the middle and lower Loup. It was a terror of a long drive, but that wasn't a circumstance compared to not hearing from Kate. I kept all this to myself, mind you. When our herd reached its destination, which it did on time, as hard luck would have it there was a hitch in the payment. The herd was turned loose and all the outfit but myself sent home. I stayed there two months longer at a little place called Broken Bow. I held the bill of sale for the herd, and would turn it over, transferring the cattle from one owner to another, on the word from my employer. At last I received a letter from Uncle Jesse saying that the payment in full had been made, so I surrendered the final document and came home. Those trains seemed to run awful slow. But I got home all too soon, for she had then been married three months.

"You see an agent for eight-day clocks came along, and being a stranger took her eye. He was one of those nice, dapper fellows, wore a red necktie, and could talk all day to a woman. He worked by the rule of three, - tickle, talk, and flatter, with a few cutes thrown in for a pelon; that gets nearly any of them. They live in town now. He's a windmill agent. I never went near them."

Meanwhile the fire kept pace with the talk, thanks to Uncle Lance's watchful eye. "That's right, Tiburcio, carry up plenty of good lena," he kept saying. "Bring in all the black-jack oak that you can find; it makes fine coals. These are both big gobblers, and to bake them until they fall to pieces like a watermelon will require a steady fire till morning. Pile up a lot of wood, and if I wake up during the night, trust to me to look after the fire. I've baked so many turkeys this way that I'm an expert at the business."

"A girl's argument," remarked Dan Happersett in a lull of talk, "don't have to be very weighty to fit any case. Anything she does is justifiable. That's one reason why I always kept shy of women. I admit that I've toyed around with some of them; have tossed my tug on one or two just to see if they would run on the rope. But now generally I keep a wire fence between them and myself if they show any symptoms of being on the marry. Maybe so I was in earnest once, back on the Trinity. But it seems that every time that I made a pass, my loop would foul or fail to open or there was brush in the way."

"Just because you have a few gray hairs in your head you think you're awful foxy, don't you?" said Uncle Lance to Dan. "I've seen lots of independent fellows like you. If I had a little widow who knew her cards, and just let her kitten up to you and act coltish, inside a week you would he following her around like a pet lamb."

"I knew a fellow," said Nancrede, lighting his pipe with a firebrand, "that when the clerk asked him, when he went for a license to marry, if he would swear that the young lady - his intended - was over twenty-one, said: 'Yes, by G - , I'll swear that she's over thirty-one.'"

At the next pause in the yarning, I inquired why a wild turkey always deceived itself by hiding its head and leaving the body exposed. "That it's a fact, we all know," volunteered Uncle Lance, "but the why and wherefore is too deep for me. I take it that it's due to running to neck too much in their construction. Now an ostrich is the same way, all neck with not a lick of sense. And the same applies to the human family. You take one of these long-necked cowmen and what does he know outside of cattle. Nine times out of ten, I can tell a sensible girl by merely looking at her neck. Now snicker, you dratted young fools, just as if I wasn't talking horse sense to you. Some of you boys haven't got much more sabe than a fat old gobbler."

"When I first came to this State," said June Deweese, who had been quietly and attentively listening to the stories, "I stopped over on the Neches River near a place called Shot-a-buck Crossing. I had an uncle living there with whom I made my home the first few years that I lived in Texas. There are more or less cattle there, but it is principally a cotton country. There was an old cuss living over there on that river who was land poor, but had a powerful purty girl. Her old man owned any number of plantations on the river - generally had lots of nigger renters to look after. Miss Sallie, the daughter, was the belle of the neighborhood. She had all the graces with a fair mixture of the weaknesses of her sex. The trouble was, there was no young man in the whole country fit to hold her horse. At least she and her folks entertained that idea. There was a storekeeper and a young doctor at the county seat, who it seems took turns calling on her. It looked like it was going to be a close race. Outside of these two there wasn't a one of us who could touch her with a twenty-four-foot fish-pole. We simply took the side of the road when she passed by.

"About this time there drifted in from out west near Fort McKavett, a young fellow named Curly Thorn. He had relatives living in that neighborhood. Out at the fort he was a common foreman on a ranch. Talk about your graceful riders, he sat a horse in a manner that left nothing to be desired. Well, Curly made himself very agreeable with all the girls on the range, but played no special favorites. He stayed in the country, visiting among cousins, until camp meeting began over at the Alabama Camp Ground. During this meeting Curly proved himself quite a gallant by carrying first one young lady and the next evening some other to camp meeting. During these two weeks of the meeting, some one introduced him to Miss Sallie. Now, remember, he didn't play her for a favorite no more than any other. That's what miffed her. She thought he ought to.

"One Sunday afternoon she intimated to him, like a girl sometimes will, that she was going home, and was sorry that she had no companion for the ride. This was sufficient for the gallant Curly to offer himself to her as an escort. She simply thought she was stealing a beau from some other girl, and he never dreamt he was dallying with Neches River royalty. But the only inequality in that couple as they rode away from the ground was an erroneous idea in her and her folks' minds. And that difference was in the fact that her old dad had more land than he could pay taxes on. Well, Curly not only saw her home, but stayed for tea - that's the name the girls have for supper over on the Neches - and that night carried her back to the evening service. From that day till the close of the session he was devotedly hers. A month afterward when he left, it was the talk of the country that they were to be married during the coming holidays.

"But then there were the young doctor and the storekeeper still in the game. Curly was off the scene temporarily, but the other two were riding their best horses to a shadow. Miss Sallie's folks were pulling like bay steers for the merchant, who had some money, while the young doctor had nothing but empty pill bags and a saddle horse or two. The doctor was the better looking, and, before meeting Curly Thorn, Miss Sallie had favored him. Knowing ones said they were engaged. But near the close of the race there was sufficient home influence used for the storekeeper to take the lead and hold it until the show down came. Her folks announced the wedding, and the merchant received the best wishes of his friends, while the young doctor took a trip for his health. Well, it developed afterwards that she was engaged to both the storekeeper and the doctor at the same time. But that's nothing. My experience tells me that a girl don't need broad shoulders to carry three or four engagements at the same time.

"Well, within a week of the wedding, who should drift in to spend Christmas but Curly Thorn. His cousins, of course, lost no time in giving him the lay of the land. But Curly acted indifferent, and never even offered to call on Miss Sallie. Us fellows joked him about his girl going to marry another fellow, and he didn't seem a little bit put out. In fact, he seemed to enjoy the sudden turn as a good joke on himself. But one morning, two days before the wedding was to take place, Miss

Sallie was missing from her home, as was likewise Curly Thorn from the neighborhood. Yes, Thorn had eloped with her and they were married the next morning in Nacogdoches. And the funny thing about it was, Curly never met her after his return until the night they eloped. But he had a girl cousin who had a finger in the pie. She and Miss Sallie were as thick as three in a bed, and Curly didn't have anything to do but play the hand that was dealt him.

"Before I came to Las Palomas, I was over round Fort McKavett and met Curly. We knew each other, and he took me home and had me stay overnight with him. They had been married then four years. She had a baby on each knee and another in her arms. There was so much reality in life that she had no time to become a dreamer. Matrimony in that case was a good leveler of imaginary rank. I always admired Curly for the indifferent hand he played all through the various stages of the courtship. He never knew there was such a thing as difference. He simply coppered the play to win, and the cards came his way."

"Bully for Curly!" said Uncle Lance, arising and fixing the fire, as the rest of us unrolled our blankets. "If some of my rascals could make a ten strike like that it would break a streak of bad luck which has overshadowed Las Palomas for over thirty years. Great Scott! - but those gobblers smell good. I can hear them blubbering and sizzling in their shells. It will surely take an axe to crack that clay in the morning. But get under your blankets, lads, for I'll call you for a turkey breakfast about dawn."

CHAPTER XII

SUMMER OF '77

During our trip into Mexico the fall before, Deweese contracted for three thousand cows at two haciendas on the Rio San Juan. Early in the spring June and I returned to receive the cattle. The ranch outfit under Uncle Lance was to follow some three weeks later and camp on the American side at Roma, Texas. We made arrangements as we crossed into Mexico with a mercantile house in Mier to act as our bankers, depositing our own drafts and taking letters of credit to the interior. In buying the cows we had designated Mier, which was just opposite Roma, as the place for settlement and Uncle Lance on his arrival brought drafts to cover our purchases, depositing them with the same merchant. On receiving, we used a tally mark which served as a road brand, thus preventing a second branding, and throughout - much to the disgust of the Mexican vaqueros - Deweese enforced every humane idea which Nancrede had practiced the spring before in accepting the trail herd at Las Palomas. There were endless quantities of stock cattle to select from on the two haciendas, and when ready to start, under the specifications, a finer lot of cows would have been hard to find. The worst drawback was that they were constantly dropping calves on the road, and before we reached the river we had a calf-wagon in regular use. On arriving at the Rio Grande, the then stage of water was fortunately low and we crossed the herd without a halt, the import papers having been attended to in advance.

Uncle Lance believed in plenty of help, and had brought down from Las Palomas an ample outfit of men and horses. He had also anticipated the dropping of calves and had rigged up a carrier, the box of which was open framework. Thus until a calf was strong enough to follow, the mother, as she trailed along beside the wagon, could keep an eye on her offspring. We made good drives the first two or three days; but after clearing the first bottoms of the Rio Grande and on reaching the tablelands, we made easy stages of ten to twelve miles a day. When near enough to calculate on our arrival at Las Palomas, the old ranchero quit us and went on into the ranch. Several days later a vaquero met the herd about thirty miles south of Santa Maria, and brought the information that the Valverde outfit was at the ranch, and instructions to veer westward and drive down the Ganso on approaching the Nueces. By these orders the delivery on the home river would occur at least twenty miles west of the ranch headquarters.

As we were passing to the westward of Santa Maria, our employer and one of the buyers rode out from that ranch and met the herd. They had decided not to brand until arriving at their destination on the Devil's River, which would take them at least a month longer. While this deviation was nothing to us, it was a gain to them. The purchaser was delighted with the cattle and our handling of them, there being fully a thousand young calves, and on reaching their camp on the Ganso, the delivery was completed - four days in advance of the specified time. For fear of losses, we had received a few head extra, and, on counting them over, found we had not lost a single hoof. The buyers received the extra cattle, and the delivery was satisfactorily concluded. One of the partners returned with us to Las Palomas for the final settlement, while the other, taking charge of the herd, turned them up the Nueces. The receiving outfit had fourteen men and some hundred and odd horses. Aside from their commissary, they also had a calf-wagon, drawn by two yoke of oxen and driven by a strapping big negro. In view of the big calf crop, the partners concluded that an extra conveyance would not be amiss, and on Uncle Lance making them a reasonable figure on our calf-wagon and the four mules drawing it, they never changed a word but took the outfit. As it was late in the day when the delivery was made, the double outfit remained in the same camp that night, and with the best wishes, bade each other farewell in the morning. Nearly a month had passed since Deweese and I had left Las Palomas for the Rio San Juan, and, returning with the herd, had met our own outfit at the Rio Grande. During the interim, before the ranch outfit had started, the long-talked-of tournament on the Nueces had finally been arranged. The date had been set for the fifth of June, and of all the home news which the outfit brought down to the Rio Grande, none was as welcome as this. According to the programme, the contests were to include riding, roping, relay races, and handling the lance. Several of us had never witnessed a tournament; but as far as roping and riding were concerned, we all considered ourselves past masters of the arts. The relay races were simple enough, and Dan Happersett volunteered this explanation of a lance contest to those of us who were uninitiated: -

"Well," said Dan, while we were riding home from the Ganso, "a straight track is laid off about two hundred yards long. About every forty yards there is a post set up along the line with an arm reaching out over the track. From this there is suspended an iron ring about two inches in diameter. The contestant is armed with a wooden lance of regulation length, and as he rides down this track at full speed and within a time limit, he is to impale as many of these rings as possible. Each contestant is entitled to three trials and the one impaling the most rings is declared the victor. That's about all there is to it, except the award. The festivities, of course, close with a dance, in which the winner crowns the Queen of the ball. That's the reason the girls always take such an interest in the lancing, because the winner has the choosing of his Queen. I won it once, over on the Trinity, and chose a little cripple girl. Had to do it or leave the country, for it was looked upon as an engagement to marry. Oh, I tell you, if a girl is sweet on a fellow, it's a mighty strong card to play."

Before starting for the Rio Grande, the old ranchero had worked our horse stock, forming fourteen new *manadas*, so that on our return about the only work which could command our attention was the breaking of more saddle horses. We had gentled two hundred the spring before, and breaking a hundred and fifty now, together with the old *remudas*, would give Las Palomas fully five hundred saddle horses. The ranch had the geldings, the men had time, and there was no good excuse for not gentling more horses. So after a few days' rest the oldest and heaviest geldings were gathered and we then settled down to routine horse work. But not even this exciting employment could keep the coming tournament from our minds. Within a week after returning to the ranch, we laid off a lancing course, and during every spare hour the knights of Las Palomas might be seen galloping over the course, practicing. I tried using the lance several times, only to find that it was not as easy as it looked, and I finally gave up the idea of lancing honors, and turned my attention to the relay races.

Miss Jean had been the only representative of our ranch at Shepherd's on San Jacinto Day. But she had had her eyes open on that occasion, and on our return had a message for nearly every one of us. I was not expecting any, still the mistress of Las Palomas had met my old sweetheart and her sister, Mrs. Hunter, at the ferry, and the three had talked the matter over and mingled their tears in mutual sympathy. I made a blustering talk which was to cover my real feelings and to show that I had grown indifferent toward Esther, but that tactful woman had not lived in vain, and read me aright.

"Tom," said she, "I was a young woman when you were a baby. There's lots of things in which you might deceive me, but Esther McLeod is not one of them. You loved her once, and you can't tell me that in less than a year you have forgotten her. I won't say that men forget easier than women, but you have never suffered one tenth the heartaches over Esther McLeod that she has over you. You can afford to be generous with her, Tom. True, she allowed an older sister to browbeat and bully her into marrying another man, but she was an inexperienced girl then. If you were honest, you would admit that Esther of her own accord would never have married

Jack Oxenford. Then why punish the innocent? Oh, Tom, if you could only see her now! Sorrow and suffering have developed the woman in her, and she is no longer the girl you knew and loved."

Miss Jean was hewing too close to the line for my comfort. Her observations were so near the truth that they touched me in a vulnerable spot. Yet as I paced the room, I expressed myself emphatically as never wishing to meet Esther McLeod again. I really felt that way. But I had not reckoned on the mistress of Las Palomas, nor considered that her strong sympathy for my former sweetheart had moved her to more than ordinary endeavor.

The month of May passed. Uncle Lance spent several weeks at the Booth ranch on the Frio. At the home ranch practice for the contests went forward with vigor. By the first of June we had sifted the candidates down until we had determined on our best men for each entry. The old ranchero and our *segundo*, together with Dan Happersett, made up a good set of judges on our special fitness for the different contests, and we were finally picked in this order: Enrique Lopez was to rope; Pasquale Arispe was to ride; to Theodore Quayle fell the chance of handling the lance, while I, being young and nimble on my feet, was decided on as the rider in the ten-mile relay race.

In this contest I was fortunate in having the pick of over three hundred and fifty saddle horses. They were the accumulation of years of the best that Las Palomas bred, and it was almost bewildering to make the final selection. But in this I had the benefit of the home judges, and when the latter differed on the speed of a horse, a trial usually settled the point. June Deweese proved to be the best judge of the ranch horses, yet Uncle Lance never yielded his opinion without a test of speed. When the horses were finally decided on, we staked off a half-mile circular track on the first bottom of the river, and every evening the horses were sent over the course. Under the conditions, a contestant was entitled to use as many horses as he wished, but must change mounts at least twenty times in riding the ten miles, and must finish under a time limit of twenty-five minutes. Out of our abundance we decided to use ten mounts, thus allotting each horse two dashes of a half mile with a rest between.

The horse-breaking ended a few days before the appointed time. Las Palomas stood on the tiptoe of expectancy over the coming tourney. Even Miss Jean rode - having a gentle saddle horse caught up for her use, and taking daily rides about the ranch, to witness the practice, for she was as deeply interested as any of us in the forthcoming contests. Born to the soil of Texas, she was a horsewoman of no ordinary ability, and rode like a veteran. On the appointed day, Las Palomas was abandoned; even the Mexican contingent joining in the exodus for Shepherd's, and only a few old servants remaining at the ranch. As usual, Miss Jean started by ambulance the afternoon before, taking along a horse for her own saddle. The white element and the vaqueros made an early start, driving a *remuda* of thirty loose horses, several of which were outlaws, and a bell mare. They were the picked horses of the ranch - those which we expected to use in the contests, and a change of mounts for the entire outfit on reaching the martial field. We had herded the horses the night before, and the vaqueros were halfway to the ferry when we overtook them. Uncle Lance was with us and in the height of his glory, in one breath bragging on Enrique and Pasquale, and admonishing and cautioning Theodore and myself in the next.

On nearing Shepherd's, Uncle Lance preceded us, to hunt up the committee and enter a man from Las Palomas for each of the contests. The ground had been well chosen, - a large open bottom on the north side of the river and about a mile above the ferry. The lancing course was laid off; temporary corrals had been built, to hold about thirty range cattle for the roping, and an equal number of outlaw horses for the riding contests; at the upper end of the valley a half-mile circular racecourse had been staked off. Throwing our outlaws into the corral, and leaving the *remuda* in charge of two vaqueros, we galloped into

Shepherd's with the gathering crowd. From all indications this would be a red-letter day at the ferry, for the attendance drained a section of country fully a hundred miles in diameter. On the north from Campbellton on the Atascosa to San Patricio on the home river to the south, and from the Blanco on the east to well up the Frio and San Miguel on the west, horsemen were flocking by platoons. I did not know one man in twenty, but Deweese greeted them all as if they were near neighbors. Later in the morning, conveyances began to arrive from Oakville and near-by points, and the presence of women lent variety to the scene.

Under the rules, all entries were to be made before ten o'clock. The contests were due to begin half an hour later, and each contestant was expected to be ready to compete in the order of his application. There were eight entries in the relay race all told, mine being the seventh, which gave me a good opportunity to study the riding of those who preceded me. There were ten or twelve entries each in the roping and riding contests, while the knights of the lance numbered an even thirty. On account of the large number of entries the contests would require a full day, running the three classes simultaneously, allowing a slight intermission for lunch. The selection of disinterested judges for each class slightly delayed the commencement. After changing horses on reaching the field, the contests with the lance opened with a lad from Ramirena, who galloped over the course and got but a single ring. From the lateness of our entries, none of us would be called until afternoon, and we wandered at will from one section of the field to another. "Red" Earnest, from Waugh's ranch on the Frio, was the first entry in the relay race. He had a good mount of eight Spanish horses which he rode bareback, making many of his changes in less than fifteen seconds apiece, and finishing full three minutes under the time limit. The feat was cheered to the echo, I joining with the rest, and numerous friendly bets were made that the time would not be lowered that day. Two other riders rode before the noon recess, only one of whom came under the time limit, and his time was a minute over Earnest's record.

Miss Jean had camped the ambulance in sight of the field, and kept open house to all comers. Suspecting that she would have Mrs. Hunter and Esther for lunch, if they were present, I avoided our party and took dinner with Mrs. Booth. Meanwhile Uncle Lance detailed Deweese and Happersett to handle my horses, allowing us five vaqueros, and distributing the other men as assistants to our other three contestants. The day was an ideal one for the contests, rather warm during the morning, but tempered later by a fine afternoon breeze. It was after four o'clock when I was called, with Waugh's man still in the lead. Forming a small circle at the starting-point, each of our vaqueros led a pair of horses, in bridles only, around a ring, - constantly having in hand eight of my mount of ten. As handlers, I had two good men in our *segundo* and Dan Happersett. I crossed the line amid the usual shouting with a running start, determined, if possible, to lower the record of Red Earnest. In making the changes, all I asked was a good grip on the mane, and I found my seat as the horse shot away. The horses had broken into an easy sweat before the race began, and having stripped to the lowest possible ounce of clothing, I felt that I was getting out of them every fraction of speed they possessed. The ninth horse in my mount, a roan, for some unknown reason sulked at starting, then bolted out on the prairie, but got away with the loss of only about ten seconds, running the half mile like a scared wolf. Until it came the roan's turn to go again, no untoward incident happened, friendly timekeepers posting me at every change of mounts. But when this bolter's turn came again, he reared and plunged away stiff-legged, crossed the inward furrow, and before I could turn him again to the track, cut inside the course for two stakes or possibly fifty yards. By this time I was beyond recall, but as I came round and passed the starting-point, the judges attempted to stop me, and I well knew my chances were over. Uncle Lance promptly waived all rights to the award, and I was allowed to finish the race, lowering Earnest's time over twenty seconds. The eighth contestant, so I learned later, barely came under the time limit.

The vaqueros took charge of the relay mounts, and, reinvesting myself in my discarded clothing, I mounted my horse to leave the field, when who should gallop up and extend sympathy and congratulations but Miss Jean and my old sweetheart. There was no avoiding them, and discourtesy to the mistress of Las Palomas being out of the question, I greeted Esther with an affected warmth and cordiality. As I released her hand I could not help noticing how she had saddened into a serious woman, while the gentleness in her voice condemned me for my attitude toward her. But Miss Jean artfully gave us little time for embarrassment, inviting me to show them the unconcluded programme. From contest to contest, we rode the field until the sun went down, and the trials ended.

It was my first tournament and nothing escaped my notice. There were fully one hundred and fifty women and girls, and possibly double that number of men, old and young, every one mounted and galloping from one point of the field to another. Blushing maidens and their swains dropped out of the throng, and from shady vantage points watched the crowd surge back and forth across the field of action. We were sorry to miss Enrique's roping; for having snapped his saddle horn with the first cast, he recovered his rope, fastened it to the fork of his saddletree, and tied his steer in fifty-four seconds, or within ten of the winner's record. When he apologized to Miss Jean for his bad luck, hat in hand and his eyes as big as saucers, one would have supposed he had brought lasting disgrace on Las Palomas.

We were more fortunate in witnessing Pasquale's riding. For this contest outlaws and spoilt horses had been collected from every quarter. Riders drew their mounts by lot, and Pasquale drew a cinnamon-colored coyote from the ranch of "Uncle Nate" Wilson of Ramirena. Uncle Nate was feeling in fine fettle, and when he learned that his contribution to the outlaw horses had been drawn by a Las Palomas man, he hunted up the ranchero. "I'll bet you a new five-dollar hat that that cinnamon horse throws your vaquero so high that the birds build nests in his crotch before he hits the ground." Uncle Lance took the bet, and disdainfully ran his eye up and down his old friend, finally remarking, "Nate, you ought to keep perfectly sober on an occasion like this - you're liable to lose all your money."

Pasquale was a shallow-brained, clownish fellow, and after saddling up, as he led the coyote into the open to mount, he imitated a drunken vaquero. Tipsily admonishing the horse in Spanish to behave himself, he vaulted into the saddle and clouted his mount over the head with his hat. The coyote resorted to every ruse known to a bucking horse to unseat his rider, in the midst of which Pasquale, languidly lolling in his saddle, took a small bottle from his pocket, and, drinking its contents, tossed it backward over his head. "Look at that, Nate," said Uncle Lance, slapping Mr. Wilson with his hat; "that's one of the Las Palomas vaqueros, bred with just sense enough to ride anything that wears hair. We'll look at those new hats this evening."

In the fancy riding which followed, Pasquale did a number of stunts. He picked up hat and handkerchief from the ground at full speed, and likewise gathered up silver dollars from alternate sides of his horse as the animal sped over a short course. Stripping off his saddle and bridle, he rode the naked horse with the grace of an Indian, and but for his clownish indifference and the apparent ease with which he did things, the judges might have taken his work more seriously. As it was, our outfit and those friendly to our ranch were proud of his performance, but among outsiders, and even the judges, it was generally believed that he was tipsy, which was an injustice to him.

On the conclusion of the contest with the lance, among the thirty participants, four were tied on honors, one of whom was Theodore Quayle. The other contests being over, the crowd gathered round the lancing course, excitement being at its highest pitch. A lad from the Blanco was the first called for on the finals, and after three efforts failed to make good his former trial. Quayle was the next called, and as he sped down the course my heart stood still for a moment; but as he returned, holding high his lance, five rings were impaled upon it. He was entitled to two more trials, but rested on his record until it was tied or beaten, and the next man was called. Forcing her way through the crowded field, Miss Jean warmly congratulated Theodore, leaving Esther to my tender care. But at this juncture, my old sweetheart caught sight of Frances Vaux and some gallant approaching from the river's shade, and together we galloped out to meet them. Miss Vaux's escort was a neighbor lad from the Frio, but both he and I for the time being were relegated to oblivion, in the prospects of a Las Palomas man by the name of Quayle winning the lancing contest. Miss Frances, with a shrug, was for denying all interest in the result, but Esther and I doubled on her, forcing her to admit "that it would be real nice if Teddy should win." I never was so aggravated over the indifference of a girl in my life, and my regard for my former sweetheart, on account of her enthusiasm for a Las Palomas lad, kindled anew within me.

But as the third man sped over the course, we hastily returned to watch the final results. After a last trial the man threw down his lance, and, riding up, congratulated Quayle. The last contestant was a red-headed fellow from the Atascosa above Oakville, and seemed to have a host of friends. On his first trial over the course, he stripped four rings, but on neither subsequent effort did he equal his first attempt. Imitating the former contestant, the red-headed fellow broke his lance and congratulated the winner.

The tourney was over. Esther and I urged Miss Frances to ride over with us and congratulate Quayle. She demurred; but as the crowd scattered I caught Theodore's eye and, signaling to him, he rode out of the crowd and joined us. The compliments of Miss Vaux to the winner were insipid and lifeless, while Esther, as if to atone for her friend's lack of interest, beamed with happiness over Quayle's good luck. Poor Teddy hardly knew which way to turn and, nice girl as she was, I almost hated Miss Frances for her indifferent attitude. A plain, blunt fellow though he was, Quayle had noticed the coolness in the greeting of the young lady whom he no doubt had had in mind for months, in case he should win the privilege, to crown as Queen of the ball. Piqued and unsettled in his mind, he excused himself on some trivial pretense and withdrew. Every one was scattering to the picnic grounds for supper, and under the pretense of escorting Esther to the Vaux conveyance, I accompanied the young ladies. Managing to fall to the rear of Miss Frances and her gallant for the day, I bluntly asked my old sweetheart if she understood the attitude of her friend. For reply she gave me a pitying glance, saying, "Oh, you boys know so little about a girl! You see that Teddy chooses Frances for his Queen to-night, and leave the rest to me."

On reaching their picnic camp, I excused myself, promising to meet them later at the dance, and rode for our ambulance. Tiburcio had supper all ready, and after it was over I called Theodore to one side and repeated Esther's message. Quayle was still doubtful, and I called Miss Jean to my assistance, hoping to convince him that Miss Vaux was not unfriendly towards him. "You always want to judge a woman by contraries," said Miss Jean, seating herself on the log beside us. "When it comes to acting her part, always depend on a girl to conceal her true feelings, especially if she has tact. Now, from what you boys say, my judgment is that she'd cry her eyes out if any other girl was chosen Queen."

Uncle Lance had promised Mr. Wilson to take supper with his family, and as we were all sprucing up for the dance, he returned. He had not been present at the finals of the lancing contest, but from guests of the Wilsons' had learned that one of his boys had won the honors. So on riding into camp, as the finishing touches were being added to our rustic toilets, he accosted Quayle and said: "Well, Theo, they tell me that you won the elephant. Great Scott, boy, that's the best luck that has struck Las Palomas since the big rain a year ago this month! Of course, we all understand that you're to choose the oldest Vaux girl. What's that? You don't know? Well, I do. I've had that all planned out, in case you won, ever since we decided that you was to contest as the representative of Las Palomas. And now you want to balk, do you?"

Uncle Lance was showing some spirit, but his sister checked him with this explanation: "Just because Miss Frances didn't show any enthusiasm over Theo winning, he and Tom somehow have got the idea in their minds that she don't care a rap to be chosen Queen. I've tried to explain it to them, but the boys don't understand girls, that's all. Why, if Theo was to choose any other girl, she'd set the river afire."

"That's it, is it?" snorted Uncle Lance, pulling his gray mustaches. "Well, I've known for some time that Tom didn't have good sense, but I have always given you, Theo, credit for having a little. I'll gamble my all that what Jean says is Bible truth. Didn't I have my eye on you and that girl for nearly a week during the hunt a year ago, and haven't you been riding my horses over to the Frio once or twice a month ever since? You can read a brand as far as I can, but I can see that you're as blind as a bat about a girl. Now, young fellow, listen to me: when the master of ceremonies announces the winners of the day, and your name is called, throw out your brisket, stand straight on those bow-legs of yours, step forward and claim your privilege. When the wreath is tendered you, accept it, carry it to the lady of your choice, and kneeling before her, if she bids you arise, place the crown on her brow and lead the grand march. I'd gladly give Las Palomas and every hoof on it for your years and chance."

The festivities began with falling darkness. The master of ceremonies, a school teacher from Oakville, read out the successful contestants and the prizes to which they were entitled. The name of Theodore Quayle was the last to be called, and excusing himself to Miss Jean, who had him in tow, he walked forward with a military air, executing every movement in the ceremony like an actor. As the music struck up, he and the blushing Frances Vaux, rare in rustic beauty and crowned with a wreath of live-oak leaves, led the opening march. Hundreds of hands clapped in approval, and as the applause quieted down, I turned to look for a partner, only to meet Miss Jean and my former sweetheart. Both were in a seventh heaven of delight, and promptly took occasion to remind me of my lack of foresight, repeating in chorus, "Didn't I tell you?" But the music had broken into a waltz, which precluded any argument, and on the mistress remarking "You young folks are missing a fine dance," involuntarily my arm encircled my old sweetheart, and we drifted away into elysian fields.

The night after the first tournament at Shepherd's on the Nueces in June, '77, lingers as a pleasant memory. Veiled in hazy retrospect, attempting to recall it is like inviting the return of childish dreams when one has reached the years of maturity. If I danced that night with any other girl than poor Esther McLeod, the fact has certainly escaped me. But somewhere in the archives of memory there is an indelible picture of a stroll through dimly lighted picnic grounds; of sitting on a rustic settee, built round the base of a patriarchal live-oak, and listening to a broken-hearted woman lay bare the sorrows which less than a year had brought her. I distinctly recall that my eyes, though unused to weeping, filled with tears, when Esther in words of deepest sorrow and contrition begged me to forgive her heedless and reckless act. Could I harbor resentment in the face of such entreaty? The impulsiveness of youth refused to believe that true happiness had gone out of her life. She was again to me as she had been before her unfortunate marriage, and must be released from the hateful bonds that bound her. Firm in this resolve, dawn stole upon us, still sitting at the root of the old oak, oblivious and happy in each other's presence, having pledged anew our troth for time and eternity.

With the breaking of day the revelers dispersed. Quite a large contingent from those present rode several miles up the river with our party. The *remuda* had been sent home the evening before with the returning vaqueros, while the impatience of the ambulance mules frequently carried them in advance of the cavalcade. The mistress of Las Palomas had as her guest returning, Miss Jule Wilson, and the first time they passed us, some four or five miles above the ferry, I noticed Uncle Lance ride up, swaggering in his saddle, and poke Glenn Gallup in the ribs, with a wink and nod towards the conveyance as the mules dashed past. The pace we were traveling would carry us home by the middle of the forenoon, and once we were reduced to the home crowd, the old matchmaker broke out enthusiastically: -

"This tourney was what I call a success. I don't care a tinker's darn for the prizes, but the way you boys built up to the girls last night warmed the sluggish blood in my old veins. Even if Cotton did claim a dance or two with the oldest Vaux girl, if Theo and her don't make the riffle now - well, they simply can't help it, having gone so far. And did any of you notice Scales and old June and Dan cutting the pigeon wing like colts? I reckon Quirk will have to make some new resolutions this morning. Oh, I heard about your declaring that you never wanted to see Esther McLeod again. That's all right, son, but hereafter remember that a resolve about a woman is only good for the day it is made, or until you meet her. And notice, will you, ahead yonder, that sister of mine playing second fiddle as a matchmaker. Glenn, if I was you, the next time Miss Jule looks back this way, I'd play sick, and maybe they'd let you ride in the ambulance. I can see at a glance that she's being poorly entertained."

CHAPTER XIII

HIDE HUNTING

During the month of June only two showers fell, which revived the grass but added not a drop of water to our tank supply or to the river. When the coast winds which followed set in, all hope for rain passed for another year. During the residence of the old ranchero at Las Palomas, the Nueces valley had suffered several severe drouths as disastrous in their effects as a pestilence. There were places in its miles of meanderings across our range where the river was paved with the bones of cattle which had perished with thirst. Realizing that such disasters repeat themselves, the ranch was set in order. That fall we branded the calf crop with unusual care. In every possible quarter, we prepared for the worst. A dozen wells were sunk over the tract and equipped with windmills. There was sufficient water in the river and tanks during the summer and fall, but by Christmas the range was eaten off until the cattle, ranging far, came in only every other day to slake their thirst.

The social gayeties of the countryside received a check from the threatened drouth. At Las Palomas we observed only the usual Christmas festivities. Miss Jean always made it a point to have something extra for the holiday season, not only in her own household, but also among the Mexican families at headquarters and the outlying ranchites. Among a number of delicacies brought up this time from Shepherd's was a box of Florida oranges, and in assisting Miss Jean to fill the baskets for each *jacal*, Aaron Scales opened this box of oranges and found a letter, evidently placed there by some mischievous girl in the packery from which the oranges were shipped. There

ANDY ADAMS

was not only a letter but a visiting card and a small photograph of the writer. This could only be accepted by the discoverer as a challenge, for the sender surely knew this particular box was intended for shipment to Texas, and banteringly invited the recipient to reply. The missive certainly fell upon fertile soil, and Scales, by right of discovery, delegated to himself the pleasure of answering.

Scales was the black sheep of Las Palomas. Born of a rich, aristocratic family in Maryland, he had early developed into a good-natured but reckless spendthrift, and his disreputable associates had contributed no small part in forcing him to the refuge of a cattle ranch. He had been offered every opportunity to secure a good education, but during his last year in college had been expelled, and rather than face parental reproach had taken passage in a coast schooner for Galveston, Texas. Then by easy stages he drifted westward, and at last, to his liking, found a home at Las Palomas. He made himself a useful man on the ranch, but, not having been bred to the occupation and with a tendency to waywardness, gave a rather free rein to the vagabond spirit which possessed him. He was a good rider, even for a country where every one was a born horseman, but the use of the rope was an art he never attempted to master.

With the conclusion of the holiday festivities and on the return of the absentees, a feature, new to me in cattle life, presented itself - hide hunting. Freighters who brought merchandise from the coast towns to the merchants of the interior were offering very liberal terms for return cargoes. About the only local product was flint hides, and of these there were very few, but the merchant at Shepherd's Ferry offered so generous inducements that Uncle Lance investigated the matter; the result was his determination to rid his range of the old, logy, worthless bulls. Heretofore they had been allowed to die of old age, but ten cents a pound for flint hides was an encouragement to remove these cumberers of the range, and turn them to some profit. So we were ordered to kill every bull on the ranch over seven years old.

In our round-up for branding, we had driven to the home range all outside cattle indiscriminately. They were still ranging near, so that at the commencement of this work nearly all the bulls in our brand were watering from the Nueces. These old residenter bulls never ranged over a mile away from water, and during the middle of the day they could be found along the river bank. Many of them were ten to twelve years old, and were as useless on the range as drones in autumn to a colony of honey-bees. Las Palomas boasted quite an arsenal of firearms, of every make and pattern, from a musket to a repeater. The outfit was divided into two squads, one going down nearly to Shepherd's, and the other beginning operations considerably above the Ganso. June Deweese took the down-river end, while Uncle Lance took some ten of us with one wagon on the up-river trip. To me this had all the appearance of a picnic. But the work proved to be anything but a picnic. To make the kill was most difficult. Not willing to leave the carcasses near the river, we usually sought the bulls coming in to water; but an ordinary charge of powder and lead, even when well directed at the forehead, rarely killed and tended rather to aggravate the creature. Besides, as we were compelled in nearly every instance to shoot from horseback, it was almost impossible to deliver an effective shot from in front. After one or more unsuccessful shots, the bull usually started for the nearest thicket, or the river; then our ropes came into use. The work was very slow; for though we operated in pairs, the first week we did not average a hide a day to the man; after killing, there was the animal to skin, the hide to be dragged from a saddle pommel into a hide yard and pegged out to dry.

Until we had accumulated a load of hides, Tiburcio Leal, our teamster, fell to me as partner. We had with us an abundance of our best horses, and those who were reliable with the rope had first choice of the *remuda*. Tiburcio was well mounted, but, on account of his years, was timid about using a rope; and well he might be, for frequently we found ourselves in a humorous predicament, and sometimes in one so grave that hilarity was not even a remote possibility.

The second morning of the hunt, Tiburcio and I singled out a big black bull about a mile from the river. I had not yet been convinced that I could not make an effective shot from in front, and, dismounting, attracted the bull's attention and fired. The shot did not even stagger him and he charged us; our horses avoided his rush, and he started for the river. Sheathing my carbine, I took down my rope and caught him before he had gone a hundred yards. As I threw my horse on his haunches to receive the shock, the weight and momentum of the bull dragged my double-cinched saddle over my horse's head and sent me sprawling on the ground. In wrapping the loose end of the rope around the pommel of the saddle, I had given it a half hitch, and as I came to my feet my saddle and carbine were bumping merrily along after Toro. Regaining my horse, I soon overtook Tiburcio, who was attempting to turn the animal back from the river, and urged him to "tie on," but he hesitated, offering me his horse instead. As there was no time to waste, we changed horses like relay riders. I soon overtook the animal and made a successful cast, catching the bull by the front feet. I threw Tiburcio's horse, like a wheeler, back on his haunches, and, on bringing the rope taut, fetched Toro to his knees; but with the strain the half-inch manila rope snapped at the pommel like a twine string. Then we were at our wit's end, the bull lumbering away with the second rope noosed over one fore foot, and leaving my saddle far in the rear. But after a moment's hesitation my partner and I doubled on him, to make trial of our guns, Tiburcio having a favorite old musket while I had only my six-shooter. Tiburcio, on my stripped horse, overtook the bull first, and attempted to turn him, but El Toro was not to be stopped. On coming up myself, I tried the same tactics, firing several shots into the ground in front of him but without deflecting the enraged bull from his course. Then I unloosed a Mexican blanket from Tiburcio's saddle, and flaunting it in his face, led him like a matador inviting a charge. This held his attention until Tiburcio, gaining courage, dashed past him from the rear and planted a musket ball behind the base of his ear, and the patriarch succumbed.

After the first few days' work, we found that the most vulnerable spot was where the spinal cord connects with the base of the brain. A well-directed shot at this point, even from a six-shooter, never failed to bring Toro to grass; and some of us became so expert that we could deliver this favorite shot from a running horse. The trouble was to get the bull to run evenly. That was one thing he objected to, and yet unless he did we could not advantageously attack him with a six-shooter. Many of these old bulls were surly in disposition, and even when they did run, there was no telling what moment they would sulk, stop without an instant's notice, and attempt to gore a passing horse.

We usually camped two or three days at a place, taking in both sides of the river, and after the work was once well under way we kept our wagon busy hauling the dry hides to a common yard on the river opposite Las Palomas. Without apology, it can be admitted that we did not confine our killing to the Las Palomas brand alone, but all cumberers on our range met the same fate. There were numerous stray bulls belonging to distant ranches which had taken up their abode on the Nueces, all of which were fish to our net. We kept a brand tally of every bull thus killed; for the primary motive was not one of profit, but to rid the range of these drones.

When we had been at work some two weeks, we had an exciting chase one afternoon in which Enrique Lopez figured as the hero. In coming in to dinner that day, Uncle Lance told of the chase after a young *ladino* bull with which we were all familiar. The old ranchero's hatred to wild cattle had caused him that morning to risk a long shot at this outlaw, wounding him. Juan Leal and Enrique Lopez, who were there, had both tried their marksmanship and their ropes on him in vain. Dragging down horses and snapping ropes, the bull made his escape into a chaparral thicket. He must have been exceedingly nimble; for I have seen Uncle Lance kill a running deer at a hundred yards with a rifle. At any rate, the entire squad turned out after dinner to renew the attack. We saddled the best horses in our *remuda* for the occasion, and sallied forth to the lair of the *ladino* bull, like a procession of professional bull-fighters.

The chaparral thicket in which the outlaw had taken refuge lay about a mile and a half back from the river and contained about two acres. On reaching the edge of the thicket, Uncle Lance called for volunteers to beat the brush and rout out the bull. As this must be done on foot, responses were not numerous. But our employer relieved the embarrassment by assigning vaqueros to the duty, also directing Enrique to take one point of the thicket and me the other, with instructions to use our ropes should the outlaw quit the thicket for the river. Detailing Tiburcio, who was with us that afternoon, to assist him in leading the loose saddle horses, he divided the six other men into two squads under Theodore Quayle and Dan Happersett. When all was ready, Enrique and myself took up our positions, hiding in the outlying mesquite brush; leaving the loose horses under saddle in the cover at a distance. The thicket was oval in form, lying with a point towards the river, and we all felt confident if the bull were started he would make for the timber on the river. With a whoop and hurrah and a free discharge of firearms, the beaters entered the chaparral. From my position I could see Enrique lying along the neck of his horse about fifty yards distant; and I had fully made up my mind to give that bucolic vaquero the first chance. During the past two weeks my enthusiasm for roping stray bulls had undergone a change; I was now quite willing that all honors of the afternoon should fall to Enrique. The beaters approached without giving any warning that the bull had been sighted, and so great was the strain and tension that I could feel the beating of my horse's heart beneath me. The suspense was finally broken by one or two shots in rapid succession, and as the sound died away, the voice of Juan Leal rang out distinctly: "Cuidado por el toro!" and the next moment there was a cracking of brush and a pale dun bull broke cover.

For a moment he halted on the border of the thicket: then, as the din of the beaters increased, struck boldly across the prairie for the river. Enrique and I were after him without loss of time. Enrique made a successful cast for his horns, and reined in his horse; but when the slack of the rope was taken up the rear cinch broke, the saddle was jerked forward on the horse's withers, and Enrique was compelled to free the rope or have his horse dragged down. I saw the mishap, and, giving my horse the rowel, rode at the bull and threw my rope. The loop neatly encircled his front feet, and when the shock came between horse and bull, it fetched the toro a somersault in the air, but unhappily took off the pommel of my saddle. The bull was on his feet in a jiffy, and before I could recover my rope, Enrique, who had reset his saddle, passed me, followed by the entire squad. Uncle Lance had been a witness to both mishaps, and on overtaking us urged me to tie on to the bull again. For answer I could only point to my missing pommel; but every man in the squad had loosened his rope, and it looked as if they would all fasten on to the *ladino*, for they were all good ropers. Man after man threw his loop on him; but the dun outlaw snapped the ropes as if they had been cotton strings, dragging down two horses with their riders and leaving them in the rear. I rode up alongside Enrique and offered him my rope, but he refused it, knowing it would be useless to try again with only a single cinch on his saddle. The young rascal had a daring idea in mind. We were within a quarter mile of the river, and escape of the outlaw seemed probable, when Enrique rode down on the bull, took up his tail, and, wrapping the brush on the pommel of his saddle, turned his horse abruptly to the left, rolling the bull over like a hoop, and of course dismounting himself in the act. Then before the dazed animal could rise, with the agility of a panther the vaquero sprang astride his loins, and as he floundered, others leaped from their horses. Toro was pinioned, and dispatched with a shot.

Then we loosened cinches to allow our heaving horses to breathe, and threw ourselves on the ground for a moment's rest. "That's the best kill we'll make on this trip," said Uncle Lance as we mounted, leaving two vaqueros to take the hide. "I despise wild cattle, and I've been hungering to get a shot at that fellow for the last three years. Enrique, the day the baby is born, I'll buy it a new cradle, and Tom shall have a new saddle and we'll charge it to Las Palomas - she's the girl that pays the bills."

Scarcely a day passed but similar experiences were related around the camp-fire. In fact, as the end of the work came in view, they became commonplace with us. Finally the two outfits were united at the general hide yard near the home ranch. Coils of small rope were brought from headquarters, and a detail of men remained in camp, baling the flint hides, while the remainder scoured the immediate country. A crude press was arranged, and by the aid of a long lever the hides were compressed into convenient space for handling by the freighters.

When we had nearly finished the killing and baling, an unlooked-for incident occurred. While Deweese was working down near Shepherd's Ferry, report of our work circulated around the country, and his camp had been frequently visited by cattlemen. Having nothing to conceal, he had showed his list of outside brands killed, which was perfectly satisfactory in most instances. As was customary in selling cattle, we expected to make report of every outside hide taken, and settle for them, deducting the necessary expense. But in every community there are those who oppose prevailing customs, and some who can always see sinister motives. One forenoon, when the baling was nearly finished, a delegation of men, representing brands of the Frio and San Miguel, rode up to our hide yard. They were all well-known cowmen, and Uncle Lance, being present, saluted them in his usual hearty manner. In response to an inquiry - "what he thought he was doing" - Uncle Lance jocularly replied: -

"Well, you see, you fellows allow your old bulls to drift down on my range, expecting Las Palomas to pension them the remainder of their days. But that's where you get fooled. Ten cents a pound for flint hides beats letting these old stagers die of old age. And this being an idle season with nothing much to do, we wanted to have a little fun. And we've had it. But laying all jokes aside, fellows, it's a good idea to get rid of these old varmints. Hereafter, I'm going to make a killing off every two or three years. The boys have kept a list of all stray brands killed, and you can look them over and see how many of yours we got. We have baled all the stray hides separate, so they can be looked over. But it's nearly noon, and you'd better all ride up to the ranch for dinner - they feed better up there than we do in camp."

Rather than make a three-mile ride to the house, the visitors took dinner with the wagon, and about one o'clock Deweese and a vaquero came in, dragging a hide between them. June cordially greeted the callers, including Henry Annear, who represented the Las Norias ranch, though I suppose it was well known to every one present that there was no love lost between them. Uncle Lance asked our foreman for his list of outside brands, explaining that these men wished to look them over. Everything seemed perfectly satisfactory to all parties concerned, and after remaining in camp over an hour, Deweese and the vaquero saddled fresh horses and rode away. The visitors seemed in no hurry to go, so Uncle Lance sat around camp entertaining them, while the rest of us proceeded with our work of baling. Before leaving, however, the entire party in company of our employer took a stroll about the hide yard, which was some distance from camp. During this tour of inspection, Annear asked which were the bales of outside hides taken in Deweese's division, claiming he represented a number of brands outside of Las Norias. The bales were pointed out and some dozen unbaled hides looked over. On a count the baled and unbaled hides were found to tally exactly with the list submitted. But unfortunately Annear took occasion to insinuate that the list of brands rendered had been "doctored." Uncle Lance paid little attention, though he heard, but the other visitors remonstrated with Annear. This only seemed to make him more contentious. Finally matters came to an open rupture when Annear demanded that the cordage be cut on certain bales to allow him to inspect them. Possibly he was within his rights, but on the Nueces during the seventies, to question a man's word was equivalent to calling him a liar; and *liar* was a fighting word all over the cattle range.

"Well, Henry," said Uncle Lance, rather firmly, "if you are not satisfied, I suppose I'll have to open the bales for you, but before I do, I'm going to send after June. Neither you nor any one else can cast any reflections on a man in my employ. No unjust act can be charged in my presence against an absent man. The vaqueros tell me that my foreman is only around the bend of the river, and I'm going to ask all you gentlemen to remain until I can send for him."

John Cotton was dispatched after Deweese. Conversation meanwhile became polite and changed to other subjects. Those of us at work baling hides went ahead as if nothing unusual was on the tapis. The visitors were all armed, which was nothing unusual, for the wearing of six-shooters was as common as the wearing of hoots. During the interim, several level-headed visitors took Henry Annear to one side, evidently to reason with him and urge an apology, for they could readily see that Uncle Lance was justly offended. But it seemed that Annear would listen to no one, and while they were yet conversing among themselves, John Cotton and our foreman galloped around the bend of the river and rode up to the yard. No doubt Cotton had explained the situation, but as they dismounted Uncle Lance stepped between his foreman and Annear, saying: -

"June, Henry, here, questions the honesty of your list of strays killed, and insists on our cutting the bales for his inspection." Turning to Annear, Uncle Lance inquired, "Do you still insist on opening the bales?"

"Yes, sir, I do."

Deweese stepped to one side of his employer, saying to Annear: "You offer to cut a bale here to-day, and I'll cut your heart out. Behind my back, you questioned my word. Question it to my face, you dirty sneak."

Annear sprang backward and to one side, drawing a six-shooter in the movement, while June was equally active. Like a flash, two shots rang out. Following the reports, Henry turned halfway round, while Deweese staggered a step backward. Taking advantage of the instant, Uncle Lance sprang like a panther on to June and bore him to the ground, while the visitors fell on Annear and disarmed him in a flash. They were dragged struggling farther apart, and after some semblance of sanity had returned, we stripped our foreman and found an ugly flesh wound crossing his side under the armpit, the bullet having been deflected by a rib. Annear had fared worse, and was spitting blood freely, and the marks of exit and entrance of the bullet indicated that the point of one lung had been slightly chipped.

"I suppose this outcome is what you might call the *amende honorable*" smilingly said George Nathan, one of the visitors, later to Uncle Lance. "I always knew there was a little bad blood existing between the boys, but I had no idea that it would flash in the pan so suddenly or I'd have stayed at home. Shooting always lets me out. But the question now is, How are we going to get our man home?"

Uncle Lance at once offered them horses and a wagon, in case Annear would not go into Las Palomas. This he objected to, so a wagon was fitted up, and, promising to return it the next day, our visitors departed with the best of feelings, save between the two belligerents. We sent June into the ranch and a man to Oakville after a surgeon, and resumed our work in the hide yard as if nothing had happened. Somewhere I have seen the statement that the climate of California was especially conducive to the healing of gunshot wounds. The same claim might be made in behalf of the Nueces valley, for within a month both the combatants were again in their saddles.

Within a week after this incident, we concluded our work and the hides were ready for the freighters. We had spent over a month and had taken fully seven hundred hides, many of which, when dry, would weigh one hundred pounds, the total having a value of between five and six thousand dollars. Like their predecessors the buffalo, the remains of the ladinos were left to enrich the soil; but there was no danger of the extinction of the species, for at Las Palomas it was the custom to allow every tenth male calf to grow up a bull.

CHAPTER XIV

A TWO YEARS' DROUTH

The spring of '78 was an early one, but the drouth continued, and after the hide hunting was over we rode our range almost night and day. Thousands of cattle had drifted down from the Frio River country, which section was suffering from drouth as badly as the Nueces. The new wells were furnishing a limited supply of water, but we rigged pulleys on the best of them, and when the wind failed we had recourse to buckets and a rope worked from the pommel of a saddle. A breeze usually arose about ten in the morning and fell about midnight. During the lull the buckets rose and fell incessantly at eight wells, with no lack of suffering cattle in attendance to consume it as fast as it was hoisted. Many thirsty animals gorged themselves, and died in sight of the well; weak ones being frequently trampled to death by the stronger, while flint hides were corded at every watering point. The river had quit flowing, and with the first warmth of spring the pools became rancid and stagnant. In sandy and subirrigated sections, under a March sun, the grass made a sickly effort to spring; but it lacked substance, and so far from furnishing food for the cattle, it only weakened them.

This was my first experience with a serious drouth. Uncle Lance, however, met the emergency as though it were part of the day's work, riding continually with the rest of us. During the latter part of March, Aaron Scales, two vaqueros, and myself came in one night from the Ganso and announced not over a month's supply of water in that creek. We also reported to our employer that during our two days' ride, we had skinned some ten cattle, four of which were in our own brand.

ANDY ADAMS

"That's not as bad as it might be," said the old ranchero, philosophically. "You see, boys, I've been through three drouths since I began ranching on this river. The second one, in '51, was the worst; cattle skulls were as thick along the Nueces that year as sunflowers in August. In '66 it was nearly as bad, there being more cattle; but it didn't hurt me very much, as mavericking had been good for some time before and for several years following, and I soon recovered my losses. The first one lasted three years, and had there been as many cattle as there are now, half of them would have died. The spring before the second drouth, I acted as *padrino* for Tiburcio and his wife, who was at that time a mere slip of a girl living at the Mission. Before they had time to get married, the dry spell set in and they put the wedding off until it should rain. I ridiculed the idea, but they were both superstitious and stuck it out. And honest, boys, there wasn't enough rain fell in two years to wet your shirt. In my forty years on the Nueces, I've seen hard times, but that drouth was the toughest of them all. Game and birds left the country, and the cattle were too poor to eat. Whenever our provisions ran low, I sent Tiburcio to the coast with a load of hides, using six yoke of oxen to handle a cargo of about a ton. The oxen were so poor that they had to stand twice in one place to make a shadow, and we wouldn't take gold for our flint hides but insisted on the staples of life. At one point on the road, Tiburcio had to give a quart of flour for watering his team both going and coming. They say that when the Jews quit a country, it's time for the gentiles to leave. But we old timers are just like a horse that chooses a new range and will stay with it until he starves or dies with old age."

I could see nothing reassuring in the outlook. Near the wells and along the river the stock had trampled out the grass until the ground was as bare as a city street. Miles distant from the water the old dry grass, with only an occasional green blade, was the only grazing for the cattle. The black, waxy soil on the first bottom of the river, on which the mesquite grass had flourished, was as bare now as a ploughed field, while the ground had cracked open in places to an incredible depth, so that without exercising caution it was dangerous to ride across.

This was the condition of the range at the approach of April. Our horse stock, to be sure, fared better, ranging farther and not requiring anything like the amount of water needed by the cattle. It was nothing unusual to meet a Las Palomas *manada* from ten to twelve miles from the river, and coming in only every second or third night to quench their thirst. We were fortunate in having an abundance of saddle horses, which, whether under saddle or not, were always given the preference in the matter of water. They were the motive power of the ranch, and during this crisis, though worked hard, must be favored in every possible manner.

Early that spring the old ranchero sent Deweese to Lagarto in an attempt to sell Captain Byler a herd of horse stock for the trail. The mission was a failure, though our *segundo* offered to sell a thousand, in the straight Las Palomas brand, at seven dollars a head on a year's credit. Even this was no inducement to the trail drover, and on Deweese's return my employer tried San Antonio and other points in Texas in the hope of finding a market. From several places favorable replies were received, particularly from places north of the Colorado River; for the drouth was local and was chiefly confined to the southern portion of the state. There was enough encouragement in the letters to justify the old ranchero's attempt to reduce the demand on the ranch's water supply, by sending a herd of horse stock north on sale. Under ordinary conditions, every ranchman preferred to sell his surplus stock at the ranch, and Las Palomas was no exception, being generally congested with marketable animals. San Antonio was, however, beginning to be a local horse and mule market of some moment, and before my advent several small selected bunches of mares, mules, and saddle horses had been sent there, and had found a ready and profitable sale.

But this was an emergency year, and it was decided to send a herd of stock horses up the country. Accordingly, before April, we worked every *manada* which we expected to keep, cutting out all the two-year-old fillies. To these were added every mongrel-colored band to the number of twenty odd, and when ready to start the herd numbered a few over twelve hundred of all ages from yearlings up. A *remuda* of fifty saddle horses, broken in the spring of '76, were allotted to our use, and our *segundo*, myself, and five Mexican vaqueros were detailed to drive the herd. We were allowed two pack mules for our commissary, which was driven with the *remuda*. With instructions to sell and hurry home, we left our horse camp on the river, and started on the morning of the last day of March.

Live-stock commission firms in San Antonio were notified of our coming, and with six men to the herd and the seventh driving the *remuda*, we put twenty miles behind us the first day. With the exception of water for saddle stock, which we hoisted from a well, there was no hope of watering the herd before reaching Mr. Booth's ranch on the Frio. He had been husbanding his water supply, and early the second evening we watered the herd to its contentment from a single shaded pool. From the Frio we could not follow any road, but were compelled to direct our course wherever there was a prospect of water. By hobbling the bell mare of the *remuda* at evening, and making two watches of the night-herding, we easily systematized our work. Until we reached the San Antonio River, about twenty miles below the city, not over two days passed without water for all the stock, though, on account of the variations from our course, we were over a week in reaching San Antonio. Having moved the herd up near some old missions within five or six miles of the city, with an abundance of water and some grass, Deweese went into town, visiting the commission firms and looking for a buyer. Fortunately a firm, which was expecting our arrival, had a prospective purchaser from Fort Worth for about our number. Making a date with the firm to show our horses the next morning, our *segundo* returned to the herd, elated over the prospect of a sale.

On their arrival the next morning, we had the horses already watered and were grazing them along an abrupt slope between the first and second bottoms of the river. The salesman understood his business, and drove the conveyance back and forth on the down hill side, below the herd, and the rise in the ground made our range stock look as big as American horses. After looking at the animals for an hour, from a buckboard, the prospective buyer insisted on looking at the *remuda*. But as these were gentle, he gave them a more critical examination, insisting on their being penned in a rope corral at our temporary camp, and had every horse that was then being ridden unsaddled to inspect their backs. The *remuda* was young, gentle, and sound, many of them submitting to be caught without a rope. The buyer was pleased with them, and when the price came up for discussion Deweese artfully set a high figure on the saddle stock, and, to make his bluff good, offered to reserve them and take them back to the ranch. But Tuttle would not consider the herd without the *remuda*, and sparring between them continued until all three returned to town.

It was a day of expectancy to the vaqueros and myself. In examining the saddle horses, the buyer acted like a cowman; but as regarding the range stock, it was evident to me that his armor was vulnerable, and if he got any the best of our *segundo* he was welcome to it. Deweese returned shortly after dark, coming directly to the herd where I and two vaqueros were on guard, to inform us that he had sold lock, stock, and barrel, including the two pack mules. I felt like shouting over the good news, when June threw a damper on my enthusiasm by the news that he had sold for delivery at Fort Worth.

"You see," said Deweese, by way of explanation, "the buyer is foreman of a cattle company out on the forks of the Brazos in Young County. He don't sabe range horses as well as he does cows, and when we had agreed on the saddle stock, and there were only two bits between us on the herd, he offered me six bits a head all round, over and above his offer, if I would put them in Fort Worth, and I took him up so quick that I nearly bit my tongue doing it. Captain Redman tells me that it's only about three hundred miles, and grass and water is reported good. I intended to take him up at his offer, anyhow, and seventy-five cents a head extra will make the old man nearly a thousand dollars, which is worth picking up. We'll put them there easy in three weeks, learn the trail and see the country besides. Uncle Lance can't have any kick coming, for I offered them to Captain Byler for seven dollars, and here I'm getting ten six-bits - nearly four thousand dollars' advance, and we won't be gone five weeks. Any money down? Well, I should remark! Five thousand deposited with Smith & Redman, and I was particular to have it inserted in the contract between us that every saddle horse, mare, mule, gelding, and filly was to be in the straight 'horse hoof' brand. There is a possibility that when Tuttle sees them again at Fort Worth, they won't look as large as they did on that hillside this morning."

We made an early start from San Antonio the next morning, passing to the westward of the then straggling city. The vaqueros were disturbed over the journey, for Fort Worth was as foreign to them as a European seaport, but I jollied them into believing it was but a little *pasear*. Though I had never ridden on a train myself, I pictured to them the luxuriant ease with which we would return, as well as the trip by stage to Oakville. I threw enough enthusiasm into my description of the good time we were going to have, coupled with their confidence in Deweese, to convince them in spite of their forebodings. Our *segundo* humored them in various ways, and after a week on the trail, water getting plentiful, using two guards, we only herded until midnight, turning the herd loose from then until daybreak. It usually took us less than an hour to gather and count them in the morning, and encouraged by their contentment, a few days later, we loose-herded until darkness and then turned them free. From then on it was a picnic as far as work was concerned, and our saddle horses and herd improved every day.

After crossing the Colorado River, at every available chance en route we mailed a letter to the buyer, notifying him of our progress as we swept northward. When within a day's drive of the Brazos, we mailed our last letter, giving notice that we would deliver within three days of date. On reaching that river, we found it swimming for between thirty and forty yards; but by tying up the pack mules and cutting the herd into four bunches, we swam the Brazos with less than an hour's delay. Overhauling and transferring the packs to horses, throwing away everything but the barest necessities, we crossed the lightened commissary, the freed mules swimming with the *remuda*. On the morning of the twentieth day out from San Antonio, our *segundo* rode into the fort ahead of the herd. We followed at our regular gait, and near the middle of the forenoon were met by Deweese and Tuttle, who piloted us to a pasture west of the city, where an outfit was encamped to receive the herd. They numbered fifteen men, and looked at our insignificant crowd with contempt; but the count which followed showed we had not lost a hoof since we left the Nueces, although for the last ten nights the stock had had the fullest freedom.

The receiving outfit looked the brands over carefully. The splendid grass and water of the past two weeks had transformed the famishing herd of a month before, and they were received without a question. Rounding in our *remuda* for fresh mounts before starting to town, the vaqueros and I did some fancy roping in catching out the horses, partially from sheer lightness of heart because we were at our journey's end, and partially to show this north Texas outfit that we were like the proverbial singed cat - better than we looked. Two of Turtle's men rode into town with us that evening to lead back our mounts, the outfit having come in purposely to receive the horse herd and drive it to their ranch in Young County. While riding in, they thawed nicely towards us, but kept me busy interpreting for them with our Mexicans. Tuttle and Deweese rode together in the lead, and on nearing town one of the strangers bantered Pasquale to sell him a nice maguey rope which the vaquero carried. When I interpreted the other's wish to him, Pasquale loosened the lasso and made a present of it to Tuttle's man. I had almost as good a rope of the same material, which I presented to the other lad with us, and the drinks we afterward consumed over this slight testimony of the amicable relations existing between a northern and southern Texas outfit over the delivery and receiving of a horse herd, showed no evidence of a drouth. The following morning I made inquiry for Frank Nancrede and the drovers who had driven a trail herd of cattle from Las Palomas two seasons before. They were all well known about the fort, but were absent at the time, having put up two trail herds that spring in Uvalde County. Deweese did not waste an hour more than was necessary in that town, and while waiting for the banks to open, arranged for our transportation to San Antonio. We were all ready to start back before noon. Fort Worth was a frontier town at the time, bustling and alert with live-stock interests; but we were anxious to get home, and promptly boarded a train for the south. After entering the train, our *segundo* gave each of the vaqueros and myself some spending money, the greater portion of which went to the "butcher" for fruits. He was an enterprising fellow and took a marked interest in our comfort and welfare. But on nearing San Antonio after midnight, he attempted to sell us our choice of three books, between the leaves of one of which he had placed a five-dollar bill and in another a ten, and offered us our choice for two dollars, and June Deweese became suddenly interested. Coming over to where we were sitting, he knocked the books on the floor, kicked them under a seat, and threatened to bend a gun over the butcher's head unless he made himself very scarce. Then reminding us that "there were tricks in all trades but ours," he kept an eye over us until we reached the city.

We were delayed another day in San Antonio, settling with the commission firm and banking the money. The next morning we took stage for Oakville, where we arrived late at night. When a short distance out of San Antonio I inquired of our driver who would relieve him beyond Pleasanton, and was gratified to hear that his name was not Jack Martin. Not that I had anything particular against Martin, but I had no love for his wife, and had no desire to press the acquaintance any further with her or her husband. On reaching Oakville, we were within forty miles of Las Palomas. We had our saddles with us, and early the next morning tried to hire horses; but as the stage company domineered the village we were unable to hire saddle stock, and on appealing to the only livery in town we were informed that Bethel & Oxenford had the first claim on their conveyances. Accordingly Deweese and I visited the offices of the stage company, where, to our surprise, we came face to face with Jack Oxenford. I do not think he knew us, though we both knew him at a glance. Deweese made known his wants, but only asked for a conveyance as far as Shepherd's. Yankeelike, Oxenford had to know who we were, where we had been, and where we were going. Our *segundo* gave him rather a short answer, but finally admitted that we belonged at Las Palomas. Then the junior member of the mail contractors became arrogant, claiming that the only conveyance capable of carrying our party was being held for a sheriff with some witnesses. On second thought he offered to send us to the ferry by two lighter vehicles in consideration of five dollars apiece, insolently remarking that we could either pay it or walk. I will not repeat Deweese's reply, which I silently endorsed.

With the soil of the Nueces valley once more under our feet we felt independent. On returning to the vaqueros, we found a stranger among them, Bernabe Cruze by name, who was a *muy amigo* of Santiago Ortez, one of our Mexicans. He belonged at the Mission, and when he learned of our predicament offered to lend us his horse, as he expected to be in town a few days. The offer was gratefully accepted, and within a quarter of an hour Manuel Flores had started for Shepherd's with an order to the merchant to send in seven horses for us. It was less than a two hours' ride to the ferry, and with the early start we expected Manuel to return before noon. Making ourselves at home in a coffeehouse conducted by a Mexican, Deweese ordered a few bottles of wine to celebrate properly our drive and to entertain Cruze and our vaqueros. Before the horses arrived, those of us who had any money left spent it in the *cantina*, not wishing to carry it home, where it would be useless. The result was that on the return of Flores with mounts we were all about three sheets in the wind, reckless and defiant.

After saddling up, I suggested to June that we ride by the stage office and show Mr. Oxenford that we were independent of him. The stage stand and office were on the outskirts of the scattered village, and while we could have avoided it, our *segundo* willingly led the way, and called for the junior member of the firm. A hostler came to the door and informed us that Mr. Oxenford was not in.

"Then I'll just leave my card," said Deweese, dismounting. Taking a brown cigarette paper from his pocket, he wrote his name on it; then pulling a tack from a notice pasted beside the office door, he drew his six-shooter, and with it deftly tacked the cigarette paper against the office door jamb. Remounting his horse, and perfectly conscious that Oxenford was within hearing, he remarked to the hostler: "When your boss returns, please tell him that those fellows from Las Palomas will neither walk with him nor ride with him. We thought he might fret as to how we were to get home, and we have just ridden by to tell him that he need feel no uneasiness. Since I have never had the pleasure of an introduction to him, I've put my name on that cigarette paper. Good-day, sir."

Arriving at Shepherd's, we rested several hours, and on the suggestion of the merchant changed horses before starting home. At the ferry we learned that there had been no serious loss of cattle so far, but that nearly all the stock from the Frio and San Miguel had drifted across to the Nueces. We also learned that the attendance on San Jacinto Day had been extremely light, not a person from Las Palomas being present, while the tournament for that year had been abandoned. During our ride up the river before darkness fell, we passed a strange medley of brands, many of which Deweese assured me were owned from fifty to a hundred miles to the north and west. Riding leisurely, it was nearly midnight when we sighted the ranch and found it astir. An extra breeze had been blowing, and the vaqueros were starting to their work at the wells in order to be on hand the moment the wind slackened. Around the two wells at headquarters were over a thousand cattle, whose constant moaning reached our ears over a mile from the ranch.

Our return was like entering a house of mourning. Miss Jean barely greeted Deweese and myself, while Uncle Lance paced the gallery without making a single inquiry as to what had become of the horse herd. On the mistress's orders, servants set out a cold luncheon, and disappeared, as if in the presence of death, without a word of greeting. Ever thoughtful, Miss Jean added several little delicacies to our plain meal, and, seating herself at the table with us, gave us a clear outline of the situation. In seventy odd miles of the meanderings of the river across our range, there was not a pool to the mile with water enough for a hundred cattle. The wells were gradually becoming weaker, yielding less water every week, while of four new ones which were commenced before our departure, two were dry and worthless. The vaqueros were then skinning on an average forty dead cattle a day, fully a half of which were in the Las Palomas brand. Sympathetically as a sister could, she accounted for her brother's lack of interest in our return by his anxiety and years, and she cautioned us to let no evil report reach his ears, as this drouth had unnerved him.

Deweese at once resumed his position on the ranch, and the next morning the ranchero held a short council with him, authorizing him to spare no expense to save the cattle. Deweese returned the borrowed horses by Enrique, and sent a letter to the merchant at the ferry, directing him to secure and send at least twenty men to Las Palomas. The first day after our return, we rode the mills and the river. Convinced that to sink other wells on the mesas would be fruitless, the foreman decided to dig a number of shallow ones in the bed of the river, in the hope of catching seepage water. Accordingly the next morning, I was sent with a commissary wagon and seven men to the mouth of the Ganso, with instructions to begin sinking wells about two miles apart. Taking with us such tools as we needed, we commenced our first well at the confluence of the Ganso with the Nueces, and a second one above. From timber along the river we cut the necessary temporary curbing, and put it in place as the wells were sunk. On the third day both wells became so wet as to impede our work, and on our foreman riding by, he ordered them curbed to the bottom and a tripod set up over them on which to rig a rope and pulley. The next morning troughs and rigging, with a *remuda* of horses and a watering crew of four strange vaqueros, arrived. The wells were only about twenty feet deep; but by drawing the water as fast as the seepage accumulated, each was capable of watering several hundred head of cattle daily. By this time Deweese had secured ample help, and started a second crew of well diggers opposite the ranch, who worked down the river while my crew followed some fifteen miles above. By the end of the month of May, we had some twenty temporary wells in operation, and these, in addition to what water the pools afforded, relieved the situation to some extent, though the ravages of death by thirst went on apace among the weaker cattle.

With the beginning of June, we were operating nearly thirty wells. In some cases two vaqueros could hoist all the water that accumulated in three wells. We had a string of camps along the river, and at every windmill on the mesas men were stationed night and day. Among the cattle, the death rate was increasing all over the range. Frequently we took over a hundred skins in a single day, while at every camp cords of fallen flint hides were accumulating. The heat of summer was upon us, the wind arose daily, sand storms and dust clouds swept across the country, until our once prosperous range looked like a desert, withered and accursed. Young cows forsook their offspring in the hour of their birth. Motherless calves wandered about the range, hollow-eyed, their piteous appeals unheeded, until some lurking wolf sucked their blood and spread a feast to the vultures, constantly wheeling in great flights overhead. The prickly pear, an extremely arid plant, affording both food and drink to herds during drouths, had turned white, blistered by the torrid sun until it had fallen down, lifeless. The chaparral was destitute of foliage, and on the divides and higher mesas, had died. The native women stripped their *jacals* of every sacred picture, and hung them on the withered trees about their doors, where they hourly prayed to their patron saints. In the humblest homes on Las Palomas, candles burned both night and day to appease the frowning Deity.

The white element on the ranch worked almost unceasingly, stirring the Mexicans to the greatest effort. The middle of June passed without a drop of rain, but on the morning of the twentieth, after working all night, as Pasquale Arispe and I were drawing water from a well on the border of the encinal I felt a breeze spring up, that started the windmill. Casting my eyes upward, I noticed that the wind had veered to a quarter directly opposite to that of the customary coast breeze. Not being able to read aright the portent of the change in the wind, I had to learn from that native-born son of the soil: "Tomas," he cried, riding up excitedly, "in three days it will rain! Listen to me: Pasquale Arispe says that in three days the *arroyos* on the hacienda of Don Lancelot will run like a mill-race. See, *companero*, the wind has changed. The breeze is from the northwest this morning. Before three days it will rain! Madre de Dios!"

The wind from the northwest continued steadily for two days, relieving us from work. On the morning of the third day the signs in sky and air were plain for falling weather. Cattle, tottering with weakness, came into the well, and after drinking, playfully kicked up their heels on leaving. Before noon the storm struck us like a cloud-burst. Pasquale and I took refuge under the wagon to avoid the hailstones. In spite of the parched ground drinking to its contentment, water flooded under the wagon, driving us out. But we laughed at the violence of the deluge, and after making everything secure, saddled our horses and set out for home, taking our relay mounts with us. It was fifteen miles to the ranch and in the eye of the storm; but the loose horses faced the rain as if they enjoyed it, while those under saddle followed the free ones as a hound does a scent. Within two hours after leaving the well, we reined in at the gate, and I saw Uncle Lance and a number of the boys promenading the gallery. But the old ranchero leisurely walked down the pathway to the gate, and amid the downpour shouted to us: "Turn those horses loose; this ranch is going to take a month's holiday."

CHAPTER XV

IN COMMEMORATION

A heavy rainfall continued the greater portion of two days. None of us ventured away from the house until the weather settled, and meantime I played the fiddle almost continuously. Night work and coarse living in camps had prepared us to enjoy the comforts of a house, as well as to do justice to the well-laden table. Miss Jean prided herself, on special occasions and when the ranch had company, on good dinners; but in commemoration of the breaking of this drouth, with none but us boys to share it, she spread a continual feast. The Mexican contingent were not forgotten by master or mistress, and the ranch supplies in the warehouse were drawn upon, delicacies as well as staples, not only for the *jacals* about headquarters but also for the outlying ranchitas. The native element had worked faithfully during the two years in which no rain to speak of had fallen, until the breaking hour, and were not forgotten in the hour of deliverance. Even the stranger vaqueros were compelled to share the hospitality of Las Palomas like invited guests.

While the rain continued falling, Uncle Lance paced the gallery almost night and day. Fearful lest the downpour might stop, he stood guard, noting every change in the rainfall, barely taking time to eat or catch an hour's sleep. But when the grateful rain had continued until the evening of the second day, assuring a bountiful supply of water all over our range, he joined us at supper, exultant as a youth of twenty. "Boys," said he, "this has been a grand rain. If our tanks hold, we will be independent for the next eighteen months, and if not another drop falls, the river ought to flow for a year. I have seen worse drouths since I lived here, but what hurt us now was the amount of cattle and the heavy drift which flooded down on us from up the river and north on the Frio. The loss is nothing; we won't notice it in another year. I have kept a close tally of the hides taken, and our brand will be short about two thousand, or less than ten per cent of our total numbers. They were principally old cows and will not be missed. The calf crop this fall will be short, but taking it up one side and down the other, we got off lucky."

The third day after the rain began the sun rose bright and clear. Not a hoof of cattle or horses was in sight, and though it was midsummer, the freshness of earth and air was like that of a spring morning. Every one felt like riding. While awaiting the arrival of saddle horses, the extra help hired during the drouth was called in and settled with. Two brothers, Fidel and Carlos Trujillo, begged for permanent employment. They were promising young fellows, born on the Aransas River, and after consulting with Deweese Uncle Lance took both into permanent service on the ranch. A room in an outbuilding was allotted them, and they were instructed to get their meals in the kitchen. The *remudas* had wandered far, but one was finally brought in by a vaquero, and by pairs we mounted and rode away. On starting, the tanks demanded our first attention, and finding all four of them safe, we threw out of gear all the windmills. Theodore Quayle and I were partners during the day's ride to the south, and on coming in at evening fell in with Uncle Lance and our *segundo*, who had been as far west as the Ganso. Quayle and I had discussed during the day the prospect of a hunt at the Vaux ranch, and on meeting our employer, artfully interested the old ranchero regarding the amount of cat sign seen that day along the Arroyo Sordo.

"It's hard luck, boys," said he, "to find ourselves afoot, and the hunting so promising. But we haven't a horse on the ranch that could carry a man ten miles in a straightaway dash after the hounds. It will be a month yet before the grass has substance enough in it to strengthen our *remudas*. Oh, if it hadn't been for the condition of saddle stock, Don Pierre would have come right through the rain yesterday. But when Las Palomas can't follow the hounds for lack of mounts, you can depend on it that other ranches can't either. It just makes me sick to think of this good hunting, but what can we do for a month but fold our hands and sit down? But if you boys are itching for an excuse to get over on the Frio, why, I'll make you a good one. This drouth has knocked all the sociability out of the country; but now the ordeal is past, Theodore is in honor bound to go over to the Vaux ranch. I don't suppose you boys have seen the girls on the Frio and San Miguel in six months. Time? That's about all we have got right now. Time? - we've got time to burn."

Our feeler had borne fruit. An excuse or permission to go to the Frio was what Quayle and I were after, though no doubt the old matchmaker was equally anxious to have us go. In expressing our thanks for the promised vacation, we included several provisos - in case there was nothing to do, or if we concluded to go - when Uncle Lance turned in his saddle and gave us a withering look. "I've often wondered," said he, "if the blood in you fellows is really red, or if it's white like a fish's. Now, when I was your age, I had to steal chances to go to see my girl. But I never gave her any show to forget me, and worried her to a fare-ye-well. And if my observation and years go for anything, that's just the way girls like to have a fellow act. Of course they'll bluff and let on they must be wooed and all that, just like Frances did at the tournament a year ago. I contend that with a clear field the only way to make any progress in sparking a girl, is to get one arm around her waist, and with the other hand keep her from scratching you. That's the very way they like to be courted."

Theodore and I dropped behind after this lecture, and before we reached the ranch had agreed to ride over to the Frio the next morning. During our absence that day, there had arrived at Las Palomas from the Mission, a *padrino* in the person of Don Alejandro Travino. Juana Leal, only daughter of

Tiburcio, had been sought in marriage by a nephew of Don Alejandro, and the latter, dignified as a Castilian noble, was then at the house negotiating for the girl's hand. Juana was nearly eighteen, had been born at the ranch, and after reaching years of usefulness had been adopted into Miss Jean's household. To ask for her hand required audacity, for to master and mistress of Las Palomas it was like asking for a daughter of the house. Miss Jean was agitated and all in a flutter; Tiburcio and his wife were struck dumb; for Juana was the baby and only unmarried one of their children, and to take her from Las Palomas - they could never consent to that. But Uncle Lance had gone through such experiences before, and met the emergency with promptness.

"That's all right, little sister," said the old matchmaker to Miss Jean, who had come out to the gate where we were unsaddling. "Don't you borrow any trouble in this matter - leave things to me. I've handled trifles like this among these natives for nearly forty years now, and I don't see any occasion to try and make out a funeral right after the drouth's been broken by a fine rain. Shucks, girl, this is a time for rejoicing! You go back in the house and entertain Don Alejandro with your best smiles till I come in. I want to have a talk with Tiburcio and his wife before I meet the *padrino*. There's several families of those Travinos over around the Mission and I want to locate which tribe this *oso* comes from. Some of them are good people and some of them need a rope around their necks, and in a case of keeps like getting married, it's always safe to know what's what and who's who. Now, Sis, go on back in the house and entertain the Don. Come with me, Tom."

I saw our plans for the morrow vanish into thin air. On arriving at the jacal, we were admitted, but a gloom like the pall of death seemed to envelop the old Mexican couple. When we had taken seats around a small table, Tia Inez handed the ranchero the formal written request. As it was penned in Spanish, it was passed to me to read, and after running through it hastily, I read it aloud, several times stopping to interpret to Uncle Lance certain extravagant phrases. The salutatory was in the usual form; the esteem which each family had always entertained for the other was dwelt upon at length, and choicer language was never used than the *padrino* penned in asking for the hand of Dona Juana. This dainty missive was signed by the godfather of the swain, Don Alejandro Travino, whose rubric riotously ran back and forth entirely across the delicately tinted sheet. On the conclusion of the reading, Uncle Lance brushed the letter aside as of no moment, and, turning to the old couple, demanded to know to which branch of the Travino family young Don Blas belonged.

The account of Tiburcio and his wife was definite and clear. The father of the swain conducted a small country store at the Mission, and besides had landed and cattle interests. He was a younger brother of Don Alejandro, who was the owner of a large land grant, had cattle in abundance, and was a representative man among the Spanish element. No better credentials could have been asked. But when their patron rallied them as to the cause of their gloom, Tia Inez burst into tears, admitting the match was satisfactory, but her baby would be carried away from Las Palomas and she might never see her again. Her two sons who lived at the ranch, allowed no day to pass without coming to see their mother, and the one who lived at a distant ranchita came at every opportunity. But if her little girl was carried away to a distant ranch - ah! that made it impossible! Let Don Lance, worthy patron of his people, forbid the match, and win the gratitude of an anguished mother. Invoking the saints to guide her aright, Dona Inez threw herself on the bed in hysterical lamentation. Realizing it is useless to argue with a woman in tears, the old matchmaker suggested to Tiburcio that we delay the answer the customary fortnight.

Promising to do nothing further without consulting them, we withdrew from the *jacal*. On returning to the house, we found Miss Jean entertaining the Don to the best of her ability, and, commanding my presence, the old matchmaker advanced to meet the *padrino*, with whom he had a slight acquaintance. Bidding his guest welcome to the ranch, he listened to the Don's apology for being such a stranger to Las Palomas until a matter of a delicate nature had brought him hither.

Don Alejandro was a distinguished-looking man, and spoke his native tongue in a manner which put my efforts as an interpreter to shame. The conversation was allowed to drift at will, from the damages of the recent drouth to the prospect of a market for beeves that fall, until supper was announced. After the evening repast was over we retired to the gallery, and Uncle Lance reopened the matchmaking by inquiring of Don Alejandro if his nephew proposed taking his bride to the Mission. The Don was all attention. Fortunately, anticipating that the question might arise, he had discussed that very feature with his nephew. At present the young man was assisting his father at the Mission, and in time, no doubt, would succeed to the business. However, realizing that her living fifty miles distant might be an objection to the girl's parents, he was not for insisting on that point, as no doubt Las Palomas offered equally good advantages for business. He simply mentioned this by way of suggestion, and invited the opinion of his host.

"Well, now, Don Alejandro," said the old matchmaker, in flutelike tones, "we are a very simple people here at Las Palomas. Breeding a few horses and mules for home purposes, and the rearing of cattle has been our occupation. As to merchandising here at the ranch, I could not countenance it, as I refused that privilege to the stage company when they offered to run past Las Palomas. At present our few wants are supplied by a merchant at Shepherd's Ferry. True, it's thirty miles, but I sometimes wish it was farther, as it is quite a temptation to my boys to ride down there on various pretexts. We send down every week for our mail and such little necessities as the ranch may need. If there was a store here, it would attract loafers and destroy the peace and contentment which we now enjoy. I would object to it; 'one man to his trade and another to his merchandise.'"

The *padrino*, with good diplomacy, heartily agreed that a store was a disturbing feature on a ranch, and instantly went off on a tangent on the splendid business possibilities of the Mission. The matchmaker in return agreed as heartily with him, and grew reminiscent. "In the spring of '51," said he, "I made the match between Tiburcio and Dona Inez, father and mother of Juana. Tiburcio was a vaquero of mine at the time, Inez being a Mission girl, and I have taken a great interest in the couple ever since. All their children were born here and still live on the ranch. Understand, Don Alejandro, I have no personal feeling in the matter, beyond the wishes of the parents of the girl. My sister has taken a great interest in Juana, having had the girl under her charge for the past eight years. Of course, I feel a pride in Juana, and she is a fine girl. If your nephew wins her, I shall tell the lucky rascal when he comes to claim her that he has won the pride of Las Palomas. I take it, Don Alejandro, that your visit and request was rather unexpected here, though I am aware that Juana has visited among cousins at the Mission several times the past few years. But that she had lost her heart to some of your gallants comes as a surprise to me, and from what I learn, to her parents also. Under the circumstances, if I were you, I would not urge an immediate reply, but give them the customary period to think it over. Our vaqueros will not be very busy for some time to come, and it will not inconvenience us to send a reply by messenger to the Mission. And tell Don Blas, even should the reply be unfavorable, not to be discouraged. Women, you know, are peculiar. Ah, Don Alejandro, when you and I were young and went courting, would we have been discouraged by a first refusal?"

Senor Travino appreciated the compliment, and, with a genial smile, slapped his host on the back, while the old matchmaker gave vent to a vociferous guffaw. The conversation thereafter took several tacks, but always reverted to the proposed match. As the hour grew late, the host apologized to his guest, as no doubt he was tired by his long ride, and offered to show him his room. The *padrino* denied all weariness, maintaining that the enjoyable evening had rested him, but reluctantly allowed himself to be shown to his apartment. No sooner were the good-nights spoken, than the old ranchero returned, and, snapping his fingers for attention, motioned me to follow. By a circuitous route we reached the *jacal* of Tiburcio. The old couple had not yet retired, and Juana blushingly admitted us. Uncle Lance jollied the old people like a robust, healthy son amusing his elders. We took seats as before around the small table, and Uncle Lance scattered the gloom of the *jacal* with his gayety.

"Las Palomas forever!" said he, striking the table with his bony fist. "This *padrino* from the Mission is a very fine gentleman but a poor matchmaker. Just because young Don Blas is the son of a Travino, the keeper of a picayune *tienda* at the Mission, was that any reason to presume for the hand of a daughter of Las Palomas? Was he any better than a vaquero just because he doled out *frijoles* by the quart, and never saw a piece of money larger than a *media real*? Why, a Las Palomas vaquero was a prince compared to a fawning attendant in a Mission store. Let Tia Inez stop fretting herself about losing Juana - it would not be yet awhile. Just leave matters to him, and he'd send Don Alejandro home, pleased with his visit and hopeful over the match, even if it never took place. And none of those frowns from the young lady!"

As we all arose at parting, the old matchmaker went over to Juana and, shaking his finger at her, said: "Now, look here, my little girl, your mistress, your parents, and myself are all interested in you, and don't think we won't act for your best interests. You've seen this young fellow ride by on a horse several times, haven't you? Danced with him a few times under the eyes of a chaperon at the last *fiesta*, haven't you? And that's all you care to know, and are ready to marry him. Well, well, it's fortunate that the marriage customs of the Mexicans protect such innocents as you. Now, if young Don Blas had worked under me for a year as a vaquero, I might be as ready to the match as you are; for then I'd know whether he was worthy of you. What does a girl of your age know about a man? But when you have as many gray hairs in your head as your mother has, you'll thank me for cautioning every one to proceed slowly in this match. Now dry those tears and go to your mother."

The next morning Don Alejandro proposed returning to the Mission. But the old ranchero hooted the idea, and informed his guest that he had ordered the ambulance, as he intended showing him the recent improvements made on Las Palomas. When the guest protested against a longer absence from home, the host artfully intimated that by remaining another day a favorable reply might possibly go with him. Don Alejandro finally consented. I was pressed in as driver and interpreter, and our team tore away from the ranch with a flourish. To put it mildly, I was disgusted at having my plans for the day knocked in the head, yet knew better than protest. As we drove along, myriads of grass-blades were peeping up since the rain, giving every view a greenish cast. Nearly every windmill on the ranch on our circuit was pointed out, and we passed three of our four tanks, one of which was over half a mile in length. After stopping at an outlying ranchita for refreshment, we spent the afternoon in a similar manner. From a swell of the prairie some ten miles to the westward of the ranch, we could distinctly see an outline of the Ganso. Halting the ambulance, the old ranchero pointed out to his guest the meanderings of that creek from its confluence with the parent stream until it became lost in the hills to the southward.

"That tract of ground," said he, "is my last landed addition to Las Palomas. It lies north and south, giving me six miles' frontage on the Nueces. and extending north of the river about four miles, Don Alejandro, when I note the great change which has come over this valley since I settled here, it convinces me that if one wishes to follow ranching he had better acquire title to what range he needs. Land has advanced in price from a few cents an acre to four bits, and now they say the next generation will see it worth a dollar. This Ganso grant contains a hundred and fourteen sections, and I have my eye on one or two other adjoining tracts. My generation will not need it, but the one who succeeds me may. Now, as we drive home, I'll try to show you the northern boundary of our range; it's fairly well outlined by the divide between the Nueces and the Frio rivers."

From the conversation which followed until we reached headquarters, I readily understood that the old matchmaker was showing the rose and concealing its thorn. His motive was not always clear to me, for one would have supposed from his almost boastful claims regarding its extent and carrying capacity for cattle, he was showing the ranch to a prospective buyer. But as we neared home, the conversation innocently drifted to the Mexican element and their love for the land to which they were born. Then I understood why I was driving four mules instead of basking in the smiles of my own sweetheart on the San Miguel. Nor did this boasting cease during the evening, but alternated from lands and cattle to the native people, and finally centred about a Mexican girl who had been so fortunate as to have been born to the soil of Las Palomas.

When Don Alejandro asked for his horse the following morning on leaving, Uncle Lance, Quayle, and myself formed a guard of honor to escort our guest a distance on his way. He took leave of the mistress of Las Palomas in an obeisance worthy of an old-time cavalier. Once we were off, Uncle Lance pretended to have had a final interview with the parents, in which they had insisted on the customary time in which to consider the proposal. The *padrino* graciously accepted the situation, thanking his host for his interest in behalf of his nephew. On reaching the river, where our ways separated, all halted for a few minutes at parting.

"Well, Don Alejandro," said the old ranchero, "this is my limit of escort to guests of the ranch. Now, the only hope I have in parting is, in case the reply should he unfavorable, that Don Blas will not be discouraged and that we may see you again at Las Palomas. Tender my congratulations to your nephew, and tell him that a welcome always awaits him in case he finds time and inclination to visit us. I take some little interest in matches. These boys of mine are going north to the Frio on a courting errand to-day. But our marriage customs are inferior to yours, and our young people, left to themselves, don't seem to marry. Don Alejandro, if you and I had the making of the matches, there'd be a cradle rocking in every *jacal.*" Both smiled, said their "Adios, amigos," and he was gone.

As our guest cantered away, down the river road, Quayle and I began looking for a ford. The river had been on a rampage, and while we were seeking out a crossing our employer had time for a few comments. "The Don's tickled with his prospects. He thinks he's got a half inch rope on Juana right now; but if I thought your prospects were no better than I know his are, you wouldn't tire any horse-flesh of mine by riding to the Frio and the San Miguel. But go right on, and stay as long as you want to, for I'm in no hurry to see your faces again. Tom, with the ice broken as it is, as soon as Esther can remove her disabilities - well, you won't have to run off the next time. And Theodore, remember what I told you the other day about sparking a girl. You're too timid and backward for a young fellow. I don't care if you come home with one eye scratched out, just so you and Frances have come to an understanding and named the day."

CHAPTER XVI

MATCHMAKING

After our return to the Frio, my first duty was writing, relative to the proposed match, an unfavorable reply to Don Alejandro Travino.

On resuming work, we spent six weeks baling hides, thus occupying our time until the beginning of the branding season. A general round-up of the Nueces valley, commencing on the coast at Corpus Christi Bay, had been agreed upon among the cowmen of the country. In pursuance of the plan four well-mounted men were sent from our ranch with Wilson's wagon to the coast, our *segundo* following a week later with the wagon, *remuda* and twelve men, to meet the rodeo at San Patricio as they worked up the river. Our cattle had drifted in every direction during the drouth and though many of them had returned since the range had again become good, they were still widely scattered. So Uncle Lance took the rest of us and started for the Frio, working down that river and along the Nueces, until we met the round-up coming up from below. During this cow hunt, I carried my fiddle with me in the wagon, and at nearly every ranch we passed we stopped and had a dance. Not over once a week did we send in cattle to the ranch to brand, and on meeting the rodeo from below, Deweese had over three thousand of our cattle. After taking these in and branding the calves, we worked over our home range until near the holidays.

On our return to the ranch, we learned that young Blas Travino from the Mission had passed Las Palomas some days before. He had stopped in passing; but, finding the ranchero absent, plead a matter of business at Santa Maria, promising to call on his return. He was then at the ranch on the Tarancalous, and hourly expecting his reappearance, the women of the household were in an agitated state of mind. Since the formal answer had been sent, no word had come from Don Blas and a rival had meanwhile sprung up in the person of Fidel Trujillo. Within a month after his employment I noticed the new vaquero casting shy glances at Juana, but until the cow hunt on the Frio I did not recognize the fine handwriting of the old matchmaker. Though my services were never called for as interpreter between Uncle Lance and the new man, any one could see there was an understanding between them. That the old ranchero was pushing Fidel forward was evident during the fall cow hunting by his sending that Mexican into Las Palomas with every bunch of cattle gathered.

That evening Don Blas rode into the ranch, accompanied by Father Norquin. The priest belonged at the Mission, and their meeting at Santa Maria might, of course, have been accidental. None of the padre's parishioners at headquarters were expecting him, however, for several months, and padres are able *padrinos*, - sometimes, among their own faith, even despotic. Taking account, as it appeared, of the ulterior motive, Uncle Lance welcomed the arrivals with a hearty hospitality, which to a stranger seemed so genuine as to dispel any suspicion. Not in many a day had a visitor at Las Palomas received more courteous consideration than did Father Norquin. The choicest mint which grew in the inclosures about the wells was none too good for the juleps which were concocted by Miss Jean. Had the master and mistress of the ranch been communicants of his church, the rosy-cheeked padre could have received no more marked attention.

The conversation touched lightly on various topics, until Santa Maria ranch was mentioned, when Uncle Lance asked the padre if Don Mateo had yet built him a chapel. The priest shrugged his shoulders deprecatingly and answered the question with another, - when Las Palomas proposed building a place of worship.

"Well, Father, I'm glad you've brought the matter up again," replied the host. "That I should have lived here over forty years and never done anything for your church or my people who belong to your faith, is certainly saying little in my behalf. I never had the matter brought home to me so clearly as during last summer's drouth. Do you remember that old maxim regarding when the devil was sick? Well, I was good and sick. If you had happened in then and had asked for a chapel, - not that I have any confidence in your teaching, - you could have got a church with a steeple on it. I was in such sore straits that the women were kept busy making candles, and we burnt them in every *jacal* until the hour of deliverance."

Helping himself from the proffered snuffbox of the padre, the host turned to his guest, and in all sincerity continued: "Yes, Father, I ought to build you a nice place of worship. We could quarry the rock during idle time, and burn our own lime right here on the ranch. While you are here, give me some plans, and we'll show you that the white element of Las Palomas are not such hopeless heretics as you suppose. Now, if we build the chapel, I'm just going to ask one favor in return: I expect to die and be buried on this ranch. You're a younger man by twenty years and will outlive me, and on the day of my burial I want you to lay aside your creed and preach my funeral in this little chapel which you and I are going to build. I have been a witness to the self-sacrifice of you and other priests ever since I lived here. Father, I like an honest man, and the earnestness of your cloth for the betterment of my people no one can question. And my covenant is, that you are to preach a simple sermon, merely commemorating the fact that here lived a man named Lovelace, who died and would be seen among his fellow men no more. These being facts, you can mention them; but beyond that, for fear our faiths might differ, the less said the better. Won't you have another mint julep before supper? No? You will, won't you, Don Blas?"

That the old ranchero was in earnest about building a chapel on Las Palomas there was no doubt. In fact, the credit should be given to Miss Jean, for she had been urging the matter ever since my coming to the ranch. At headquarters and outlying ranchitas on the land, there were nearly twenty families, or over a hundred persons of all ages. But that the old match-maker was going to make the most out of his opportunity by erecting the building at an opportune time, there was not the shadow of a question.

The evening passed without mention of the real errand of our guests. The conversation was allowed to wander at will, during which several times it drifted into gentle repartee between host and padre, both artfully avoiding the rock of matchmaking. But the next morning, as if anxious to begin the day's work early, Father Norquin, on arising, inquired for his host, strutted out to the corrals, and, on meeting him, promptly inquired why, during the previous summer, Don Alejandro Travino's mission to obtain the hand of Juana Leal had failed.

"That's so," assented Uncle Lance, very affably, "Don Alejandro was here as godfather to his nephew. And this young man with you is Don Blas, the bear? Well, why did we waste so much time last night talking about chapels and death when we might have made a match in less time? You priests have everything in your favor as *padrinos*, but you are so slow that a rival might appear and win the girl while you were drumming up your courage. I don't write Spanish myself, but I have boys here on the ranch who do. One of them, if I remember rightly, wrote the answer at the request of Juana's mother. If my memory hasn't failed me entirely, the parents objected to being separated from their only daughter. You know how that is among your people; and I never like to interfere in family matters. But from what I hear Don Blas has a rival now. Yes; young Travino failed to press his suit, and a girl will stand for nearly anything but neglect. But that's one thing they won t stand for, not when there's a handsome fellow at hand to play the bear. Then the old lover is easily forgotten for the new. Eh, Father?"

"Ah, Don Lance, I know your reputation as a matchmaker," replied Father Norquin, in a rich French accent. "Report says had you not had a hand in it the match would have been successful. The supposition is that it only lacked your approval. The daughter of a vaquero refusing a Travino? Tut, tut, man!"

A hearty guffaw greeted these aspersions. "And so you've heard I was a matchmaker, have you? Of course, you believed it just like any other old granny. Now, of course, when I'm asked by any of my people to act as *padrino*, I never refuse any more than you do. I've made many a match and hope to be spared to make several more. But come; they're calling us to breakfast, and after that we'll take a walk over to the ranch burying ground. It's less than a half mile - in that point of encinal yonder. I want to show you what I think would be a nice spot for our chapel."

The conversation during breakfast was artfully directed by the host to avoid the dangerous shoals, though the padre constantly kept an eye on Juana as she passed back and forth. As we arose from the table and were passing to the gallery, Uncle Lance nudged the priest, and, poking Don Blas in the ribs, said: "Isn't Juana a stunning fine cook? Got up that breakfast herself. There isn't an eighteen-year-old girl in Texas who can make as fine biscuits as she does. But Las Palomas raises just as fine girls as she does horses and cattle. The rascal who gets her for a wife can thank his lucky stars. Don Blas, you ought to have me for *padrino*. Your uncle and the padre here are too poky. Why, if I was making a match for as fine a girl as Juana is, I'd set the river afire before I'd let an unfavorable answer discourage me. Now, the padre and I are going for a short walk, and we'll leave you here at the house to work out your own salvation. Don't pay any attention to the mistress, and I want to tell you right now, if you expect to win Juana, never depend on old fogy *padrinos* like your uncle and Father Norquin. Do a little hustling for yourself."

The old ranchero and the priest were gone nearly an hour, and on their return looked at another site in the rear of the Mexican quarters. It was a pretty knoll, and as the two joined us where we were repairing a windmill at the corrals, Father Norquin, in an ecstasy of delight, said: "Well, my children, the chapel is assured at Las Palomas. Don Lance wanted to build it over in the encinal, with twice as nice a site right here in the rancho. We may need the building for a school some day, and if we should, we don't want it a mile away. The very idea! And the master tells me that a chapel has been the wish of his sister for years. Poor woman - to have such a brother. I must hasten to the house and thank her."

No sooner had the padre started than I was called aside by my employer. "Tom," said he, "you slip around to Tia Inez's *jacal* and tell her that I'm going to send Father Norquin over to see her. Tell her to stand firm on not letting Juana leave the ranch for the Mission. Tell her that I've promised the padre a chapel for Las Palomas, and rather than miss it, the priest would consign the whole Travino family to endless perdition. Tell her to laugh at his scoldings and inform him that Juana can get a husband without going so far. And that you heard me say that I was going to give Fidel, the day he married her daughter, the same number of heifers that all her brothers got. Impress it on Tia Inez's mind that it means something to be born to Las Palomas."

I set out on my errand and he hastened away to overtake the padre before the latter reached the house. Tia Inez welcomed me, no doubt anticipating that I was the bearer of some message. When I gave her the message her eyes beamed with gratitude and she devoutly crossed her breast invoking the blessing of the saints upon the master. I added a few words of encouragement of my own - that I understood that when we quarried the rock for the chapel, there was to be enough extra cut to build a stone cottage for Juana and Fidel. This was pure invention on my part, but I felt a very friendly interest in Las Palomas, for I expected to bring my bride to it as soon as possible. Therefore, if I could help the present match forward by the use of a little fiction, why not?

Father Norquin's time was limited at Las Palomas, as he was under appointment to return to Santa Maria that evening. Therefore it became an active morning about the ranch. Long before we had finished the repairs on the windmill, a *mozo* from the house came out to the corrals to say I was wanted by the master. Returning with the servant, I found Uncle Lance and the mistress of the ranch entertaining their company before a cheerful fire in the sitting-room. On my entrance, my employer said: -

"Tom, I have sent for you because I want you to go over with the padre to the *jacal* of Juana's parents. Father Norquin here is such an old granny that he believes I interfered, or the reply of last summer would have been favorable. Now, Tom, you're not to open your mouth one way or the other. The padre will state his errand, and the old couple will answer him in your presence. Don Blas will remain here, and whatever the answer is, he and I must abide by it. Really, as I have said, I have no interest in the match, except the welfare of the girl. Go on now, Father, and let's see what you can do as a *padrino*."

As we arose to go, Miss Jean interposed and suggested that, out of deference to Father Norquin, the old couple be sent for, but her brother objected. He wanted the parents to make their own answer beneath their own roof, unembarrassed by any influence. As we left the room, the old matchmaker accompanied us as far as the gate, where he halted and said to the padre: -

"Father Norquin, in a case like the present, you will not mind my saying that your wish is not absolute, and I am sending a witness with you to see that you issue no peremptory orders on this ranch. And remember, that this old couple have been over thirty years in my employ, and temper your words to them as you would to your own parents, were they living. Juana was born here, which means a great deal, and with the approval of her parents, she'll marry the man of her choice, and no *padrino*, let him be priest or layman, can crack his whip on the soil of Las Palomas to the contrary. As my guest, you must excuse me for talking so plain, but my people are as dear to me as your church is to you."

As my employer turned and leisurely walked back to the house, Father Norquin stood stock-still. I was slightly embarrassed myself, but it was easily to be seen that the padre's plans had received a severe shock. I made several starts toward the Mexican quarters before the priest shook away his hesitations and joined me. That the old ranchero's words had agitated him was very evident in his voice and manner. Several times he stopped me and demanded explanations, finally raising the question of a rival. I told him all I knew about the matter; that Fidel, a new vaquero on the ranch, had found favor in Juana's eyes, that he was a favorite man with master and mistress, but what view the girl's parents took of the matter I was unable to say. This cleared up the situation wonderfully, and the padre brightened as we neared the *jacal.*

Tiburcio was absent, and while awaiting his return, the priest became amiable and delivered a number of messages from friends and relatives at the Mission. Tia Inez was somewhat embarrassed at first, but gradually grew composed, and before the return of her husband all three of us were chatting like cronies. On the appearance of Tio Tiburcio, coffee was ordered and the padre told several good stories, over which we all laughed heartily. Cigarettes were next, and in due time Father Norquin very good naturedly inquired why an unfavorable answer, regarding the marriage of their daughter with young Blas Travino, had been returned the previous summer. The old couple looked at each other a moment, when the husband turned in his chair, and with a shrug of his shoulders and a jerk of his head, referred the priest to his wife. Tia Inez met the padre's gaze, and in a clear, concise manner, and in her native tongue, gave her reasons. Father Norquin explained the prominence of the Travino family and their disappointment over the refusal, and asked if the decision was final, to which he received an affirmative reply. Instead of showing any displeasure, he rose to take his departure, turning in the doorway to say to the old couple: -

"My children, peace and happiness in this life is a priceless blessing. I should be untrue to my trust did I counsel a marriage that would give a parent a moment of unhappiness. My blessing upon this house and its dwellers, and upon its sons and daughters as they go forth to homes of their own." While he lifted his hand in benediction, the old couple and myself bowed our heads for a moment, after which the padre and I passed outside.

I was as solemn as an owl, yet inwardly delighted at the turn of affairs. But Father Norquin had nothing to conceal, while delight was wreathed all over his rosy countenance. Again and again he stopped me to make inquiries about Fidel, the new vaquero. That lucky rascal was a good-looking native, a much larger youth than the aspiring Don Blas, and I pictured him to the padre as an Adonis. To the question if he was in the ranch at present, fortune favored me, as Fidel and nearly all the regular vaqueros were cutting timbers in the encinal that day with which to build new corrals at one of the outlying tanks. As he would not return before dark, and I knew the padre was due at Santa Maria that evening, my description of him made Don Blas a mere pigmy in comparison. But we finally reached the house, and on our reentering the sitting-room, young Travino very courteously arose and stood until Father Norquin should be seated. But the latter faced his parishioner, saying: -

"You young simpleton, what did you drag me up here for on a fool's errand? I was led to believe that our generous host was the instigator of the unfavorable answer to your uncle's negotiations last summer. Now I have the same answer repeated from the lips of the girl's parents. Consider the predicament in which you have placed a servant of the Church. Every law of hospitality has been outraged through your imbecility. And to complete my humiliation, I have received only kindness on every hand. The chapel which I have desired for years is now a certainty, thanks to the master and mistress of Las Palomas. What apology can I offer for your" -

"Hold on there, Father," interrupted Uncle Lance. "If you owe

ANDY ADAMS

this ranch any apology, save your breath for a more important occasion. Don Blas is all right; any suitor who would not be jealous over a girl like Juana is not welcome at Las Palomas. Why, when I was his age I was suspicious of my sweetheart's own father, and you should make allowance for this young man's years and impetuosity. Sit down, Father, and let's have a talk about this chapel - that's what interests me most right now. You see, within a few days my boys will have all the palisades cut for the new corrals, and then we can turn our attention to getting out the rock for the chapel. We have a quarry of nice soft stone all opened up, and I'll put a dozen vaqueros to blocking out the rock in a few days. We always have a big stock of *zacahuiste* grass on hand for thatching *jacals*, plenty of limestone to burn for the lime, sand in abundance, and all we lack is the masons. You'll have to send them out from the Mission, but I'll pay them. Oh, I reckon the good Lord loves Las Palomas, for you see He's placed everything convenient with which to build the chapel."

Father Norquin could not remain seated, but paced the room enumerating the many little adornments which the mother church would be glad to supply. Enthusiastic as a child over a promised toy, no other thought entered the simple padre's mind, until dinner was announced. And all during the meal, the object of our guest's mission was entirely lost sight of, in contemplation of the coming chapel. The padre seemed as anxious to avoid the subject of matchmaking as his host, while poor Don Blas sat like a willing sacrifice, unable to say a word. I sympathized with him, for I knew what it was to meet disappointment. At the conclusion of the mid-day repast, Father Norquin flew into a great bustle in preparing to start for Santa Maria, and I was dispatched for the horses. Our guests and my employer were waiting at the stile when I led up their mounts, and at final parting the old matchmaker said to the priest: -

"Now, remember, I expect you to have this chapel completed by Easter Sunday, when I want you to come out and spend at least two weeks with us and see that it is finished to suit you, and arrange for the dedication. Las Palomas will build the chapel, but when our work is done yours commences. And I want to tell you right now, there's liable to be several weddings in it before the mortar gets good and dry. I have it on pretty good authority that one of my boys and Pierre Vaux's eldest girl are just about ready to have you pronounce them man and wife. No, he's not of any faith, but she's a good Catholic. Now, look here, Father Norquin, if I have to proselyte you to my way of thinking, it'll never hurt you any. I was never afraid to do what was right, and when at Las Palomas you needn't be afraid either, even if we have to start a new creed. Well, good-by to both of you."

We had a windmill to repair that afternoon, some five miles from the ranch, so that I did not return to the house until evening; but when all gathered around the supper table that night, Uncle Lance was throwing bouquets at himself for the crafty manner in which he had switched the padre from his mission, and yet sent him away delighted. He admitted that he was scared on the appearance of Father Norquin as a *padrino*, on account of the fact that a priest was usually supreme among his own people. That he had early come to the conclusion if there was to be any coercion used in this case, he was determined to get in his bluff first. But Miss Jean ridiculed the idea that there was any serious danger.

"Goodness me, Lance," said she, "I could have told you there was no cause for alarm. In this case between Fidel and Juana, I've been a very liberal chaperon. Oh, well, now, never mind about the particulars. Once, to try his nerve, I gave him a chance, and I happen to know the rascal kissed her the moment my back was turned. Oh, I think Juana will stay at Las Palomas."

CHAPTER XVII

WINTER AT LAS PALOMAS

The winter succeeding the drouth was an unusually mild one, frost and sleet being unseen at Las Palomas. After the holidays several warm rains fell, affording fine hunting and assuring enough moisture in the soil to insure an early spring. The preceding winter had been gloomy, but this proved to be the most social one since my advent, for within fifty miles of the ranch no less than two weddings occurred during Christmas week. As to little neighborhood happenings, we could hear of half a dozen every time we went to Shepherd's after the mail.

When the native help on the ranch was started at blocking out the stone for the chapel, Uncle Lance took the hounds and with two of the boys went down to Wilson's ranch for a hunt. Gallup went, of course, but just why he took Scales along, unless with the design of making a match between one of the younger daughters of this neighboring ranchman and the Marylander, was not entirely clear. When he wanted to, Scales could make himself very agreeable, and had it not been for his profligate disposition, his being taken along on the hunt would have been no mystery. Every one on the ranch, including the master and mistress, were cognizant of the fact that for the past year he had maintained a correspondence with a girl in Florida - the one whose letter and photograph had been found in the box of oranges. He hardly deserved the confidence of the roguish girl, for he showed her letters to any one who cared to read them. I had read every line of the whole correspondence, and it was plain that Scales had deceived the girl into believing that he was a prominent ranchman, when in reality the best that could be said of him was that he was a lovable vagabond. From the last letter, it was clear that he had promised to marry the girl during the Christmas week just past, but he had asked for a postponement on the ground that the drouth had prevented him from selling his beeves.

When Uncle Lance made the discovery, during a cow hunt the fall before, of the correspondence between Scales and the Florida girl, he said to us around the camp-fire that night: "Well, all I've got to say is that that girl down in Florida is hard up. Why, it's entirely contrary to a girl's nature to want to be wooed by letter. Until the leopard changes his spots, the good old way, of putting your arm around the girl and whispering that you love her, will continue to be popular. If I was to hazard an opinion about that girl, Aaron, I'd say that she was ambitious to rise above her surroundings. The chances are that she wants to get away from home, and possibly she's as much displeased with the young men in the orange country as I sometimes get with you dodrotted cow hands. Now, I'm not one of those people who're always harping about the youth of his day and generation being so much better than the present. That's all humbug. But what does get me is, that you youngsters don't profit more by the experience of an old man like me who's been married three times. Line upon line and precept upon precept, I have preached this thing to my boys for the last ten years, and what has it amounted to? Not a single white bride has ever been brought to Las Palomas. They can call me a matchmaker if they want to, but the evidence is to the contrary." This was on the night after we passed Shepherd's, where Scales had received a letter from the Florida girl. But why he should accompany the hunt now to Remirena, unless the old ranchero proposed reforming him, was too deep a problem for me.

On leaving for Wilson's, there was the usual bustle; hounds responding to the horn and horses under saddle champing their bits. I had hoped that permission to go over to the Frio and San Miguel would be given John and myself, but my employer's mind was too absorbed in something else, and we were overlooked in the hurry to get away. Since the quarrying of the rock had commenced, my work had been overseeing the native help, of which we had some fifteen cutting and hauling. In numerous places within a mile of headquarters, a soft porous rock cropped out. By using a crowbar with a tempered chisel point, the Mexicans easily channeled the rock into blocks, eighteen by thirty inches, splitting each stone a foot in thickness, so that when hauled to the place of use, each piece was ready to lay up in the wall. The ranch house at headquarters was built out of this rock, and where permanency was required, it was the best material available, whitening and apparently becoming firmer with time and exposure.

I had not seen my sweetheart in nearly a month, but there I was, chained to a rock quarry and mule teams. The very idea of Gallup and the profligate Scales riding to hounds and basking in the society of charming girls nettled me. The remainder of the ranch outfit was under Deweese, building the new corrals, so that I never heard my own tongue spoken except at meals and about the house. My orders included the cutting of a few hundred rock extra above the needs of the chapel, and when this got noised among the help, I had to explain that there was some talk of building a stone cottage, and intimated that it was for Juana and Fidel. But that lucky rascal was one of the crew cutting rock, and from some source or other he had learned that I was liable to need a cottage at Las Palomas in the near future. The fact that I was acting *segundo* over the quarrying outfit, was taken advantage of by Fidel to clear his skirts and charge the extra rock to my matrimonial expectations. He was a fast workman, and on every stone he split from the mother ledge, he sang out, "Otro piedra por Don Tomas!" And within a few minutes' time some one else would cry out, "Otro cillar por Fidel y Juana," or "Otro piedra por padre Norquin."

A week passed and there was no return of the hunters. We had so systematized our work at the quarry that my presence was hardly needed, so every evening I urged Cotton to sound the mistress for permission to visit our sweethearts. John was a good-natured fellow who could be easily led or pushed forward, and I had come to look upon Miss Jean as a ready supporter of any of her brother's projects. For that reason her permission was as good as the master's; but she parried all Cotton's hints, pleading the neglect of our work in the absence of her brother. I was disgusted with the monotony of quarry work, and likewise was John over building corrals, as no cow hand ever enthuses over manual labor, when an incident occurred which afforded the opportunity desired. The mistress needed some small article from the store at Shepherd's, and a Mexican boy had been sent down on this errand and also to get the mail of the past two weeks. On the boy's return, he brought a message from the merchant, saying that Henry Annear had been accidentally killed by a horse that day, and that the burial would take place at ten o'clock the next morning.

The news threw the mistress of Las Palomas into a flutter. Her brother was absent, and she felt a delicacy in consulting Deweese, and very naturally turned to me for advice. Funerals in the Nueces valley were so very rare that I advised going, even if the unfortunate man had stood none too high in our estimation. Annear lived on the divide between Shepherd's and the Frio at a ranch called Las Norias. As this ranch was not over ten miles from the mouth of the San Miguel, the astute mind can readily see the gleam of my ax in attending. Funerals were such events that I knew to a certainty that all the countryside within reach would attend, and the Vaux ranch was not over fifteen miles distant from Las Norias. Acting on my advice, the mistress ordered the ambulance to be ready to start by three o'clock the next morning, and gave every one on the ranch who cared, permission to go along. All of us took advantage of the offer, except Deweese, who, when out of hearing of the mistress, excused himself rather profanely.

The boy had returned late in the day, but we lost no time in acting on Miss Jean's orders. Fortunately the ambulance teams were in hand hauling rock, but we rushed out several vaqueros to bring in the *remuda* which contained our best saddle horses. It was after dark when they returned with the mounts wanted, and warning Tiburcio that we would call him at an early hour, every one retired for a few hours' rest. I would resent the charge that I am selfish or unsympathetic, yet before falling asleep that night the deplorable accident was entirely overlooked in the anticipated pleasure of seeing Esther.

As it was fully a thirty-five-mile drive we started at daybreak, and to encourage the mules Quayle and Happersett rode in the lead until sun-up, when they dropped to the rear with Cotton and myself. We did not go by way of Shepherd's, but crossed the river several miles above the ferry, following an old cotton road made during the war, from the interior of the state to Matamoras, Mexico. It was some time before the hour named for the burial when we sighted Las Norias on the divide, and spurred up the ambulance team, to reach the ranch in time for the funeral. The services were conducted by a strange minister who happened to be visiting in Oakville, but what impressed me in particular was the solicitude of Miss Jean for the widow. She had been frequently entertained at Las Palomas by its mistress, as the sweetheart of June Deweese, though since her marriage to Annear a decided coolness had existed between the two women. But in the present hour of trouble, the past was forgotten and they mingled their tears like sisters.

On our return, which was to be by way of the Vauxes', I joined those from the McLeod ranch, while Happersett and Cotton accompanied the ambulance to the Vaux home. Nearly every one going our way was on horseback, and when the cavalcade was some distance from Las Norias, my sweetheart dropped to the rear for a confidential chat and told me that a lawyer from Corpus Christi, an old friend of the family, had come up for the purpose of taking the preliminary steps for securing her freedom, and that she expected to be relieved of the odious tie which bound her to Oxenford at the May term of court. This was pleasant news to me, for there would then be no reason for delaying our marriage.

Happersett rode down to the San Miguel the next morning to inform Quayle and myself that the mistress was then on the way to spend the night with the widow Annear, and that the rest of us were to report at home the following evening. She had apparently inspected the lines on the Frio, and, finding everything favorable, turned to other fields. I was disappointed, for Esther and I had planned to go up to the Vaux ranch during the visit. Dan suggested that we ride home together by way of the Vauxes'. But Quayle bitterly refused even to go near the ranch. He felt very sore and revengeful over being jilted by Frances after she had let him crown her Queen of the ball at the tournament dance. So, agreeing to meet on the divide the next day for the ride back to Las Palomas, we parted.

The next afternoon, on reaching the divide between the Frio and the home river, Theodore and I scanned the horizon in vain for any horsemen. We dismounted, and after waiting nearly an hour, descried two specks to the northward which we knew must be our men. On coming up they also threw themselves on the ground, and we indulged in a cigarette while we compared notes. I had nothing to conceal, and frankly confessed that Esther and I expected to marry during the latter part of May. Cotton, though, seemed reticent, and though Theodore cross-questioned him rather severely, was non-committal and dumb as an oyster; but before we recrossed the Nueces that evening, John and I having fallen far to the rear of the other two, he admitted to me that his wedding would occur within a month after Lent. It was to be a confidence between us, but I advised him to take Uncle Lance into the secret at once.

But on reaching the ranch we learned that the hunting party had not returned, nor had the mistress. The next morning we resumed our work, Quayle and Cotton at corral building and I at the rock quarry. The work had progressed during my absence, and the number of pieces desired was nearing completion, and with but one team hauling the work-shop was already congested with cut building stone. By noon the quarry was so cluttered with blocks that I ordered half the help to take axes and go to the encinal to cut dry oak wood for burning the lime. With the remainder of my outfit we cleaned out and

ANDY ADAMS

sealed off the walls of an old lime kiln, which had served ever since the first rock buildings rose on Las Palomas. The oven was cut in the same porous formation, the interior resembling an immense jug, possibly twelve feet in diameter and fifteen feet in height to the surface of the ledge. By locating the kiln near the abrupt wall of an abandoned quarry, ventilation was given from below by a connecting tunnel some twenty feet in length. Layers of wood and limestone were placed within until the interior was filled, when it was fired, and after burning for a few hours the draft was cut off below and above, and the heat retained until the limestone was properly burned.

Near the middle of the afternoon, the drivers hauling the blocks drove near the kiln and shouted that the hunters had returned. Scaling off the burnt rock in the interior and removing the debris made it late before our job was finished; then one of the vaqueros working on the outside told us that the ambulance had crossed the river over an hour before, and was then in the ranch. This was good news, and mounting our horses we galloped into headquarters and found the corral outfit already there. Miss Jean soon had our *segundo* an unwilling prisoner in a corner, and from his impatient manner and her low tones it was plain to be seen that her two days' visit with Mrs. Annear had resulted in some word for Deweese. Not wishing to intrude, I avoided them in search of my employer, finding him and Gallup at an outhouse holding a hound while Scales was taking a few stitches in an ugly cut which the dog had received from a *javeline*. Paying no attention to the two boys, I gave him the news, and bluntly informed him that Esther and I expected to marry in May.

"Bully for you, Tom," said he. "Here, hold this fore foot, and look out he don't bite you. So she'll get her divorce at the May term, and then all outdoors can't stand in your way the next time. Now, that means that you'll have to get out fully two hundred more of those building rock, for your cottage will need three rooms. Take another stitch, knot your thread well, and be quick about it. I tell you the *javeline* were pretty fierce: this is the fifth dog we've doctored since we returned."

On freeing the poor hound, we both looked the pack over carefully, and as no others needed attention, Aaron and Glenn were excused. No sooner were they out of hearing than I suggested that the order be made for five hundred stone, as no doubt John Cotton would also need a cottage shortly after Lent. The old matchmaker beamed with smiles. "Is that right, Tom?" he inquired. "Of course, you boys tell each other what you would hardly tell me. And so they have made the riffle at last? Why, of course they shall have a cottage, and have it so near that I can hear the baby when it cries. Bully for tow-headed John. Oh, I reckon Las Palomas is coming to the front this year. Three new cottages and three new brides is not to be sneezed at! Does your mistress know all this good news?"

I informed him that I had not seen Miss Jean to speak to since the funeral, and that Cotton wished his intentions kept a secret. "Of course," he said; "that's just like a sap-headed youth, as if getting married was anything to be ashamed of. Why, when I was the age of you boys I'd have felt proud over the fact. Wants it kept a secret, does he? Well, I'll tell everybody I meet, and I'll send word to the ferry and to every ranch within a hundred miles, that our John Cotton and Frank Vaux are going to get married in the spring. There's nothing disgraceful in matrimony, and I'll publish this so wide that neither of them will dare back out. I've had my eye on that girl for years, and now when there's a prospect of her becoming the wife of one of my boys, he wants it kept a secret? Well, I don't think it'll keep."

After that I felt more comfortable over my own confession. Before we were called to supper every one in the house, including the Mexicans about headquarters, knew that Cotton and I were soon to be married. And all during the evening the same subject was revived at every lull in the conversation, though Deweese kept constantly intruding the corral building and making inquiries after the hunt. "What difference does it make if we hunted or not?" replied Uncle Lance to his foreman with some little feeling. "Suppose we did only hunt every third or fourth day? Those Wilson folks have a way of entertaining friends which makes riding after hounds seem commonplace. Why, the girls had Glenn and Aaron on the go until old man Nate and myself could hardly get them out on a hunt at all. And when they did, provided the girls were along, they managed to get separated, and along about dusk they'd come slouching in by pairs, looking as innocent as turtle-doves. Not that those Wilson girls can't ride, for I never saw a better horsewoman than Susie - the one who took such a shine to Scales."

I noticed Miss Jean cast a reproving glance at her brother on his connecting the name of Susie Wilson with that of his vagabond employee. The mistress was a puritan in morals. That Scales fell far below her ideal there was no doubt, and the brother knew too well not to differ with her on this subject. When all the boys had retired except Cotton and me, the brother and sister became frank with each other.

"Well, now, you must not blame me if Miss Susie was attentive to Aaron," said the old matchmaker, in conciliation, pacing the room. "He was from Las Palomas and their guest, and I see no harm in the girls being courteous and polite. Susie was just as nice as pie to me, and I hope you don't think I don't entertain the highest regard for Nate Wilson's family. Suppose one of the girls did smile a little too much on Aaron, was that my fault? Now, mind you, I never said a word one way or the other, but I'll bet every cow on Las Palomas that Aaron Scales, vagabond that he is, can get Susie Wilson for the asking. I know your standard of morals, but you must make allowance for others who look upon things differently from you and me. You remember Katharine Vedder who married Carey Troup at the close of the war. There's a similar case for you. Katharine married Troup just because he was so wicked, at least that was the reason she gave, and she and you were old run-togethers. And you remember too that getting married was the turning-point in Carey Troup's life. Who knows but Aaron might sober down if he was to marry? Just because a man has sown a few wild oats in his youth, does that condemn him for all time? You want to be more liberal. Give me the man who has stood the fire tests of life in preference to one who has never been tempted."

"Now, Lance, you know you had a motive in taking Aaron down to Wilson's," said the sister, reprovingly. "Don't get the idea that I can't read you like an open book. Your argument is as good as an admission of your object in going to Ramirena. Ever since Scales got up that flirtation with Suzanne Vaux last summer, it was easy to see that Aaron was a favorite with you. Why don't you take Happersett around and introduce him to some nice girls? Honest, Lance, I wouldn't give poor old Dan for the big beef corral full of rascals like Scales. Look how he trifled with that silly girl in Florida."

Instead of continuing the argument, the wily ranchero changed the subject.

"The trouble with Dan is he's too old. When a fellow begins to get a little gray around the edges, he gets so foxy that you couldn't bait him into a matrimonial trap with sweet grapes. But, Sis, what's the matter with your keeping an eye open for a girl for Dan, if he's such a favorite with you? If I had half the interest in him that you profess, I certainly wouldn't ask any one to help. It wouldn't surprise me if the boys take to marrying freely after John and Tom bring their brides to Las Palomas. Now that Mrs. Annear is a widow, there's the same old chance for June. If Glenn don't make the riffle with Miss Jule, he ought to be shot on general principles. And I don't know, little sister, if you and I were both to oppose it, that we could prevent that rascal of an Aaron from marrying into the Wilson family. You have no idea what a case Susie and Scales scared up during our ten days' hunt. That only leaves Dan and Theodore. But what's the use of counting the chickens so soon? You go to bed, for I'm going to send to the Mission to-morrow after the masons. There's no use in my turning in, for I won't sleep a wink to-night, thinking all this over."

CHAPTER XVIII

AN INDIAN SCARE

Near the close of January, '79, the Nueces valley was stirred by an Indian scare. I had a distinct recollection of two similar scares in my boyhood on the San Antonio River, in which I never caught a glimpse of the noble red man. But whether the rumors were groundless or not, Las Palomas set her house in order. The worst thing we had to fear was the loss of our saddle stock, as they were gentle and could be easily run off and corralled on the range by stretching lariats. At this time the ranch had some ten *remudas* including nearly five hundred saddle horses, some of them ranging ten or fifteen miles from the ranch, and on receipt of the first rumor, every *remuda* was brought in home and put under a general herd, night and day.

"These Indian scares," said Uncle Lance, "are just about as regular as drouths. When I first settled here, the Indians hunted up and down this valley every few years, but they never molested anything. Why, I got well acquainted with several bucks, and used to swap rawhide with them for buckskin. Game was so abundant then that there was no temptation to kill cattle or steal horses. But the rascals seem to be getting worse ever since. The last scare was just ten years ago next month, and kept us all guessing. The renegades were Kickapoos and came down the Frio from out west. One Sunday morning they surprised two of Waugh's vaqueros while the latter were dressing a wild hog which they had killed. The Mexicans had only one horse and one gun between them. One of them took the horse and the other took the carbine. Not daring to follow the one with the gun for fear of ambuscade, the Indians gave chase to the vaquero on horseback, whom they easily captured. After stripping him of all his clothing, they tied his hands with thongs, and pinned the poor devil to a tree with spear thrusts through the back.

"The other Mexican made his escape in the chaparral, and got back to the ranch. As it happened, there was only a man or two at Waugh's place at the time, and no attempt was made to follow the Indians, who, after killing the vaquero, went on west to Altita Creek - the one which puts into the Nueces from the north, just about twenty miles above the Ganso. Waugh had a sheep camp on the head of Altito, and there the Kickapoos killed two of his *pastors* and robbed the camp. From that creek on westward, their course was marked with murders and horse stealing, but the country was so sparsely settled that little or no resistance could be offered, and the redskins escaped without punishment. At that time they were armed with bow and arrow and spears, but I have it on good authority that all these western tribes now have firearms. The very name of Indians scares women and children, and if they should come down this river, we must keep in the open and avoid ambush, as that is an Indian's forte."

All the women and children at the outlying ranchitas were brought into headquarters, the men being left to look after the houses and their stock and flocks. In the interim, Father Norquin and the masons had arrived and the chapel was daily taking shape. But the rumors of the Indian raid thickened. Reports came in of shepherds shot with their flocks over near Espontos Lake and along the Leona River, and Las Palomas took on the air of an armed camp. Though we never ceased to ride the range wherever duty called, we went always in squads of four or five.

The first abatement of the scare took place when one evening a cavalcade of Texas Rangers reached our ranch from DeWitt County. They consisted of fifteen mounted men under Lieutenant Frank Barr, with a commissary of four pack mules. The detachment was from one of the crack companies of the state, and had with them several half-blood trailers, though every man in the squad was more or less of an expert in that line. They were traveling light, and had covered over a hundred miles during the day and a half preceding their arrival at headquarters. The hospitality of Las Palomas was theirs to command, and as their most urgent need was mounts, they were made welcome to the pick of every horse under herd. Sunrise saw our ranger guests on their way, leaving the high tension relaxed and every one on the ranch breathing easier. But the Indian scare did not prove an ill wind to the plans of Father Norquin. With the concentration of people from the ranchitas and those belonging at the home ranch, the chapel building went on by leaps and bounds. A native carpenter had been secured from Santa Maria, and the enthusiastic padre, laying aside his vestments, worked with his hands as a common laborer. The energy with which he inspired the natives made him a valuable overseer. From assisting the carpenter in hewing the rafters, to advising the masons in laying a keystone, or with his own hands mixing the mortar and tamping the earth to give firm foundation to the cement floor, he was the directing spirit. Very little lumber was used in the construction of buildings at Las Palomas. The houses were thatched with a coarse salt grass, called by the natives *zacahuiste*. Every year in the overflowed portions of the valley, great quantities of this material were cut by the native help and stored against its need. The grass sometimes grew two feet in height, and at cutting was wrapped tightly and tied in "hands" about two inches in diameter. For fastening to the roofing lath, green blades of the Spanish dagger were used, which, after being roasted over a fire to toughen the fibre, were split into thongs and bound the hands securely in a solid mass, layer upon layer like shingles. Crude as it may appear, this was a most serviceable roof, being both rain proof and impervious to heat, while, owing to its compactness, a live coal of fire laid upon it would smoulder but not ignite.

No sooner had the masons finished the plastering of the inner walls and cementing the floor, than they began on a two-roomed cottage. As its white walls arose conjecture was rife as to who was to occupy it. I made no bones of the fact that I expected to occupy a *jacal* in the near future, but denied that this was to be mine, as I had been promised one with three rooms. Out of hearing of our employer, John Cotton also religiously denied that the tiny house was for his use. Fidel, however, took the chaffing without a denial, the padre and Uncle Lance being his two worst tormentors.

During the previous visit of the padre, when the chapel was decided on, the order for the finishing material for the building had been placed with the merchant at Shepherd's, and was brought up from Corpus Christi through his freighters. We now had notice from the merchant that his teamsters had returned, and two four-mule teams went down to the ferry for the lumber, glassware, sash and doors. Miss Jean had been importuning the padre daily to know when the dedication would take place, as she was planning to invite the countryside.

"Ah, my daughter," replied the priest, "we must learn to cultivate patience. All things that abide are of slow but steady growth, and my work is for eternity. Therefore I must be an earnest servant, so that when my life's duty ends, it can be said in truth, 'Well done, thou good and faithful servant.' But I am as anxious to consecrate this building to the Master's service as any one. My good woman, if I only had a few parishioners like you, we would work wonders among these natives."

On the return of the mule teams, the completion of the building could be determined, and the padre announced the twenty-first of February as the date of dedication. On reaching this decision, the ranch was set in order for an occasion of more than ordinary moment. Fidel and Juana were impatient to be married, and the master and mistress had decided that the ceremony should be performed the day after the dedication, and all the guests of the ranch should remain for the festivities. The padre, still in command, dispatched a vaquero to the Mission, announcing the completion of the chapel, and asking for a brother priest to bring out certain vestments and assist in the dedicatory exercises. The Indian scare was subsiding, and as no word had come from the rangers confidence grew that the worst was over, so we scattered in every direction inviting guests. From the Booths on the Frio to the Wilsons of Ramirena, and along the home river as far as Lagarto, our friends were bidden in the name of the master and mistress of Las Palomas.

On my return from taking the invitations to the ranches north, the chapel was just receiving the finishing touches. The cross crowning the front glistened in fresh paint, while on the interior walls shone cheap lithographs of the Madonna and Christ. The old padre, proud and jealous as a bridegroom over his bride, directed the young friar here and there, himself standing aloof and studying with an artist's eye every effect in color and drapery. The only discordant note in the interior was the rough benches, in the building of which Father Norquin himself had worked, thus following, as he repeatedly admonished us, in the footsteps of his Master, the carpenter of Galilee.

The ceremony of dedication was to be followed by mass at high noon. Don Mateo Gonzales of Santa Maria sent his regrets, as did likewise Don Alejandro Travino of the Mission, but the other invited guests came early and stayed late. The women and children of the outlying ranchitas had not yet returned to their homes, and with our invited guests made an assembly of nearly a hundred and fifty persons. Unexpectedly, and within two hours of the appointed time for the service to commence, a cavalcade was sighted approaching the ranch from the west. As they turned in towards headquarters, some one recognized the horses, and a shout of welcome greeted our ranger guests of over two weeks before. Uncle Lance met them as if they had been expected, and invited the lieutenant and his men to dismount and remain a few days as guests of Las Palomas. When they urged the importance of continuing on their journey to report to the governor, the host replied: -

"Lieutenant Barr, that don't go here. Fall out of your saddles and borrow all the razors and white shirts on the ranch, for we need you for the dedication of a chapel to-day, and for a wedding and infare for to-morrow. We don't see you along this river as often as we'd like to, and when you do happen along in time for a peaceful duty, you can't get away so easily. If you have any special report to make to your superiors, why, write her out, and I'll send a vaquero with it to Oakville this afternoon, and it'll go north on the stage to-morrow. But, lieutenant, you mustn't think you can ride right past Las Palomas when you're not under emergency orders. Now, fall off those horses and spruce up a little, for I intend to introduce you to some as nice girls as you ever met. You may want to quit rangering some day, and I may need a man about your size, and I'm getting tired of single ones."

Lieutenant Barr surrendered. Saddles were stripped from horses, packs were unlashed from mules, and every animal was sent to our *remudas* under herd. The accoutrements were stacked inside the gate like haycocks, with slickers thrown over them; the carbines were thrown on the gallery, and from every nail, peg, or hook on the wall belts and six-shooters hung in groups. These rangers were just ordinary looking men, and might have been mistaken for an outfit of cow hands. In age they ranged from a smiling youth of twenty to grizzled men of forty, yet in every countenance was written a resolute determination. All the razors on the ranch were brought into immediate use, while every presentable shirt, collar, and tie in the house was unearthed and placed at their disposal. While arranging hasty toilets, the men informed us that when they reached Espontos Lake the redskins had left, and that they had trailed them south until the Indians had crossed the Rio Grande into Mexico several days in advance of their arrival. The usual number of isolated sheepherders killed, and of horses stolen, were the features of the raid.

The guests had been arriving all morning. The Booths had reached the ranch the night before, and the last to put in an appearance was the contingent from the Frio and San Miguel. Before the appearance of the rangers, they had been sighted across the river, and they rode up with Pierre Vaux, like a captain of the Old Guard, in the lead.

"Ah, Don Lance," he cried, "vat you tink? Dey say Don Pierre no ride fas' goin' to church. Dese youngsters laff all time and say I never get here unless de dogs is 'long. Sacre! Act all time lak I vas von ol' man. *Humbre*, keep away from dis horse; he allow nobody but me to lay von han' on him - keep away, I tol' you!"

I helped the girls to dismount, Miss Jean kissing them right and left, and bustling them off into the house to tidy up as fast as possible; for the hour was almost at hand. On catching sight of Mrs. Annear, fresh and charming in her widow's weeds, Uncle Lance brushed Don Pierre aside and cordially greeted her. Vaqueros took the horses, and as I strolled up the pathway with Esther, I noticed an upper window full of ranger faces peering down on the girls. Before this last contingent had had time to spruce up, Pasquale's eldest boy rode around all the *jacals*, ringing a small handbell to summon the population to the dedication. Outside of our home crowd, we had forty white guests, not including the two Booth children and the priests. As fast as the rangers were made presentable, the master and mistress introduced them to all the girls present. Of course, there were a few who could not be enticed near a woman, but Quayle and Happersett, like kindred spirits, took the backward ones under their wing, and the procession started for the chapel.

The audience was typical of the Texas frontier at the close of the '70's. Two priests of European birth conducted the services. Pioneer cowmen of various nationalities and their families intermingled and occupied central seats. By the side of his host, a veteran of '36, when Mexican rule was driven from the land, sat Lieutenant Barr, then engaged in accomplishing a second redemption of the state from crime and lawlessless. Lovable and esteemed men were present, who had followed the fortunes of war until the Southern flag, to which they had rallied, went down in defeat. The younger generation of men were stalwart in physique, while the girls were modest in their rustic beauty. Sitting on the cement floor on three sides of us were the natives of the ranch, civilized but with little improvement over their Aztec ancestors.

The dedicatory exercises were brief and simple. Every one was invited to remain for the celebration of the first mass in the newly consecrated building. Many who were not communicants accepted, but noticing the mistress and my sweetheart taking their leave, I joined them and assisted in arranging the tables so that all our guests could be seated at two sittings. At the conclusion of the services, dinner was waiting, and Father Norquin and Mr. Nate Wilson were asked to carve at one table, while the young friar and Lieutenant Barr, in a similar capacity, officiated at the other. There was so much volunteer help in the kitchen that I was soon excused, and joined the younger people on the gallery. As to whom Cotton and Gallup were monopolizing there was no doubt, but I had a curiosity to notice what Scales would do when placed between two fires. But not for nothing had he cultivated the acquaintance of a sandy-mustached young ranger, who was at that moment entertaining Suzanne Vaux in an alcove at the farther end of the veranda. Aaron, when returning from the chapel with Susie Wilson, had succeeded in getting no nearer the house than a clump of oak trees which sheltered an old rustic settee. And when the young folks were called in to dinner, the vagabond Scales and Miss Wilson of Ramirena had to be called the second time.

In seating the younger generation, Miss Jean showed her finesse. Nearly all the rangers had dined at the first tables, but the widow Annear waited for the second one - why, only a privileged few of us could guess. Artfully and with seeming unconsciousness on the part of every one, Deweese was placed beside the charming widow, though I had a suspicion that June was the only innocent party in the company. Captain Byler and I were carving at the same table at which our foreman and the widow were seated, and, being in the secret, I noted step by step the progress of the widow, and the signs of gradual surrender of the corporal *segundo*. I had a distinct recollection of having once smashed some earnest resolves, and of having capitulated under similar circumstances, and now being happily in love, I secretly wished success to the little god Cupid in the case in hand. And all during the afternoon and evening, it was clearly apparent to any one who cared to notice that success was very likely.

The evening was a memorable one at Las Palomas. Never before in my knowledge had the ranch had so many and such amiable guests. The rangers took kindly to our hospitality, and Father Norquin waddled about, God-blessing every one, old and young, frivolous and sedate. Owing to the nature of the services of the day, the evening was spent in conversation among the elders, while the younger element promenaded the spacious gallery, or occupied alcoves, nooks, and corners about the grounds. On retiring for the night, the men yielded the house to the women guests, sleeping on the upper and lower verandas, while the ranger contingent, scorning beds or shelter, unrolled their blankets under the spreading live-oaks in the yard.

But the real interest centred in the marriage of Fidel and Juana, which took place at six o'clock the following evening. Every one, including the native element, repaired to the new chapel to attend the wedding. Uncle Lance and his sister had rivaled each other as to whether man or maid should have the better outfit. Fidel was physically far above the average of the natives, slightly bow-legged, stolid, and the coolest person in the church. The bride was in quite a flutter, but having been coached and rehearsed daily by her mistress, managed to get through the ordeal. The young priest performed the ceremony, using his own native tongue, the rich, silvery accents of Spanish. At the conclusion of the service, every one congratulated the happy couple, the women and girls in tears, the sterner sex without demonstration of feeling. When we were outside the chapel, and waiting for our sweethearts to dry their tears and join us, Uncle Lance came swaggering' over to John Cotton and me, and, slapping us both on the back, said: -

"Boys, that rascal of a Fidel has a splendid nerve. Did you notice how he faced the guns without a tremor; never batted an eye but took his medicine like a little man. I hope both of you boys will show equally good nerve when your turn comes. Why, I doubt if there was a ranger in the whole squad, unless it was that red-headed rascal who kissed the bride, who would have stood the test like that vaquero - without a shiver. And it's something you can't get used to. Now, as you all know, I've been married three times. The first two times I was as cool as most, but the third whirl I trembled all over. Quavers ran through me, my tongue was palsied, my teeth chattered, my knees knocked together, and I felt like a man that was sent for and couldn't go. Now, mind you, it was the third time and I was only forty-five."

What a night that was! The contents of the warehouse had been shifted, native musicians had come up from Santa Maria, and every one about the home ranch who could strum a guitar was pressed into service. The storeroom was given over to the natives, and after honoring the occasion with their presence as patrons, the master and mistress, after the opening dance, withdrew in company with their guests. The night had then barely commenced. Claiming two guitarists, we soon had our guests waltzing on veranda, hall, and spacious dining-room to the music of my fiddle. Several of the rangers could play, and by taking turns every one had a joyous time, including the two priests. Among the Mexicans the dancing continued until daybreak. Shortly after midnight our guests retired, and the next morning found all, including the priests, preparing to take their departure. As was customary, we rode a short distance with our guests, bidding them again to Las Palomas and receiving similar invitations in return. With the exception of Captain Byler, the rangers were the last to take their leave. When the mules were packed and their mounts saddled, the old ranchero extended them a welcome whenever they came that way again.

"Well, now, Mr. Lovelace," said Lieutenant Barr, "you had better not press that invitation too far. The good time we have had with you discounts rangering for the State of Texas. Rest assured, sir, that we will not soon forget the hospitality of Las Palomas, nor its ability to entertain. Push on with the packs, boys, and I'll take leave of the mistress in behalf of you all, and overtake the squad before it reaches the river."

CHAPTER XIX

HORSE BRANDS

Before gathering the fillies and mares that spring, and while riding the range, locating our horse stock, Pasquale brought in word late one evening that a *ladino* stallion had killed the regular one, and was then in possession of the *manada*. The fight between the outlaw and the ranch stallion had evidently occurred above the mouth of the Ganso and several miles to the north of the home river, for he had accidentally found the carcass of the dead horse at a small lake and, recognizing the animal by his color, had immediately scoured the country in search of the band. He had finally located the *manada*, many miles off their range; but at sight of the vaquero the *ladino* usurper had deserted the mares, halting, however, out of gunshot, yet following at a safe distance as Pasquale drifted them back. Leaving the *manada* on their former range, Pasquale had ridden into the ranch and reported. It was then too late in the day to start against the interloper, as the range was fully twenty-five miles away, and we were delayed the next morning in getting up speedy saddle horses from distant and various *remudas*, and did not get away from the ranch until after dinner. But then we started, taking the usual pack mules, and provisioned for a week's outing.

Included in the party was Captain Frank Byler, the regular home crowd, and three Mexicans. With an extra saddle horse for each, we rode away merrily to declare war on the *ladino* stallion. "This is the third time since I've teen ranching here," said Uncle Lance to Captain Frank, as we rode along, "that I've had stallions killed. There always have been bands of wild

ANDY ADAMS

horses, west here between the Leona and Nueces rivers and around Espontos Lake. Now that country is settling up, the people walk down the bands and the stallions escape, and in drifting about find our range. They're wiry rascals, and our old stallions don't stand any more show with them than a fat hog would with a *javaline*. That's why I take as much pride in killing one as I do a rattlesnake."

We made camp early that evening on the home river, opposite the range of the *manada*. Sending out Pasquale to locate the band and watch them until dark, Uncle Lance outlined his idea of circling the band and bagging the outlaw in the uncertain light of dawn. Pasquale reported on his return after dark that the *manada* were contentedly feeding on their accustomed range within three miles of camp. Pasquale had watched the band for an hour, and described the *ladino* stallion as a cinnamon-colored coyote, splendidly proportioned and unusually large for a mustang.

Naturally, in expectation of the coming sport, the horses became the topic around the camp-fire that night. Every man present was a born horseman, and there was a generous rivalry for the honor in telling horse stories. Aaron Scales joined the group at a fortunate time to introduce an incident from his own experience, and, raking out a coal of fire for his pipe, began: -

"The first ranch I ever worked on," said he, "was located on the Navidad in Lavaca County. It was quite a new country then, rather broken and timbered in places and full of bear and wolves. Our outfit was working some cattle before the general round-up in the spring. We wanted to move one brand to another range as soon as the grass would permit, and we were gathering them for that purpose. We had some ninety saddle horses with us to do the work, - sufficient to mount fifteen men. One night we camped in a favorite spot, and as we had no cattle to hold that night, all the horses were thrown loose, with the usual precaution of hobbling, except two or three on picket. All but about ten head wore the bracelets, and those ten were pals, their pardners wearing the hemp. Early in the evening, probably nine o'clock, with a bright fire burning, and the boys spreading down their beds for the night, suddenly the horses were heard running, and the next moment they hobbled into camp like a school of porpoise, trampling over the beds and crowding up to the fire and the wagon. They almost knocked down some of the boys, so sudden was their entrance. Then they set up a terrible nickering for mates. The boys went amongst them, and horses that were timid and shy almost caressed their riders, trembling in limb and muscle the while through fear, like a leaf. We concluded a bear had scented the camp, and in approaching it had circled round, and run amuck our saddle horses. Every horse by instinct is afraid of a bear, but more particularly a range-raised one. It's the same instinct that makes it impossible to ride or drive a range-raised horse over a rattlesnake. Well, after the boys had petted their mounts and quieted their fears, they were still reluctant to leave camp, but stood around for several hours, evidently feeling more secure in our presence. Now and then one of the free ones would graze out a little distance, cautiously sniff the air, then trot back to the others. We built up a big fire to scare away any bear or wolves that might he in the vicinity, but the horses stayed like invited guests, perfectly contented as long as we would pet them and talk to them. Some of the boys crawled under the wagon, hoping to get a little sleep, rather than spread their bed where a horse could stampede over it. Near midnight we took ropes and saddle blankets and drove them several hundred yards from camp. The rest of the night we slept with one eye open, expecting every moment to hear them take fright and return. They didn't, but at daylight every horse was within five hundred yards of the wagon, and when we unhobbled them and broke camp that morning, we had to throw riders in the lead to hold them back."

On the conclusion of Scales's experience, there was no lack of volunteers to take up the thread, though an unwritten law forbade interruptions. Our employer was among the group, and out of deference to our guest, the boys remained silent. Uncle Lance finally regaled us with an account of a fight between range stallions which he had once witnessed, and on its conclusion Theodore Quayle took his turn.

"The man I was working for once moved nearly a thousand head of mixed range stock, of which about three hundred were young mules, from the San Saba to the Concho River. It was a dry country and we were compelled to follow the McKavett and Fort Chadbourne trail. We had timed our drives so that we reached creeks once a day at least, sometimes oftener. It was the latter part of summer, and was unusually hot and drouthy. There was one drive of twenty-five miles ahead that the owner knew of without water, and we had planned this drive so as to reach it at noon, drive halfway, make a dry camp over night, and reach the pools by noon the next day. Imagine our chagrin on reaching the watering place to find the stream dry. We lost several hours riding up and down the *arroyo* in the hope of finding relief for the men, if not for the stock. It had been dusty for weeks. The cook had a little water in his keg, but only enough for drinking purposes. It was twenty miles yet to the Concho, and make it before night we must. Turning back was farther than going ahead, and the afternoon was fearfully hot. The heat waves looked like a sea of fire. The first part of the afternoon drive was a gradual ascent for fifteen miles, and then came a narrow plateau of a divide. As we reached this mesa, a sorrier-looking lot of men, horses, and mules can hardly be imagined. We had already traveled over forty miles without water for the stock, and five more lay between us and the coveted river.

"The heat was oppressive to the men, but the herd suffered most from the fine alkali dust which enveloped them. Their eyebrows and nostrils were whitened with this fine powder, while all colors merged into one. On reaching this divide, we could see the cotton-woods that outlined the stream ahead. Before we had fully crossed this watershed and begun the descent, the mules would trot along beside the riders in the lead, even permitting us to lay our hands on their backs. It was getting late in the day before the first friendly breeze of the afternoon blew softly in our faces. Then, Great Scott! what a change came over man and herd. The mules in front threw up their heads and broke into a grand chorus. Those that were strung out took up the refrain and trotted forward. The horses set up a rival concert in a higher key. They had scented the water five miles off.

"All hands except one man on each side now rode in the lead. Every once in a while, some enthusiastic mule would break through the line of horsemen, and would have to be brought back. Every time we came to an elevation where we could catch the breeze, the grand horse and mule concert would break out anew. At the last elevation between us and the water, several mules broke through, and before they could be brought back the whole herd had broken into a run which was impossible to check. We opened out then and let them go.

"The Concho was barely running, but had long, deep pools here and there, into which horses and mules plunged, dropped down, rolled over, and then got up to nicker and bray. The young mules did everything but drink, while the horses were crazy with delight. When the wagon came up we went into camp and left them to play out their hands. There was no herding to do that night, as the water would hold them as readily as a hundred men."

"Well, I'm going to hunt my blankets," said Uncle Lance, rising. "You understand, Captain, that you are to sleep with me to-night. Davy Crockett once said that the politest man he ever met in Washington simply set out the decanter and glasses, and then walked over and looked out of the window while he took a drink. Now I want to be equally polite and don't want to hurry you to sleep, but whenever you get tired of yarning, you'll find the bed with me in it to the windward of that live-oak tree top over yonder."

Captain Frank showed no inclination to accept the invitation just then, but assured his host that he would join him later. An hour or two passed by.

"Haven't you fellows gone to bed yet?" came an inquiry from out of a fallen tree top beyond the fire in a voice which we all recognized. "All right, boys, sit up all night and tell fool stories if you want to. But remember, I'll have the last rascal of you in the saddle an hour before daybreak. I have little sympathy for a man who won't sleep when he has a good chance. So if you don't turn in at all it will be all right, but you'll be routed out at three in the morning, and the man who requires a second calling will get a bucket of water in his face."

Captain Frank and several of us rose expecting to take the hint of our employer, when our good intentions were arrested by a query from Dan Happersett, "Did any of you ever walk down a wild horse?" None of us had, and we turned back and reseated ourselves in the group.

"I had a little whirl of it once when I was a youngster," said Dan, "except we didn't walk. It was well known that there were several bands of wild horses ranging in the southwest corner of Tom Green County. Those who had seen them described one band as numbering forty to fifty head with a fine chestnut stallion as a leader. Their range was well located when water was plentiful, but during certain months of the year the shallow lagoons where they watered dried up, and they were compelled to leave. It was when they were forced to go to other waters that glimpses of them were to be had, and then only at a distance of one or two miles. There was an outfit made up one spring to go out to their range and walk these horses down. This season of the year was selected, as the lagoons would be full of water and the horses would be naturally reduced in flesh and strength after the winter, as well as weak and thin blooded from their first taste of grass. We took along two wagons, one loaded with grain for our mounts. These saddle horses had been eating grain for months before we started and their flesh was firm and solid.

"We headed for the lagoons, which were known to a few of our party, and when we came within ten miles of the water holes, we saw fresh signs of a band - places where they had apparently grazed within a week. But it was the second day before we caught sight of the wild horses, and too late in the day to give them chase. They were watering at a large lake south of our camp, and we did not disturb them. We watched them until nightfall, and that night we planned to give them chase at daybreak. Four of us were to do the riding by turns, and imaginary stations were allotted to the four quarters of our camp. If they refused to leave their range and circled, we could send them at least a hundred and fifty miles the first day, ourselves riding possibly a hundred, and this riding would be divided among four horses, with plenty of fresh ones at camp for a change.

"Being the lightest rider in the party, it was decided that I was to give them the first chase. We had a crafty plainsman for our captain, and long before daylight he and I rode out and waited for the first peep of day. Before the sun had risen, we sighted the wild herd within a mile of the place where darkness had settled over them the night previous. With a few parting instructions from our captain, I rode leisurely between them and the lake where they had watered the evening before. At first sight of me they took fright and ran to a slight elevation. There they halted a moment, craning their necks and sniffing the air. This was my first fair view of the chestnut stallion. He refused to break into a gallop, and even stopped before the rest, turning defiantly on this intruder of his domain. From the course I was riding, every moment I was expecting them to catch the wind of me. Suddenly they scented me, knew me for an enemy, and with the stallion in the lead they were off to the south.

"It was an exciting ride that morning. Without a halt they ran twenty miles to the south, then turned to the left and there halted on an elevation; but a shot in the air told them that all was not well and they moved on. For an hour and a half they kept their course to the east, and at last turned to the north. This was, as we had calculated, about their range. In another hour at the farthest, a new rider with a fresh horse would take up the running. My horse was still fresh and enjoying the chase, when on a swell of the plain I made out the rider who was to relieve me; and though it was early yet in the day the mustangs had covered sixty miles to my forty. When I saw my relief locate the band, I turned and rode leisurely to camp. When the last two riders came into camp that night, they reported having left the herd at a new lake, to which the mustang had led them, some fifteen miles from our camp to the westward.

"Each day for the following week was a repetition of the first with varying incident. But each day it was plain to be seen that they were fagging fast. Toward the evening of the eighth day, the rider dared not crowd them for fear of their splitting into small bands, a thing to be avoided. On the ninth day two riders took them at a time, pushing them unmercifully but preventing them from splitting, and in the evening of this day they could be turned at the will of the riders. It was then agreed that after a half day's chase on the morrow, they could be handled with ease. By noon next day, we had driven them within a mile of our camp.

"They were tired out and we turned them into an impromptu corral made of wagons and ropes. All but the chestnut stallion. At the last he escaped us; he stopped on a little knoll and took a farewell look at his band.

"There were four old United States cavalry horses among our captive band of mustangs, gray with age and worthless - no telling where they came from. We clamped a mule shoe over the pasterns of the younger horses, tied toggles to the others, and the next morning set out on our return to the settlements."

Under his promise the old ranchero had the camp astir over an hour before dawn. Horses were brought in from picket ropes, and divided into two squads, Pasquale leading off to the windward of where the band was located at dusk previous. The rest of the men followed Uncle Lance to complete the leeward side of the circle. The location of the *manada*, had been described as between a small hill covered with Spanish bayonet on one hand, and a *zacahuiste* flat nearly a mile distant on the other, both well-known landmarks. As we rode out and approached the location, we dropped a man every half mile until the hill and adjoining salt flat had been surrounded. We had divided what rifles the ranch owned between the two squads, so that each side of the circle was armed with four guns. I had a carbine, and had been stationed about midway of the leeward half-circle. At the first sign of dawn, the signal agreed upon, a turkey call, sounded back down the line, and we advanced. The circle was fully two miles in diameter, and on receiving the signal I rode slowly forward, halting at every sound. It was a cloudy morning and dawn came late for clear vision. Several times I dismounted and in approaching objects at a distance drove my horse before me, only to find that, as light increased, I was mistaken.

When both the flat and the dagger crowned hill came into view, not a living object was in sight. I had made the calculation that, had the *manada* grazed during the night, we should be far to the leeward of the band, for it was reasonable to expect that they would feed against the wind. But there was also the possibility that the outlaw might have herded the band several miles distant during the night, and while I was meditating on this theory, a shot rang out about a mile distant and behind the hill. Giving my horse the rowel, I rode in the direction of the report; but before I reached the hill the *manada* tore around it, almost running into me. The coyote mustang was leading the band; but as I halted for a shot, he turned inward, and, the mares intervening, cut off my opportunity. But the warning shot had reached every rider on the circle, and as I plied rowel and quirt to turn the band, Tio Tiburcio cut in before me and headed them backward. As the band whirled away from us the stallion forged to the front and, by biting and a free use of his heels, attempted to turn the *manada* on their former course. But it mattered little which way they turned now, for our cordon was closing round them, the windward line then being less than a mile distant.

As the band struck the eastward or windward line of horsemen, the mares, except for the control of the stallion, would have yielded, but now, under his leadership, they recoiled like a band of *ladinos*. But every time they approached the line of the closing circle they were checked, and as the cordon closed to less than half a mile in diameter, in spite of the outlaw's lashings, the *manada* quieted down and halted. Then we unslung our carbines and rifles and slowly closed in upon the quarry. Several times the mustang stallion came to the outskirts of the band, uttering a single piercing snort, but never exposed himself for a shot. Little by little as we edged in he grew impatient, and finally trotted out boldly as if determined to forsake his harem and rush the line. But the moment he cleared the band Uncle Lance dismounted, and as he knelt the stallion stopped like a statue, gave a single challenging snort, which was answered by a rifle report, and he fell in his tracks.

CHAPTER XX

SHADOWS

Spring was now at hand after an unusually mild winter. With the breaking of the drouth of the summer before there had sprung up all through the encinal and sandy lands an immense crop of weeds, called by the natives *margoso*, fallow-weed. This plant had thriven all winter, and the cattle had forsaken the best mesquite grazing in the river bottoms to forage on it. The results showed that their instinct was true; for with very rare exceptions every beef on the ranch was fit for the butcher's block. Truly it was a year of fatness succeeding a lean one. Never during my acquaintance with Las Palomas had I seen the cattle come through a winter in such splendid condition. But now there was no market. Faint rumors reached us of trail herds being put up in near-by counties, and it was known that several large ranches in Nueces County were going to try the experiment of sending their own cattle up the trail. Lack of demand was discouraging to most ranchmen, and our range was glutted with heavy steer cattle.

The first spring work of any importance was gathering the horses to fill a contract we had with Captain Byler. Previous to the herd which Deweese had sold and delivered at Fort Worth the year before, our horse stock had amounted to about four thousand head. With the present sale the ranch holdings would be much reduced, and it was our intention to retain all *manadas* used in the breeding of mules. When we commenced gathering we worked over every one of our sixty odd bands, cutting out all the fillies and barren mares. In disposing of whole *manadas* we kept only the geldings and yearlings, throwing in the old stallions for good measure, as they would be worthless to us when separated from their harems. In less than a week's time we had made up the herd, and as they were all in the straight 'horse hoof' we did not road-brand them. While gathering them we put them under day and night herd, throwing in five *remudas* as we had agreed, but keeping back the bell mares, as they were gentle and would be useful in forming new bands of saddle horses. The day before the appointed time for the delivery, the drover brought up saddle horses and enough picked mares to make his herd number fifteen hundred.

The only unpleasant episode of the sale was a difference between Theodore Quayle and my employer. Quayle had cultivated the friendship of the drover until the latter had partially promised him a job with the herd, in case there was no objection. But when Uncle Lance learned that Theodore expected to accompany the horses, he took Captain Frank to task for attempting to entice away his men. The drover entered a strong disclaimer, maintaining that he had promised Quayle a place only in case it was satisfactory to all concerned; further, that in trail work with horses he preferred Mexican vaqueros, and had only made the conditional promise as a favor to the young man. Uncle Lance accepted the explanation and apologized to the drover, but fell on Theodore Quayle and cruelly upbraided him for forsaking the ranch without cause or reason. Theodore was speechless with humiliation, but no sooner were the hasty words spoken than my employer saw that he had grievously hurt another's feelings, and humbly craved Quayle's pardon.

The incident passed and was apparently forgotten. The herd started north on the trail on the twenty-fifth of March, Quayle stayed on at Las Palomas, and we resumed our regular spring work on the ranch. While gathering the mares and fillies, we had cut out all the geldings four years old and upward to the number of nearly two hundred, and now our usual routine of horse breaking commenced. The masons had completed their work on all three of the cottages and returned to the Mission, but the carpenter yet remained to finish up the woodwork. Fidel and Juana had begun housekeeping in their little home, and the cosy warmth which radiated from it made me impatient to see my cottage finished. Through the mistress, arrangements had been made for the front rooms in both John's cottage and mine to be floored instead of cemented.

Some two weeks before Easter Sunday, Cotton returned from the Frio, where he had been making a call on his intended. Uncle Lance at once questioned him to know if they had set the day, and was informed that the marriage would occur within ten days after Lent, and that he expected first to make a hurried trip to San Antonio for a wedding outfit.

"That's all right, John," said the old ranchero approvingly, "and I expect Quirk might as well go with you. You can both draw every cent due you, and take your time, as wages will go right on the same as if you were working. There will not be much to do except the usual horse breaking and a little repairing about the ranch. It's quite likely I shan't be able to spare Tom in the early summer, for if no cattle buyers come along soon, I'm going to send June to the coast and let him sniff around for one. I'd like the best in the world to sell about three thousand beeves, and we never had fatter ones than we have to-day. If we can make a sale, it'll keep us busy all the fore part of the summer. So both you fellows knock off any day you want to and go up to the city. And go horseback, for this ranch don't give Bethel & Oxenford's stages any more of its money."

With this encouragement, we decided to start for the city the next morning. But that evening I concluded to give a certain roan gelding a final ride before turning him over to the vaqueros. He was a vicious rascal, and after trying a hundred manoeuvres to unhorse me, reared and fell backward, and before I could free my foot from the stirrup, caught my left ankle, fracturing several of the small bones in the joint. That settled my going anywhere on horseback for a month, as the next morning I could not touch my foot to the ground. John did not like to go alone, and the mistress insisted that

ANDY ADAMS

Theodore was well entitled to a vacation. The master consented, each was paid the wages due him, and catching up their own private horses, the old cronies started off to San Antonio. They expected to make Mr. Booth's ranch in a little over half a day, and from there a sixty-mile ride would put them in the city.

After the departure of the boys the dull routine of ranch work went heavily forward. The horse breaking continued, vaqueros rode the range looking after the calf crop, while I had to content myself with nursing a crippled foot and hobbling about on crutches. Had I been able to ride a horse, it is quite possible that a ranch on the San Miguel would have had me as its guest; but I must needs content myself with lying around the house, visiting with Juana, or watching the carpenter finishing the cottages. I tried several times to interest my mistress in a scheme to invite my sweetheart over for a week or two, but she put me off on one pretext and another until I was vexed at her lack of enthusiasm. But truth compels me to do that good woman justice, and I am now satisfied that my vexation was due to my own peevishness over my condition and not to neglect on her part. And just then she was taking such an absorbing interest in June and the widow, and likewise so sisterly a concern for Dan Happersett, that it was little wonder she could give me no special attention when I was soon to be married. It was the bird in the bush that charmed Miss Jean.

Towards the close of March a number of showers fell, and we had a week of damp, cloudy weather. This was unfortunate, as it called nearly every man from the horse breaking to ride the range and look after the young calves. One of the worst enemies of a newly born calf is screw worms, which flourish in wet weather, and prove fatal unless removed; for no young calf withstands the pest over a few days. Clear dry weather was the best preventive against screw worms, but until the present damp spell abated every man in the ranch was in the saddle from sunrise to sunset.

In the midst of this emergency work a beef buyer by the name of Wayne Orahood reached the ranch. He was representing the lessees of a steamship company plying between New Orleans and Texas coast points. The merchant at the ferry had advised Orahood to visit Las Palomas, but on his arrival about noon there was not a white man on the ranch to show him the cattle. I knew the anxiety of my employer to dispose of his matured beeves, and as the buyer was impatient there was nothing to do but get up horses and ride the range with him. Miss Jean was anxious to have the stock shown, and in spite of my lameness I ordered saddle horses for both of us. Unable to wear a boot and still hobbling on crutches, I managed to Indian mount an old horse, my left foot still too inflamed to rest in the stirrup. From the ranch we rode for the encinal ridges and sandy lands to the southeast, where the fallow-weed still throve in rank profusion, and where our heaviest steers were liable to range. By riding far from the watering points we encountered the older cattle, and within an hour after leaving the ranch I was showing some of the largest beeves on Las Palomas.

How that beef buyer did ride! Scarcely giving the cattle a passing look, he kept me leading the way from place to place where our salable stock was to be encountered. Avoiding the ranchitos and wells, where the cows and younger cattle were to be found, we circled the extreme outskirts of our range, only occasionally halting, and then but for a single glance over some prime beeves. We turned westward from the encinal at a gallop, passing about midway between Santa Maria and the home ranch. Thence we pushed on for the hills around the head of the Ganso. Not once in the entire ride did we encounter any one but a Mexican vaquero, and there was no relief for my foot in meeting him! Several times I had an inclination to ask Mr. Orahood to remember my sore ankle, and on striking the broken country I suggested we ride slower, as many of our oldest beeves ranged through these hills. This suggestion enabled me to ease up and to show our best cattle to advantage until the sun set. We were then twenty-five miles from the ranch. But neither distance nor approaching darkness checked Wayne Orahood's enthusiasm. A dozen times he remarked, "We'll look at a few more cattle, son, and then ride in home." We did finally turn homeward, and at a leisurely gait, but not until it was too dark to see cattle, and it was several hours after darkness when we sighted the lamps at headquarters, and finished the last lap in our afternoon's sixty-mile ride.

My employer and Mr. Orahood had met before, and greeted each other with a rugged cordiality common among cowmen. The others had eaten their supper; but while the buyer and I satisfied the inner man, Uncle Lance sat with us at the table and sparred with Orahood in repartee, or asked regarding mutual friends, artfully avoiding any mention of cattle. But after we had finished Mr. Orahood spoke of his mission, admitted deprecatingly that he had taken a little ride south and west that afternoon, and if it was not too much trouble he would like to look over our beeves on the north of the Nueces in the morning. He showed no enthusiasm, but acknowledged that he was buying for shipment, and thought that another month's good grass ought to put our steers in fair condition. I noticed Uncle Lance clouding up over the buyer's lack of appreciation, but he controlled himself, and when Mr. Orahood expressed a wish to retire, my employer said to his guest, as with candle in hand the two stood in parting: -

"Well, now, Wayne, that's too bad about the cattle being so thin. I've been working my horse stock lately, and didn't get any chance to ride the range until this wet spell. But since the screw worms got so bad, being short-handed, I had to get out and rustle myself or we'd lost a lot of calves. Of course, I have noticed a steer now and then, and have been sorry to find them so spring-poor. Actually, Wayne, if we were expecting company, we'd have to send to the ferry and get a piece of bacon, as I haven't seen a hoof fit to kill. That roast beef which you had for supper - well, that was sent us by a neighbor who has fat cows. About a year ago now, water was awful scarce with us, and a few old cows died up and down this valley. I suppose you didn't hear of it, living so far away. Heretofore, every time we had a drouth there was such a volunteer growth of fallow-weed that the cattle got mud fat following every dry spell. Still I'll show you a few cattle among the guajio brush and sand hills on the divide in the morning and see what you think of them. But of course, if they lack flesh, in case you are buying for shipment I shan't expect you to bid on them."

The old ranchero and the buyer rode away early the next morning, and did not return until near the middle of the afternoon, having already agreed on a sale. I was asked to write in duplicate the terms and conditions. In substance, Las Palomas ranch agreed to deliver at Rockport on the coast, on the twentieth of May, and for each of the following three months, twelve hundred and fifty beeves, four years old and upward. The consideration was $27.50 per head, payable on delivery. I knew my employer had oversold his holdings, but there would be no trouble in making up the five thousand head, as all our neighbors would gladly turn in cattle to fill the contract. The buyer was working on commission, and the larger the quantity he could contract for, the better he was suited. After the agreement had been signed in duplicate, Mr. Orahood smilingly admitted that ours were the best beeves he had bought that spring. "I knew it," said Uncle Lance; "you don't suppose I've been ranching in this valley over forty years without knowing a fat steer when I see one. Tom, send a *muchacho* after a bundle of mint. Wayne, you haven't got a lick of sense in riding - I'm as tired as a dog."

The buyer returned to Shepherd's the next morning. The horse breaking was almost completed, except allotting them into *remudas*, assigning bell mares, and putting each band under herd for a week or ten days. The weather was fairing off, relieving the strain of riding the range, and the ranch once more relaxed into its languid existence. By a peculiar coincidence, Easter Sunday occurred on April the 13th that year, it being also the sixty-sixth birthday of the ranchero. Miss Jean usually gave a little home dinner on her brother's birthday, and had planned one for this occasion, which was but a few days distant. In the mail which had been sent for on

Saturday before Easter, a letter had come from John Cotton to his employer, saying he would start home in a few days, and wanted Father Norquin sent for, as the wedding would take place on the nineteenth of the month. He also mentioned the fact that Theodore expected to spend a day or two with the Booths returning, but he would ride directly down to the Vaux ranch, and possibly the two would reach home about the same time.

I doubt if Uncle Lance ever enjoyed a happier birthday than this one. There was every reason why he should enjoy it. For a man of his age, his years rested lightly. The ranch had never been more prosperous. Even the drouth of the year before had not proved an ill wind; for the damage then sustained had been made up by conditions resulting in one of the largest sales of cattle in the history of the ranch. A chapel and three new cottages had been built without loss of time and at very little expense. A number of children had been born to the soil, while the natives were as loyal to their master as subjects in the days of feudalism. There was but one thing lacking to fill the cup to overflowing - the ranchero was childless. Possessed with a love of the land so deep as to be almost his religion, he felt the need of an heir.

"Birthdays to a man of my years," said Uncle Lance, over Easter dinner, "are food for reflection. When one nears the limit of his allotted days, and looks back over his career, there is little that satisfies. Financial success is a poor equivalent for other things. But here I am preaching when I ought to be rejoicing. Some one get John's letter and read it again. Let's see, the nineteenth falls on Saturday. Lucky day for Las Palomas! Well, we'll have the padre here, and if he says barbecue a beef, down goes the fattest one on the ranch. This is the year in which we expect to press our luck. I begin to feel it in my old bones that the turning-point has come. When Father Norquin arrives, I think I'll have him preach us a sermon on the evils of single life. But then it's hardly necessary, for most of you boys have got your eye on some girl right now. Well, hasten the day, every rascal of you, and you'll find a cottage ready at a month's notice."

The morning following Easter opened bright and clear, while on every hand were the signs of spring. A vaquero was dispatched to the Mission to summon the padre, carrying both a letter and the compliments of the ranch. Among the jobs outlined for the week was the repairing of a well, the walls of which had caved in, choking a valuable water supply with debris. This morning Deweese took a few men and went to the well, to raise the piping and make the necessary repairs, curbing being the most important. But while the foreman and Santiago Ortez were standing on a temporary platform some thirty feet down, a sudden and unexpected cave-in occurred above them. Deweese saw the danger, called to his companion, and, in a flash laid hold of a rope with which materials were being lowered. The foreman's warning to his companion reached the helpers above, and Deweese was hastily windlassed to the surface, but the unfortunate vaquero was caught by the falling debris, he and the platform being carried down into the water beneath. The body of Ortez was recovered late that evening, a coffin was made during the night, and the next morning the unfortunate man was laid in his narrow home.

The accident threw a gloom over the ranch. Yet no one dreamt that a second disaster was at hand. But the middle of the week passed without the return of either of the absent boys. Foul play began to be suspected, and meanwhile Father Norquin arrived, fully expecting to solemnize within a few days the marriage of one of the missing men. Aaron Scales was dispatched to the Vaux ranch, and returned the next morning by daybreak with the information that neither Quayle nor Cotton had been seen on the Frio recently. A vaquero was sent to the Booth ranch, who brought back the intelligence that neither of the missing boys had been seen since they passed northward some two weeks before. Father Norquin, as deeply affected as any one, returned to the Mission, unable to offer a word of consolation. Several days passed without tidings. As the days lengthened into a week, the master, as deeply mortified over the incident as if the two had been his own sons, let his suspicion fall on Quayle. And at last when light was thrown on the mystery, the old ranchero's intuition proved correct.

My injured foot improved slowly, and before I was able to resume my duties on the ranch, I rode over one day to the San Miguel for a short visit. Tony Hunter had been down to Oakville a few days before my arrival, and while there had met Clint Dansdale, who was well acquainted with Quayle and Cotton. Clint, it appeared, had been in San Antonio and met our missing men, and the three had spent a week in the city chumming together. As Dansdale was also on horseback, the trio agreed to start home the same time, traveling in company until their ways separated. Cotton had told Dansdale what business had brought him to the city, and received the latter's congratulations. The boys had decided to leave for home on the ninth, and on the morning of the day set forth, moneyless but rich in trinkets and toggery. But some where about forty miles south of San Antonio they met a trail herd of cattle from the Aransas River. Some trouble had occurred between the foreman and his men the day before, and that morning several of the latter had taken French leave. On meeting the travelers, the trail boss, being short-handed, had offered all three of them a berth. Quayle had accepted without a question. The other two had stayed all night with the herd, Dansdale attempting to dissuade Cotton, and Quayle, on the other hand, persuading him to go with the cattle. In the end Quayle's persuasions won. Dansdale admitted that the opportunity appealed strongly to him, but he refused the trail foreman's blandishments and returned to his ranch, while the two Las Palomas lads accompanied the herd, neither one knowing or caring where they were going.

When I returned home and reported this to my employer, he was visibly affected. "So that explains all," said he, "and my surmises regarding Theodore were correct. I have no particular right to charge him with ingratitude, and yet this ranch was as much his home as mine. He had the same to eat, drink, and wear as I had, with none of the concern, and yet he deserted me. I never spoke harshly to him but once, and now I wish I had let him go with Captain Byler. That would have saved me Cotton and the present disgrace to Las Palomas. I ought to have known that a good honest boy like John would be putty in the hands of a fellow like Theodore. But it's just like a fool boy to throw away his chances in life. They still sell their birthright for a mess of pottage. And there stands the empty cottage to remind me that I have something to learn. Old as I am, my temper will sometimes get away from me. Tom, you are my next hope, and I am almost afraid some unseen obstacle will arise as this one did. Does Frances know the facts?" I answered that Hunter had kept the facts to himself, not even acquainting his own people with them, so that aside from myself he was the first to know the particulars. After pacing the room for a time in meditation, Uncle Lance finally halted and asked me if Scales would be a capable messenger to carry the news to the Vaux family. I admitted that he was the most tactful man on the ranch. Aaron was summoned, given the particulars, and commanded to use the best diplomacy at his command in transmitting the facts, and to withhold nothing; to express to the ranchman and his family the deep humiliation every one at Las Palomas felt over the actions of John Cotton.

Years afterward I met Quayle at a trail town in the north. In the limited time at our command, the old days we spent together in the Nueces valley occupied most of our conversation. Unmentioned by me, his desertion of Las Palomas was introduced by himself, and in attempting to apologize for his actions, he said: -

"Quirk, that was the only dirty act I was ever guilty of. I never want to meet the people the trick was practiced on. Leaving Las Palomas was as much my privilege as going there was. But I was unfortunate enough to incur a few debts while living there that nothing but personal revenge could ever repay. Had it been any other man than Lance Lovelace, he or I would have died the morning Captain Byler's horse herd started from the Nueces River. But he was an old man, and my hand was held and my tongue was silent. You know the tricks of a certain girl who, with her foot on my neck, stretched forth a welcoming hand to a rival. Tom, I have lived to pay her my last obligation in a revenge so sweet that if I die an outcast on the roadside, all accounts are square."

CHAPTER XXI

INTERLOCUTORY PROCEEDINGS

A big summer's work lay before us. When Uncle Lance realized the permanent loss of three men from the working force of Las Palomas, he rallied to the situation. The ranch would have to run a double outfit the greater portion of the summer, and men would have to be secured to fill our ranks. White men who were willing to isolate themselves on a frontier ranch were scarce; but the natives, when properly treated, were serviceable and, where bred to the occupation and inclined to domesticity, made ideal vaqueros. My injured foot improved slowly, and as soon as I was able to ride, it fell to me to secure the extra help needed. The desertion of Quayle and Cotton had shaken my employer's confidence to a noticeable degree, and in giving me my orders to secure vaqueros, he said: -

"Tom, you take a good horse and go down the Tarancalous and engage five vaqueros. Satisfy yourself that the men are fit for the work, and hire every one by the year. If any of them are in debt, a hundred dollars is my limit of advance money to free them. And hire no man who has not a family, for I'm losing confidence every minute in single ones, especially if they are white. We have a few empty *jacals*, and the more children that I see running naked about the ranch, the better it suits me. I'll never get my money back in building that Cotton cottage until I see a mother, even though she is a Mexican, standing in the door with a baby in her arms. The older I get, the more I see my mistake in depending on the white element."

I was gone some three days in securing the needed help. It was a delicate errand, for no ranchero liked to see people leave his lands, and it was only where I found men unemployed that I applied for and secured them. We sent wagons from Las Palomas after their few effects, and had all the families contentedly housed, either about headquarters or at the outlying ranchitas, before the first contingent of beeves was gathered. But the attempt to induce any of the new families to occupy the stone cottage proved futile, as they were superstitious. There was a belief among the natives, which no persuasion could remove, regarding houses that were built for others and never occupied. The new building was tendered to Tio Tiburcio and his wife, instead of their own palisaded *jacal*, but it remained tenantless - an eyesore to its builder.

Near the latter end of April, a contract was let for two new tanks on the Ganso grant of land. Had it not been for the sale of beef, which would require our time the greater portion of the summer, it was my employer's intention to have built these reservoirs with the ranch help. But with the amount of work we had in sight, it was decided to let the contract to parties who made it their business and were outfitted for the purpose. Accordingly in company with the contractor, Uncle Lance and myself spent the last few days of the month laying off and planning the reservoir sites on two small tributaries which formed the Ganso. We were planning to locate these tanks several miles above the juncture of the small rivulets, and as far apart as possible. Then the first rainfall which would make running water, would assure us a year's supply on the extreme southwestern portion of our range. The contractor had a big outfit of oxen and mules, and the conditions called for one of the reservoirs to be completed before June 15th. Thus, if rains fell when they were expected, one receptacle at least would be in readiness.

When returning one evening from starting the work, we found Tony Hunter a guest of the ranch. He had come over for the special purpose of seeing me, but as the matter was not entirely under my control, my employer was brought into the consultation. In the docket for the May term of court, the divorce proceedings between Esther and Jack Oxenford would come up for a hearing at Oakville on the seventh of the month. Hunter was anxious, if possible, to have all his friends present at the trial. But dates were getting a little close, for our first contingent of beeves was due on the coast on the twentieth, and to gather and drive them would require not less than ten days. A cross-bill had been filed by Oxenford's attorney at the last hour, and a fight was going to be made to prevent the decree from issuing. The judge was a hold-over from the reconstruction regime, having secured his appointment through the influence of congressional friends, one of whom was the uncle of the junior stage man. Unless the statutory grounds were clear, there was a doubt expressed by Esther's attorney whether the court would grant the decree. But that was the least of Hunter's fears, for in his eyes the man who would willfully abuse a woman had no rights, in court or out. Tony, however, had enemies; for he and Oxenford had had a personal altercation, and since the separation the Martin family had taken the side of Jack's employer and severed all connections with the ranch. That the mail contractors had the village of Oakville under their control, all agreed, as we had tested that on our return from Fort Worth the spring before. In all the circumstances, though Hunter had no misgivings as to the ultimate result, yet being a witness and accused of being the main instigator in the case, he felt that he ought, as a matter of precaution, to have a friend or two with him.

"Well, now, Tony," said my employer, "this is crowding the mourners just a trifle, but Las Palomas was never called on in a good cause but she could lend a man or two, even if they had to get up from the dinner table and go hungry. I don't suppose the trial will last over a day or two at the furthest, and even if it did, the boys could ride home in the night. In our first bunch and in half a day, we'll gather every beef in two rodeos and start that evening. Steamships won't wait, and if we were a day behind time, they might want to hold out demurrage on us. If it wasn't for that, the boys could stay a week and you would be welcome to them. Of course, Tom will want to go, and about the next best man I could suggest would be June. I'd like the best in the world to go myself, but you see how I'm situated, getting these cattle off and a new tank building at the same time. Now, you boys make your own arrangements among yourselves, and this ranch stands ready to back up anything you say or do."

Tony remained overnight, and we made arrangements to meet him, either at Shepherd's the evening before or in Oakville on the morning of the trial. Owing to the behavior of Quayle and Cotton, none of us had attended the celebration of San Jacinto Day at the ferry. Nor had any one from the Vaux or McLeod ranches, for while they did not understand the situation, it was obvious that something was wrong, and they had remained away as did Las Palomas. But several of Hunter's friends from the San Miguel had been present, as likewise had Oxenford, and reports came back to the ranch of the latter's conduct and of certain threats he had made when he found there was no one present to resent them. The next morning, before starting home, Tony said to our *segundo* and myself; -

"Then I'll depend on you two, and I may have a few other friends who will want to attend. I don't need very many for a coward like Jack Oxenford. He is perfectly capable of abusing an unprotected woman, or an old man if he had a crowd of friends behind to sick him on. Oh, he's a cur all right; for when I told him that he was whelped under a house, he never resented it. He loves me all right, or has good cause to. Why, I bent the cylinder pin of a new six-shooter over his head when he had a gun on him, and he forgot to use it. I don't expect any trouble, but if you don't look a sneaking cur right in the eye, he may slip up behind and bite you."

After making arrangements to turn in two hundred beeves on our second contingent, and send a man with them to the coast, Hunter returned home. There was no special programme for the interim until gathering the beeves commenced, yet on a big ranch like Las Palomas there is always work. While Deweese finished curbing the well in which Ortez lost his life, I sawed off and cut new threads on all the rods and piping belonging to that particular windmill. With a tireless energy for one of his years, Uncle Lance rode the range, until he could have told at a distance one half his holdings of cattle by flesh marks alone. A few days before the date set for the trial, Enrique brought in word one evening that an outfit of strange men were encamped north of the river on the Ganso Tract. The vaquero was unable to make out their business, but was satisfied they were not there for pleasure, so my employer and I made an early start the next morning to see who the campers were. On the extreme northwestern corner of our range, fully twenty-five miles from headquarters, we met them and found they were a corps of engineers, running a preliminary survey for a railroad. They were in the employ of the International and Great Northern Company, which was then contemplating extending their line to some point on the Rio Grande. While there was nothing definite in this prior survey, it sounded a note of warning; for the course they were running would carry the line up the Ganso on the south side of the river, passing between the new tanks, and leaving our range through a sag in the hills on the south end of the grant. The engineer in charge very courteously informed my employer that he was under instructions to run, from San Antonio to different points on the river, three separate lines during the present summer. He also informed us that the other two preliminary surveys would be run farther west, and there was a possibility that the Las Palomas lands would be missed entirely, a prospect that was very gratifying to Uncle Lance.

"Tom," said he, as we rode away, "I've been dreading this very thing for years. It was my wish that I would never live to see the necessity of fencing our lands, and to-day a railroad survey is being run across Las Palomas. I had hoped that when I died, this valley would be an open range and as primitive as the day of my coming to it. Here a railroad threatens our peace, and the signs are on every hand that we'll have to fence to protect ourselves. But let it come, for we can't stop it. If I'm spared, within the next year, I'll secure every tract of land for sale adjoining the ranch if it costs me a dollar an acre. Then if it comes to the pinch, Las Palomas will have, for all time, land

and to spare. You haven't noticed the changes in the country, but nearly all this chaparral has grown up, and the timber is twice as heavy along the river as when I first settled here. I hate the sight even of a necessity like a windmill, and God knows we have no need of a railroad. To a ranch that doesn't sell fat beeves over once in ten years, transportation is the least of its troubles."

About dusk on the evening of the day preceding the trial, June Deweese and I rode into Shepherd's, expecting to remain overnight. Shortly after our arrival, Tony Hunter hastily came in and informed us that he had been unable to get hotel accommodations for his wife and Esther in Oakville, and had it not been that they had old friends in the village, all of them would have had to return to the ferry for the night. These friends of the McLeod family told Hunter that the stage people had coerced the two hotels into refusing them, and had otherwise prejudiced the community in Oxenford's favor. Hunter had learned also that the junior member of the stage firm had collected a crowd of hangers-on, and being liberal in the use of money, had convinced the rabble of the village that he was an innocent and injured party. The attorney for Esther had arrived, and had cautioned every one interested on their side of the case to be reserved and careful under every circumstance, as they had a bitter fight on their hands.

The next morning all three of us rode into the village. Court had been in session over a week, and the sheriff had sworn in several deputies to preserve the peace, as there was considerable bitterness between litigants outside the divorce case. These under-sheriffs made it a point to see that every one put aside his arms on reaching the town, and tried as far as lay in their power to maintain the peace. During the early days of the reconstruction regime, before opening the term the presiding judge had frequently called on the state for a company of Texas Rangers to preserve order and enforce the mandates of the court. But in '79 there seemed little occasion for such a display of force, and a few fearless officers were considered sufficient. On reaching the village, we rode to the house where the women were awaiting us. Fortunately there was ample corral room at the stable, so we were independent of hostelries and liveries. Mrs. Hunter was the very reverse of her husband, being a timid woman, while poor Esther was very nervous under the dread of the coming trial. But we cheered them with our presence, and by the time court opened, they had recovered their composure.

Our party numbered four women and five men. Esther lacked several summers of being as old as her sister, while I was by five years the youngest of the men, and naturally looked to my elders for leadership. Having left our arms at the house, we entered the court-room in as decorous and well-behaved a manner as if it had been a house of worship and this a Sabbath morning. A peculiar stillness pervaded the room, which could have been mistaken as an omen of peace, or the tension similar to the lull before a battle. Personally I was composed, but as I allowed my eyes from time to time to rest upon Esther, she had never seemed so near and dear to me as in that opening hour of court. She looked very pale, and moved by the subtle power of love, I vowed that should any harm come to or any insulting word be spoken of her, my vengeance would be sure and swift.

Court convened, and the case was called. As might have been expected, the judge held that under the pleadings it was not a jury case. The panel was accordingly excused for the day, and joined those curiously inclined in the main body of the room. The complaining witnesses were called, and under direct examination the essential facts were brought forth, laying the foundation for a legal separation. The plaintiff was the last witness to testify. As she told her simple story, a hushed silence fell over the room, every spectator, from the judge on the bench to the sheriff, being eager to catch every syllable of the recital. But as in duty bound to a client, the attorney for the defendant, a young man who had come from San Antonio to conduct the case, opened a sharp cross-questioning. As the examination proceeded, an altercation between the attorneys was prevented only by the presence of the sheriff and deputies.

Before the inquiry progressed, the attorney for the plaintiff apologized to the court, pleading extenuating circumstances in the offense offered to his client. Under his teachings, he informed the court, the purity of womanhood was above suspicion, and no man who wished to be acknowledged as a gentleman among his equals would impugn or question the statement of a lady. The witness on the stand was more to him than an ordinary client, as her father and himself had been young men together, had volunteered under the same flag, his friend offering up his life in its defense, and he spared to carry home the news of an unmarked grave on a Southern battle-field. It was a privilege to him to offer his assistance and counsel to-day to a daughter of an old comrade, and any one who had the temerity to offer an affront to this witness would be held to a personal account for his conduct.

The first day was consumed in taking testimony. The defense introduced much evidence in rebuttal. Without regard to the truth or their oaths, a line of witnesses were introduced who contradicted every essential point of the plaintiff's case. When the credibility of their testimony was attacked, they sought refuge in the technicalities of the law, and were supported by rulings of the presiding judge. When Oxenford took the stand in his own behalf, there were not a dozen persons present who believed the perjured statements which fell from his lips. Yet when his testimony was subjected to a rigid cross-questioning, every attempt to reach the truth precipitated a controversy between attorneys as bitter as it was personal. That the defendant at the bar had escaped prosecution for swindling the government out of large sums of money for a mail service never performed was well known to every one present, including the judge, yet he was allowed to testify against the character of a woman pure as a child, while his own past was protected from exposure by rulings from the bench.

When the evidence was all in, court adjourned until the following day. That evening our trio, after escorting the women to the home of their friend, visited every drinking resort, hotel, and public house in the village, meeting groups of

Oxenford's witnesses, even himself as he dispensed good cheer to his henchmen. But no one dared to say a discourteous word, and after amusing ourselves by a few games of billiards, we mounted our horses and returned to Shepherd's for the night. As we rode along leisurely, all three of us admitted misgivings as to the result, for it was clear that the court had favored the defense. Yet we had a belief that the statutory grounds were sufficient, and on that our hopes hung.

The next morning found our party in court at the opening hour. The entire forenoon was occupied by the attorney for the plaintiff in reviewing the evidence, analyzing and weighing every particle, showing an insight into human motives which proved him a master in his profession. After the noon recess, the young lawyer from the city addressed the court for two hours, his remarks running from bombast to flights of oratory, and from eulogies upon his client to praise of the unimpeachable credibility of the witnesses for the defense. In concluding, the older lawyer prefaced his remarks by alluding to the divine intent in the institution of marriage, and contending that of the two, women were morally the better. In showing the influence of the stronger upon the weaker sex, he asserted that it was in the power of the man to lift the woman or to sink her into despair. In his peroration he rose to the occasion, and amid breathless silence, facing the court, who quailed before him, demanded whether this was a temple of justice. Replying to his own interrogatory, he dipped his brush in the sunshine of life, and sketched a throne with womanhood enshrined upon it. While chivalry existed among men, it mattered little, he said, as to the decrees of courts, for in that higher tribunal, human hearts, woman would remain forever in control. At his conclusion, women were hysterical, and men were aroused from their usual languor by the eloquence of the speaker. Had the judge rendered an adverse decision at that moment, he would have needed protection; for to the men of the South it was innate to be chivalrous to womanhood. But the court was cautious, and after announcing that he would take the case under advisement until morning, adjourned for the day.

ANDY ADAMS

All during the evening men stood about in small groups and discussed the trial. The consensus of opinion was favorable to the plaintiff. But in order to offset public opinion, Oxenford and a squad of followers made the rounds of the public places, offering to wager any sum of money that the decree would not be granted. Since feeling was running rather high, our little party avoided the other faction, and as we were under the necessity of riding out to the ferry for accommodation, concluded to start earlier than the evening before. After saddling, we rode around the square, and at the invitation of Deweese dismounted before a public house for a drink and a cigar before starting. We were aware that the town was against us, and to maintain a bold front was a matter of necessity. Unbuckling our belts in compliance with the sheriff's orders, we hung our six-shooters on the pommels of our saddles and entered the bar-room. Other customers were being waited on, and several minutes passed before we were served. The place was rather crowded, and as we were being waited on, a rabble of roughs surged through a rear door, led by Jack Oxenford. He walked up to within two feet of me where I stood at the counter, and apparently addressing the barkeeper, as we were charging our glasses, said in a defiant tone: -

"I'll bet a thousand dollars Judge Thornton refuses to grant a separation between my wife and me."

The words flashed through me like an electric shock, and understanding the motive, I turned on the speaker and with the palm of my hand dealt him a slap in the face that sent him staggering back into the arms of his friends. Never before or since have I felt the desire to take human life which possessed me at that instant. With no means of defense in my possession but a penknife, I backed away from him, he doing the like, and both keeping close to the bar, which was about twenty feet long. In one hand I gripped the open-bladed pocket knife, and, with the other behind my back, retreated to my end of the counter as did Oxenford to his, never taking our eyes off each other. On reaching his end of the bar, I noticed the barkeeper going through motions that looked like passing him a gun, and in the same instant some friend behind me laid the butt of a pistol in my hand behind my back. Dropping the knife, I shifted the six-shooter to my right hand, and, advancing on the object of my hate, fired in such rapid succession that I was unable to tell even whether my fire was being returned. When my gun was empty, the intervening clouds of smoke prevented any view of my adversary; but my lust for his life was only intensified when, on turning to my friends, I saw Deweese supporting Hunter in his arms. Knowing that one or the other had given me the pistol, I begged them for another to finish my work. But at that moment the smoke arose sufficiently to reveal my enemy crippling down at the farther end of the bar, a smoking pistol in his hand. As Oxenford sank to the floor, several of his friends ran to his side, and Deweese, noticing the movement, rallied the wounded man in his arms. Shaking him until his eyes opened, June, exultingly as a savage, cried, "Tony, for God's sake stand up just a moment longer. Yonder he lies. Let me carry you over so you can watch the cur die." Turning to me he continued: "Tom, you've got your man. Run for your life; don't let them get you."

Passing out of the house during the excitement, I was in my saddle in an instant, riding like a fiend for Shepherd's. The sun was nearly an hour high, and with a good horse under me, I covered the ten miles to the ferry in less than an hour. Portions of the route were sheltered by timber along the river, but once as I crossed a rise opposite a large bend, I sighted a posse in pursuit several miles to the rear. On reaching Shepherd's, fortunately for me a single horse stood at the hitch-rack. The merchant and owner of the horse came to the door as I dashed up, and never offering a word of explanation, I changed horses. Luckily the owner of the horse was Red Earnest, a friend of mine, and feeling that they would not have long to wait for explanations, I shook out the reins and gave him the rowel. I knew the country, and soon left the river road, taking an air-line course for Las Palomas, which I reached within two hours after nightfall. In few and profane words, I explained the situation to my employer, and asked for a horse that would put the Rio Grande behind me before morning. A number were on picket near by, and several of the boys ran for the best mounts available. A purse was forced into my pocket, well filled with gold. Meanwhile I had in my possession an extra six-shooter, and now that I had a moment's time to notice it, recognized the gun as belonging to Tony Hunter. Filling the empty chambers, and waving a farewell to my friends, I passed out by the rear and reached the saddle shed, where a well-known horse was being saddled by dexterous hands. Once on his back, I soon passed the eighty miles between me and the Rio Grande, which I swam on my horse the next morning within an hour after sunrise.

CHAPTER XXII

SUNSET

Of my exile of over two years in Mexico, little need be said. By easy stages, I reached the haciendas on the Rio San Juan where we had received the cows in the summer of '77. The reception extended me was all one could ask, but cooled when it appeared that my errand was one of refuge and not of business. I concealed my offense, and was given employment as corporal *segundo* over a squad of vaqueros. But while the hacienda to which I was attached was larger than Las Palomas, with greater holdings in live-stock, yet my life there was one of penal servitude. I strove to blot out past memories in the innocent pleasures of my associates, mingling in all the social festivities, dancing with the dark-eyed senoritas and gambling at every *fiesta*. Yet in the midst of the dissipation, there was ever present to my mind the thought of a girl, likewise living a life of loneliness at the mouth of the San Miguel.

During my banishment, but twice did any word or message reach me from the Nueces valley. Within a few months after my locating on the Rio San Juan, Enrique Lopez, a trusted vaquero from Las Palomas, came to the hacienda, apparently seeking employment. Recognizing me at a glance, at the first opportunity he slipped me a letter unsigned and in an unknown hand. After reading it I breathed easier, for both Hunter and Oxenford had recovered, the former having been shot through the upper lobe of a lung, while the latter had sustained three wounds, one of which resulted in the loss of an arm. The judge had reserved his decision until the recovery of both men was assured, but before the final adjournment of court, refused the decree. I had had misgivings that this would be the result, and the message warned me to remain away, as the stage company was still offering a reward for my arrest. Enrique loitered around the camp several days, and on being refused employment, made inquiry for a ranch in the south and rode away in the darkness of evening. But we had had several little chats together, in which the rascal delivered many oral messages, one of which he swore by all the saints had been intrusted to him by my own sweetheart while visiting at the ranch. But Enrique was capable of enriching any oral message, and I was compelled to read between the lines; yet I hope the saints, to whom he daily prayed, will blot out any untruthful embellishments.

The second message was given me by Frank Nancrede, early in January, '81. As was his custom, he was buying saddle horses at Las Palomas during the winter for trail purposes, when he learned of my whereabouts in Mexico. Deweese had given him directions where I could be found, and as the Rio San Juan country was noted for good horses, Nancrede and a companion rode directly from the Nueces valley to the hacienda where I was employed. They were on the lookout for a thousand saddle horses, and after buying two hundred from the ranch where I was employed, secured my services as interpreter in buying the remainder. We were less than a month in securing the number wanted, and I accompanied the herd to the Rio Grande on its way to Texas. Nancrede offered me every encouragement to leave Mexico, assuring me that Bethel & Oxenford had lost their mail contract between San Antonio and Brownsville, and were now operating in other sections of the state. He was unable to give me the particulars, but frauds had been discovered in Star Route lines, and the government had revoked nearly all the mail contracts in southern Texas. The trail boss promised me a job with any of their herds, and assured me that a cow hand of my abilities would never want a situation in the north. I was anxious to go with him, and would have done so, but felt a compunction which I did not care to broach to him, for I was satisfied he would not understand.

The summer passed, during which I made it a point to meet other drovers from Texas who were buying horses and cattle. From several sources the report of Nancrede, that the stage line south from San Antonio was now in new hands, was confirmed. One drover assured me that a national scandal had grown out of the Star Route contracts, and several officials in high authority had been arraigned for conspiracy to defraud. He further asserted that the new contractor was now carrying the mail for ten per cent, of what was formerly allowed to Bethel & Oxenford, and making money at the reduced rate. This news was encouraging, and after an exile of over two years and a half, I recrossed the Rio Grande on the same horse on which I had entered. Carefully avoiding ranches where I was known, two short rides put me in Las Palomas, reaching headquarters after nightfall, where, in seclusion, I spent a restless day and night.

A few new faces were about the ranch, but the old friends bade me a welcome and assured me that my fears were groundless. During the brief time at my disposal, Miss Jean entertained me with numerous disclosures regarding my old sweetheart. The one that both pleased and interested me was that she was contented and happy, and that her resignation was due to religious faith. According to my hostess's story, a camp meeting had been held at Shepherd's during the fall after my banishment, by a sect calling themselves Predestinarians. I have since learned that a belief in a predetermined state is entertained by a great many good people, and I admit it seems as if fate had ordained that Esther McLeod and I should never wed. But it was a great satisfaction to know that she felt resigned and could draw solace from a spiritual source, even though the same was denied to me. During the last meeting between Esther and Miss Jean, but a few weeks before, the former had confessed that there was now no hope of our ever marrying.

As I had not seen my parents for several years, I continued my journey to my old home on the San Antonio River. Leaving Las Palomas after nightfall, I passed the McLeod ranch after midnight. Halting my horse to rest, I reviewed the past, and

ANDY ADAMS

the best reasoning at my command showed nothing encouraging on the horizon. That Esther had sought consolation from a spiritual source did not discourage me; for, under my observation, where it had been put to the test, the love of man and wife overrode it. But to expect this contented girl to renounce her faith and become my wife, was expecting her to share with me nothing, unless it was the chance of a felon's cell, and I remounted my horse and rode away under a starry sky, somewhat of a fatalist myself. But I derived contentment from my decision, and on reaching home no one could have told that I had loved and lost. My parents were delighted to see me after my extended absence, my sisters were growing fast into womanhood, and I was bidden the welcome of a prodigal son. During this visit a new avenue in life opened before me, and through the influence of my eldest brother I secured a situation with a drover and followed the cattle trail until the occupation became a lost one. My last visit to Las Palomas was during the winter of 1894-95. It lacked but a few months of twenty years since my advent in the Nueces valley. After the death of Oxenford by small-pox, I had been a frequent visitor at the ranch, business of one nature and another calling me there. But in this last visit, the wonderful changes which two decades had wrought in the country visibly impressed me, and I detected a note of decay in the old ranch. A railroad had been built, passing within ten miles of the western boundary line of the Ganso grant. The Las Palomas range had been fenced, several large tracts of land being added after my severing active connections with the ranch. Even the cattle, in spite of all the efforts made for their improvement, were not so good as in the old days of the open range, or before there was a strand of wire between the Nueces and Rio Grande rivers. But the alterations in the country were nothing compared to the changes in my old master and mistress. Uncle Lance was nearing his eighty-second birthday, physically feeble, but mentally as active as the first morning of our long acquaintance. Miss Jean, over twenty years the junior of the ranchero, had mellowed into a ripeness consistent with her days, and in all my aimless wanderings I never saw a brother and sister of their ages more devoted to, or dependent on each other.

On the occasion of this past visit, I was in the employ of a live-stock commission firm. A member of our house expected to attend the cattle convention at Forth Worth in the near future, and I had been sent into the range sections to note the conditions of stock and solicit for my employers. The spring before, our firm had placed sixty thousand cattle for customers. Demand continued, and the house had inquiry sufficient to justify them in sending me out to secure, of all ages, not less than a hundred thousand steer cattle. And thus once more I found myself a guest of Las Palomos.

"Don't talk cattle to me," said Uncle Lance, when I mentioned my business; "go to June - he'll give you the ages and numbers. And whatever you do, Tom, don't oversell us, for wire fences have cut us off, until it seems like old friends don't want to neighbor any more. In the days of the open range, I used to sell every hoof I had a chance to, but since then things have changed. Why, only last year a jury indicted a young man below here on the river for mavericking a yearling, and sent him to Huntsville for five years. That's a fair sample of these modern days. There isn't a cowman in Texas to-day who amounts to a pinch of snuff, but got his start the same way, but if a poor fellow looks out of the corner of his eye now at a critter, they imagine he wants to steal it. Oh, I know them; and the bigger rustlers they were themselves on the open range, the bitterer their persecution of the man who follows their example."

June Deweese was then the active manager of the ranch, and after securing a classification of their salable stock, I made out a memorandum and secured authority in writing, to sell their holdings at prevailing prices for Nueces river cattle. The remainder of the day was spent with my old friends in a social visit, and as we delved into the musty past, the old man's love of the land and his matchmaking instincts constantly cropped out.

"Tom," said he, in answer to a remark of mine, "I was an awful fool to think my experience could be of any use to you boys.

Every last rascal of you went off on the trail and left me here with a big ranch to handle. Gallup was no better than the rest, for he kept Jule Wilson waiting until now she's an old maid. Sis, here, always called Scales a vagabond, but I still believe something could have been made of him with a little encouragement. But when the exodus of the cattle to the north was at its height, he went off with a trail herd just like the rest of you. Then he followed the trail towns as a gambler, saved money, and after the cattle driving ended, married an adventuress, and that's the end of him. The lack of a market was one of the great drawbacks to ranching, but when the trail took every hoof we could breed and every horse we could spare, it also took my boys. Tom, when you get old, you'll understand that all is vanity and vexation of spirit. But I am perfectly resigned now. In my will, Las Palomas and everything I have goes to Jean. She can dispose of it as she sees fit, and if I knew she was going to leave it to Father Norquin or his successor, my finger wouldn't be raised to stop it. I spent a lifetime of hard work acquiring this land, and now that there is no one to care for the old ranch, I wash my hands of it."

Knowing the lifetime of self-sacrifice in securing the land of Las Palomas, I sympathized with the old ranchero in his despondency.

"I never blamed you much, Tom," he resumed after a silence; "but there's something about cattle life which I can't explain. It seems to disqualify a man for ever making a good citizen afterward. He roams and runs around, wasting his youth, and gets so foxy he never marries."

"But June and the widow made the riffle finally," I protested.

"Yes, they did, and that's something to the good, but they never had any children. Waited ten years after Annear was killed, and then got married. That was one of Jean's matches. Tom, you must go over and see Juana before you go. There was a match that I made. Just think of it, they have eight children, and Fidel is prouder over them than I ever was of this ranch. The natives have never disappointed me, but the Caucasian seems to be played out."

I remained overnight at the ranch. After supper, sitting in his chair before a cheerful fire, Uncle Lance dozed off to sleep, leaving his sister and myself to entertain each other. I had little to say of my past, and the future was not encouraging, except there was always work to do. But Miss Jean unfolded like the pages of an absorbing chronicle, and gave me the history of my old acquaintances in the valley. Only a few of the girls had married. Frances Vaux, after flirting away her youth, had taken the veil in one of the orders in her church. My old sweetheart was contentedly living a life of seclusion on the ranch on which she was born, apparently happy, but still interested in any word of me in my wanderings. The young men of my acquaintance, except where married, were scattered wide, the whereabouts of nearly all of them unknown. Tony Hunter had held the McLeod estate together, and it had prospered exceedingly under his management. My old friend, Red Earnest, who outrode me in the relay race at the tournament in June, '77, was married and serving in the Customs Service on the Rio Grande as a mounted river guard.

The next morning, I made the round of the Mexican quarters, greeting my old friends, before taking my leave and starting for the railroad. The cottage which had been built for Esther and me stood vacant and windowless, being used only for a storehouse for *zacahuiste*. As I rode away, the sight oppressed me; it brought back the June time of my youth, even the hour and instant in which our paths separated. On reaching the last swell of ground, several miles from the ranch, which would give me a glimpse of headquarters, I halted my horse in a farewell view. The sleepy old ranch cosily nestled among the encinal oaks revived a hundred memories, some sad, some happy, many of which have returned in retrospect during lonely hours since.

Choose from Thousands of 1stWorldLibrary Classics By

Adolphus WilliamWard
Aesop
Agatha Christie
Alexander Aaronsohn
Alexander Kielland
Alexandre Dumas
Alfred Gatty
Alfred Ollivant
Alice Duer Miller
Alice Turner Curtis
Alice Dunbar
Ambrose Bierce
Amelia E. Barr
Andrew Lang
Andrew McFarland Davis
Anna Sewell
Annie Besant
Annie Hamilton Donnell
Annie Payson Call
Anton Chekhov
Arnold Bennett
Arthur Conan Doyle
Arthur Ransome
Atticus
B. M. Bower
Basil King
Bayard Taylor
Ben Macomber
Booth Tarkington
Bram Stoker
C. Collodi
C. E. Orr
C. M. Ingleby
Carolyn Wells
Catherine Parr Traill
Charles A. Eastman
Charles Dickens
Charles Dudley Warner
Charles Farrar Browne
Charles Ives
Charles Kingsley
Charles Lathrop Pack
Charles Whibley
Charles Willing Beale
Charlotte M. Braeme
Charlotte M.Yonge
Clair W. Hayes
Clarence Day Jr.
Clarence E. Mulford

Clemence Housman
Confucius
Cornelis DeWitt Wilcox
Cyril Burleigh
D. H. Lawrence
Daniel Defoe
David Garnett
Don Carlos Janes
Donald Keyhole
Dorothy Kilner
Dougan Clark
E. Nesbit
E.P.Roe
E. Phillips Oppenheim
Edgar Allan Poe
Edgar Rice Burroughs
Edith Wharton
Edward J. O'Biren
John Cournos
Edwin L. Arnold
Eleanor Atkins
Elizabeth Cleghorn
Gaskell
Elizabeth Von Arnim
Ellem Key
Emily Dickinson
Erasmus W. Jones
Ernie Howard Pie
Ethel Turner
Ethel Watts Mumford
Eugenie Foa
Eugene Wood
Evelyn Everett-Green
Everard Cotes
F. J. Cross
Federick Austin Ogg
Ferdinand Ossendowski
Francis Bacon
Francis Darwin
Frances Hodgson Burnett
Frank Gee Patchin
Frank Harris
Frank Jewett Mather
Frank L. Packard
Frederick Trevor Hill
Frederick Winslow Taylor
Friedrich Kerst
Friedrich Nietzsche
Fyodor Dostoyevsky

Gabrielle E. Jackson
Garrett P. Serviss
Gaston Leroux
George Ade
Geroge Bernard Shaw
George Ebers
George Eliot
George MacDonald
George Orwell
George Tucker
George W. Cable
George Wharton James
Gertrude Atherton
Grace E. King
Grant Allen
Guillermo A. Sherwell
Gulielma Zollinger
Gustav Flaubert
H. A. Cody
H. B. Irving
H. G. Wells
H. H. Munro
H. Irving Hancock
H. Rider Haggard
H. W. C. Davis
Hamilton Wright Mabie
Hans Christian Andersen
Harold Avery
Harold McGrath
Harriet Beecher Stowe
Harry Houidini
Helent Hunt Jackson
Helen Nicolay
Hendy David Thoreau
Henrik Ibsen
Henry Adams
Henry Ford
Henry Frost
Henry James
Henry Jones Ford
Henry Seton Merriman
Henry Wadsworth
Longfellow
Henry W Longfellow
Herbert A. Giles
Herbert N. Casson
Herman Hesse
Homer
Honore De Balzac

Horace Walpole
Horatio Alger, Jr.
Howard Pyle
Howard R. Garis
Hugh Lofting
Hugh Walpole
Humphry Ward
Ian Maclaren
Israel Abrahams
J.G.Austin
J. Henri Fabre
J. M. Barrie
J. Macdonald Oxley
J. S. Knowles
J. Storer Clouston
Jack London
Jacob Abbott
James Allen
James Lane Allen
James Andrews
James Baldwin
James DeMille
James Joyce
James Oliver Curwood
James Oppenheim
James Otis
Jane Austen
Jens Peter Jacobsen
Jerome K. Jerome
John Burroughs
John F. Kennedy
John Gay
John Glasworthy
John Habberton
John Joy Bell
John Milton
John Philip Sousa
Jonathan Swift
Joseph Carey
Joseph Conrad
Joseph Jacobs
Julian Hawthrone
Julies Vernes
Justin Huntly McCarthy
Kakuzo Okakura
Kenneth Grahame
Kate Langley Bosher
L. A. Abbot
L. T. Meade
L. Frank Baum
Laura Lee Hope

Laurence Housman
Leo Tolstoy
Leonid Andreyev
Lewis Carroll
Lilian Bell
Lloyd Osbourne
Louis Tracy
Louisa May Alcott
Lucy Fitch Perkins
Lucy Maud Montgomery
Lydia Miller Middleton
Lyndon Orr
M. H. Adams
Margaret E. Sangster
Margaret Vandercook
Maria Edgeworth
Maria Thompson Daviess
Mariano Azuela
Marion Polk Angellotti
Mark Overton
Mark Twain
Mary Austin
Mary Cole
Mary Rowlandson
Mary Wollstonecraft
Shelley
Max Beerbohm
Myra Kelly
Nathaniel Hawthrone
O. F. Walton
Oscar Wilde
Owen Johnson
P.G.Wodehouse
Paul and Mable Thorn
Paul G. Tomlinson
Paul Severing
Peter B. Kyne
Plato
R. Derby Holmes
R. L. Stevenson
Rabindranath Tagore
Rahul Alvares
Ralph Waldo Emmerson
Rene Descartes
Rex E. Beach
Richard Harding Davis
Richard Jefferies
Robert Barr
Robert Frost
Robert Gordon Anderson
Robert L. Drake

Robert Lansing
Robert Michael Ballantyne
Robert W. Chambers
Rosa Nouchette Carey
Ross Kay
Rudyard Kipling
Samuel B. Allison
Samuel Hopkins Adams
Sarah Bernhardt
Selma Lagerlof
Sherwood Anderson
Sigmund Freud
Standish O'Grady
Stanley Weyman
Stella Benson
Stephen Crane
Stewart Edward White
Stijn Streuvels
Swami Abhedananda
Swami Parmananda
T. S. Ackland
The Princess Der Ling
Thomas A. Janvier
Thomas A Kempis
Thomas Anderton
Thomas Bailey Aldrich
Thomas Bulfinch
Thomas De Quincey
Thomas H. Huxley
Thomas Hardy
Thomas More
Thornton W. Burgess
U. S. Grant
Valentine Williams
Victor Appleton
Virginia Woolf
Walter Scott
Washington Irving
Wilbur Lawton
Wilkie Collins
Willa Cather
Willard F. Baker
William Makepeace
Thackeray
William W. Walter
Winston Churchill
Yei Theodora Ozaki
Young E. Allison
Zane Grey